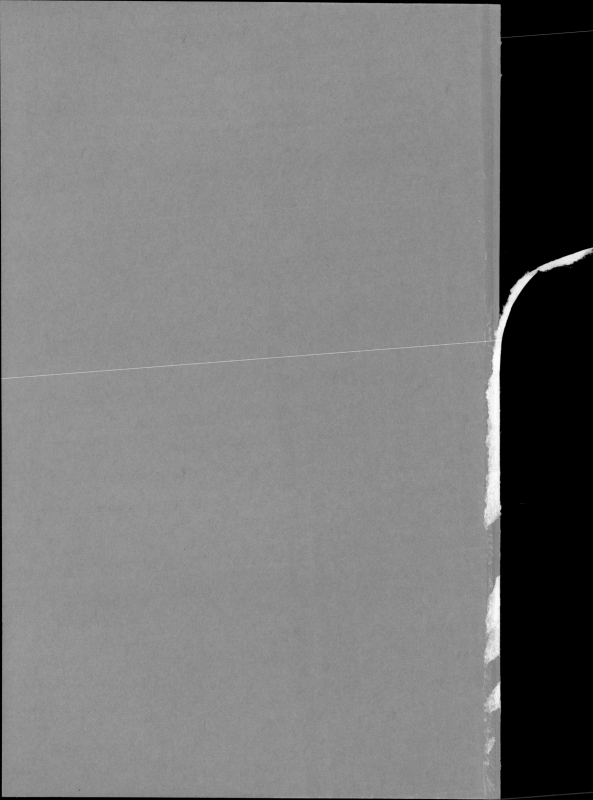

THE
ROMANCE
READER

PEARL ABRAHAM

A RIVERHEAD BOOK 1995 NEW YORK

THE ROMANCE READER

RIVERHEAD BOOKS
A DIVISION OF G. P. PUTNAM'S SONS
Publishers since 1838
200 Madison Avenue
New York, N. Y. 10016

Book design by Gretchen Achilles

Library of Congress Cataloging-in-Publication Data

Abraham, Pearl, date.
  The romance reader / Pearl Abraham.
    p.   cm.
  I. Title.
PS351.B615R66   1995   95-964-CIP
813'.54—dc20

Printed in the United States of America

1 3 5 7 9 10 8 6 4 2

This book is printed on acid-free paper ♾

FOR THEIR ENCOURAGEMENT AND WISDOM, I THANK
MONA SIMPSON, JONATHAN DEE, BRIAN MORTON,
MY AGENT, DENISE SHANNON, AND, ESPECIALLY,
MY EDITOR, CINDY SPIEGEL.

FOR HIS LOVE AND PATIENCE,
I AM GRATEFUL TO STEPHEN SPEWOCK.

PART

ONE

CHAPTER ONE

THE SOUND OF Ma's voice speaking English wakes me.

Something's wrong. She's on the phone in the middle of the night, on Shabbat. I hear Father moving around in their bedroom, and I wonder why, if something has happened, he's not on the phone.

In the hallway, the door to the kitchen is closed, and Ma's on the other side, talking. It's strange to stand there with the door closed. I'd forgotten there was a door.

Father comes out of his room, dressed, tying his black-and-gold caftan with a gartl. "It's time for Mama to go to the hospital and have the baby," he says.

"Right now? Who's taking you?"

Ma opens the door and whispers, "Shhh. Come into the kitchen. I'll explain."

She's wearing her blue maternity dress, the same one she wears whenever she goes out, but on her head is a soft quilted night kerchief, not a silk print.

Father and I follow her into the kitchen, and she closes the door. Her stomach is so big she has to step out of the way to let us in. She says she can't tell anymore how much room she needs; she wasn't this swollen with Aaron or any of us.

Ma has the phone near her ear, and I hear a man's voice at the other end.

She says, "Five minutes? Good." She hangs up. Then her hand is on her stomach as if holding it in place, and pain passes through her face, starting in her eyes.

She takes a deep breath and whispers softly, quickly, like she's afraid if she stops she won't finish. "I was going to wake you, Rachel. I have to go to the hospital to have the baby. The taxi will be here any minute. Don't wake the children. In the morning, send the boys to the synagogue. Serve lunch; maybe Father will be home by then. Don't tell people in the synagogue where Father is. They shouldn't know before. Better to avoid the evil eye."

We hear a car pull up, and Father goes out to the driver. I follow Ma into her room. There's a small suitcase ready at the foot of her bed, but she doesn't lift it. She waits for the driver.

He stoops to enter the small room and stands with his hands in his pockets, hunched over, as if otherwise he'd hit the ceiling. He makes our bungalow seem tiny. His hair is long, and under his jacket, his shirt hangs out.

Ma lifts a folded kerchief, and there's a ten-dollar bill just sitting there. The driver looks at it, and Ma says, "It's your pay. Take it. We can't touch it on Shabbat."

She points to her suitcase and asks if he would carry it. "Sure," he says, and in his hands the small suitcase is a toy.

"Can you do anything on your Sabbath?" he asks, his voice deep and rough.

"Shhh," I say before I can stop myself. If the kids wake up and see him here, they'll get scared. He looks at me and nods.

Ma puts her black coat over her shoulders; she hasn't been

able to button it for a long time now. She walks out to the car slowly, with Father at her side, not touching, just walking, the taxi driver following behind. It's not often I see Ma and Father walk this way, side by side.

The driver opens the back door, and Ma gets in, careful not to touch the car. She lowers herself onto the seat sideways, her feet still on the ground, her body facing the door. Then she uses her arms to help bring her legs in. The driver shuts the door, and the noise, so everyday, sounds sinful to me on Shabbat.

Father stands near the passenger door, not touching the handle, waiting, and finally the driver understands and opens the door for him too. Then they're all in, and the car turns around quickly; the wheels skid. If anyone saw Ma and Father in a car on Shabbat, they'd know right away where they were going.

I stand there, at the open door, and look out into the darkness. It's three o'clock. Morning is still hours away, and the street looks so different, blue and black. The silver garbage cans glow. I'm glad it was me Ma was going to wake up, that I was the one up with Ma and Father. A wind comes blowing in, and I start to feel cold standing there in my nightgown. I close and lock the door and go in to wake Leah, even though Ma said not to. Her sleep is deep; I have to shake her three times before she opens her eyes.

"What time is it?" she asks.

When she's more awake, she says, "Last year, Blumy's mother also had a baby on Shabbat."

In the morning, Aaron climbs out of his crib and comes to my bed.

"Mama," he says.

I hug him. "Mama went to buy a new baby."

He shakes his head no and says he is Mama's baby. I laugh. "Now Mama has two babies."

David, Levi, and Sarah gather around my bed in their pajamas, like I am Ma.

Leah grumbles. "It's so early. Go back to sleep, everyone. I'm tired."

"You're always tired. You're a poofer," David says.

He sits in the old oak office chair and turns and leans back so it squeaks. Leah pulls her blanket over her head.

I explain that Ma went to Good Samaritan Hospital in a taxi in the middle of the night to have a baby, and David starts everyone wondering whether it's a boy or a girl. The boys want a boy and the girls a girl. We say it's a girl because the last baby was a boy and Ma has always gone in order—girl, boy, girl, boy, girl, boy. First there's me, then David, Leah, Levi, Sarah, and Aaron. Still David says it has to be a boy, because otherwise the girls would be in the majority, and Father wouldn't allow that.

At nine o'clock, the boys go to synagogue. I tell them not to say anything and, if asked, to say they don't know where Father is, that he's just not home. It turns out there are only six men anyway, not enough for minyan, and without Father to go out and gather four more, they give up and leave. David and Levi pray without minyan. As soon as it's even a little warm out, people don't bother with Father's synagogue. In good weather, they don't mind walking all the way to Maple or Phyllis Terrace, and Ma tells Father he's wasting his time. She says, "Is this what you're killing yourself for, a rain-day synagogue for everyone's convenience?"

We go outside and wait for Father. He will be walking home all the way from Good Samaritan, seven miles. Levi is the first to see him coming up the block, and he and Sarah run to meet him. Father puts his arms around them, and they walk up the block slowly. He looks tired.

"Mazel tov," he says, smiling. "Mama had a baby girl."

"Another girl?" David says.

"A healthy child, that's what's important," Father tells him.

"Who does she look like?" Leah asks.

"Like all our babies. Very beautiful. She already sucks her finger."

We go in, and Father makes kiddish. Leah and I serve lunch, but no one wants to eat, not even Father.

He tells us there were some complications, that we have to thank God the baby is alive. He says, "Mama is weak. She lost blood."

"What complications?" I ask.

"The cord was tangled around the baby's neck, the baby couldn't breathe, and Dr. Landau wasn't there. He arrived late."

"What cord?" I ask. Father doesn't answer right away. I ask again. "Where did the cord come from?"

"The cord that attaches the child to its mother. The cord of life God provides for the child's first nine months," he explains.

"Why wasn't Dr. Landau there?" David asks.

"Why?" Father repeats, his voice higher. "Why? Because he's not a religious Yid. Because he's a murderer. That's why. Because he was out drinking at a party at such a time, when a new life is entering the world and the mother is in danger."

Father sways and talks and pulls his beard. "But enough such talk at the Shabbat table. We have a mazel tov. Let's sing."

Leah and I look at each other. It's not often we see Father angry, calling someone a murderer.

We get up to clear the table. There are too many leftovers. And we all want dessert, because we haven't eaten much else. Things don't feel the same with Ma away. The meal doesn't feel like a Shabbat meal. Father's tired; he sings some more zemiros and dozes in his chair. We wake him up for the blessing after eating. He goes into his room to lie down, and it's strange, Father in the room without Ma. David goes to Shabbat classes, and Leah and I sit on the front steps and talk about the cord. Neither of us has ever heard about a cord inside the mother. In the books we read, there is sometimes a baby but never anything about getting pregnant and growing fat and fatter. There is never anything about blood or a cord.

As soon as Father wakes up, he goes out to gather minyan. He didn't like hearing that six men had to go walking to another synagogue. "A bad precedent," he said. "That's not the way to get people used to coming regularly." He looked at David and said, "You and Levi together could've put together minyan easily; you had only four more to go."

Leah and I sit on the stairs and watch Father stop whoever walks by. He stands at the corner of Rita, where there's a real road, where people take walks. Leah and I don't say anything, just hope he gets his minyan. It means so much to him. Ma hates Father's synagogue. Every time he goes out to gather people, she starts a fight. She gets angry and yells out the window.

We watch Father walk up the block with a modern young man, almost a boy, really, except that he's wearing a suit and hat, so he's past bar mitzvah. When David, Levi, and Aaron are bar mitzvah, there will automatically be four for minyan in our family. The men Father picks up on Rita are almost always modern. Chassidic families in Monhegan belong to the Viznitz community and live on Phyllis Terrace or Maple. We watch Father walk the modern boy all the way into synagogue, as if he's afraid to let him loose. We laugh at how the boy looks like a prisoner, too polite to say no. Father comes out again to look for two more men.

From Jill Lane, David comes with a ninth man, and then Father paces up and down Rita, asking everyone. He doesn't want to lose a minyan for just one more person, a tenth. Leah and I watch anxiously now. We want a tenth. We know Father needs a tenth. He needs it more than ever today, after the failure this morning.

Five minutes go by, and I start to see why Ma gets angry. It's upsetting to see Father so needy.

Because of this morning, David must be trying harder. He brings in the tenth man. He walks with him all the way into the synagogue, the way Father does, and I send Levi to the corner to say there are already ten. But Father sees another person, another possibility. Then there's more than minyan, there are eleven now, and Father walks into the synagogue triumphant and smiling.

Leah and I stand at the back door, listening, the way Ma always does. I've never been interested before, but with Ma away, it seems someone should be. I hold the curtain aside so we can see.

Before beginning, Father turns to the congregation and announces the mazel tov. Everyone shakes his hand, even the new people who don't know him, and Mr. Dorf, one of the regulars, offers Father a ride to the hospital after Shabbat.

CHAPTER TWO

SUNDAY MORNING, LEAH and I stay home to take care of things. First I have to get Aaron to the Pals. When Gita had a baby, Itzi Pal stayed at our house for two weeks.

Aaron is excited to be out; he calls it bye-bye and doesn't ask questions about where we're going.

I stay awhile, as if we are just visiting together, playing with Zevi and Itzi Pal. Aaron wouldn't let me take off his snowsuit at first. I had to take my coat off to show him it's all right, safe.

Gita boils hot water. For herself she makes coffee, tea with milk for me. I feel grown up, like Ma, sitting here drinking tea with Gita. We sip and watch Aaron play.

"He'll be happy here," Gita says. "Don't worry."

Her Yiddish is like Ma's. Israeli.

She wants to know if we need help with food. She says, "I can cook double and send the meals in a taxi."

I thank her. Ma doesn't want us being dependent, using up so many favors. She's been saying for weeks now, "Don't let Gita cook for you. It's enough she's taking Aaron. She has enough to do for her own family."

I say, "Leah and I are home. Father's home. We don't have that much to do. We can cook."

"You're not even thirteen yet," she says. "Already cooking."

I feel much older. Ma never thinks I'm too young when it comes to doing housework.

I tell Gita about the room Father's planning as a surprise. That he's turning the front porch, where the entrance is now, into a large room. We'll have a real dining room, and the boys' room will be only a boys' room.

"Will it be finished in time?" Gita asks.

"It better be. They're making a lot of noise."

Gita claps her hands together, "Oh, I'm so happy for her. She'll love having a nice front room, always ready to receive guests. Your mother needs nice things around her."

Aaron and Zevi are on the floor, playing. Aaron looks up at me and smiles. He looks happy, as if I brought him here for playtime and will wait until he's tired, as if he is the child of a young mother who takes him to a special play group. I would give him all that if I could. But the taxi comes to pick me up, and Gita helps me leave when Aaron's not looking.

The Rickel's truck is pulled up in front of the bungalow, and the men are unloading Sheetrock, rolls of pink insulation, wood, nails. Gil and his friend are here, Gil with nails in his mouth. They carry everything into the hallway, leaving heavy boot marks and white chalk dust all over the floor.

Leah and I lean against the bales of insulation and watch. Gil's friend takes his shirt off. His skin is dark and smooth and muscu-

lar. I watch his bones and muscles move in a diagonal, back and
forth across the right side of his back when he lifts his arm and
brings the hammer down on a nail. Up. Down. I want to put my
hand on his back, feel the muscles move. His arms are large and
strong, arms I can imagine carrying me over the threshold in a
novel.

At lunch, his girlfriend shows up with sandwiches. She climbs
up on the unfinished roof, and I see them kissing. They use their
tongues.

Gil joins Father in the kitchen for a sandwich. Leah and I
serve tuna sandwiches with lettuce and tomato in the middle, like
a deli.

Gil says, "Tom and Julie were just married a few months ago."

He speaks in a singsong, a Dutch Yiddish, like Ma's aunt
Devorah.

Tom. He doesn't look like a Tom. The one simple syllable
doesn't describe this strong, beautiful man. He needs a name like
Isaiah or Daniel, something godly.

They're sitting near each other on the edge of the roof, their
boots dangling. I can't just stand out here and watch, so I walk to
the mailbox, slowly, even though the mailman hasn't come yet. I
pick up yesterday's damp *Pennysaver* from the ground, pull it out
of the plastic, and walk back up the path to our front steps, looking
and not looking at the front page. They're still kissing up there.
I'm glad Ma's not home; in two minutes she'd know exactly what
I'm doing. Father doesn't notice things.

The sun is out. It's warm for March, and I sit on the steps and
thumb through the paper, not reading.

"What time will you be finished here?" I hear Julie ask.

"I'm not sure. Seven, maybe, when it's too dark to continue, I
guess. It's a rush job, Gil says. Something about a baby and the

Sabbath. These people are very religious Jews; that man is a rabbi."

People who aren't Jewish show respect for Father, for his title, Rabbi. In the Chassidic community, Father's known as a rebbele without any followers. He doesn't belong to a great dynasty, not Satmar or Viznitz, or even to a smaller one, Karlin or Lubavitch.

"A rabbi," Julie says. "He does dress strangely."

I hate her, even though she's pretty and I like her long bell-bottom jean legs.

"You should see that man at work," Tom says and laughs. "His clothes keep getting in the way. Every time he uses a hammer, his beanie goes flying and he goes after it. I don't know how he ever gets any work done, dressed that way."

My face must be red. I feel hot even though I'm sitting outside without a coat on.

"Well, back to work," Tom says. "I'll see you later, sweetheart." I don't look up, but I know they're kissing. Sweetheart. I've never heard a real person say it. I've only seen it in books. Sweet. Heart. Julie walks to her parked car, and I like the way she throws her bag onto the passenger seat and gets in, one smooth motion. It's creamy off-white and small. She turns the car around quickly, beeps, throws Tom a kiss, and speeds up Ashley Hill. I wonder where she's going, what she will do all afternoon, until Tom comes home in his old dark-green pickup truck. I wonder what non-Jewish wives do all day. Julie doesn't look like a wife. She's married, but she looks regular, good, like a girl.

It's March, the end of winter, and the bungalows all around are still shut up. They're wet and silent, so silent. Ashley Country Club is a summer place, only we live here winters. When it snows, everything remains white and untouched, pure snow on the roofs and paths. Except for bungalow number 19. Walking turns our snow brown and muddy. Our garbage cans overflow.

Leah comes to the door. "What are you doing out here?"

"It's nice sitting here in the sun." I make room for her on the step.

"Maybe we can get a tan in the middle of winter," she says, leaning back. "I have an idea for dinner. A picnic on Francis Island. There's that salami hanging above the door. We can have salami sandwiches with mustard and pickles."

I'm sitting with my elbows on my legs, leaning, comfortable. I don't feel like moving. I turn the pages of the wet *Pennysaver* and listen to the hammers. Ma said to keep an eye out for a girls' bedroom set or a master set for her room. The Gantzes bought a beautiful five-piece bedroom set through the *Pennysaver* for only two hundred fifty dollars.

Leah's impatient. "Come on. Let's get the sandwiches ready."

"There's plenty of time. I want to sit here doing nothing for a while."

She jumps up. "I'll start."

We walk down Ashley Lane, to Rita Avenue. It's different with only the five of us plus Father, without Ma or Aaron. We're a small, happy family going on a picnic in the middle of March. If Ma were here, there'd be fighting. She doesn't lose a minute letting everyone know what she thinks. She'd be saying it's getting dark out and what are we, crazy, taking the kids out for a picnic in the middle of winter. And she'd be asking, What kind of life is this, a husband who's not working, not bringing home enough to live on, and what for do we need a synagogue?

I look at Father. He walks with his hands behind his back, the way Grandfather taught him, tall and straight, never slouched. He takes long strides, and Sarah and Levi have to skip to keep up with him. He's telling them about how he had to camp out with the sheep in the hills for whole weeks at a time, because that's where the pasture was good that year in Romania.

"What did you do at night?" Levi asks. "Weren't you afraid?"

"At night I said my prayers, rolled up in my blanket, and looked up at the stars."

"Did you play a flute, like a shepherd?" Leah asks.

"I had my books with me. I was expected to study during the day to keep up with the boys in school. Grandfather came every few days to bring food and to test me."

David and I agree it would be fun camping out, but not alone in the dark. "We should have lived on a farm," David says. "Why didn't you become a farmer like Grandfather?"

Father smiles. "We could buy a goat and keep her near the bungalow. You want a goat?"

We don't answer. We all know what Ma would say to a goat near her house. Father doesn't think of that. He's been married to her for years, but still he doesn't know her the way we do.

At Francis Lake, he leads the way across the bridge to the island. "What if I bought this whole island and built a house for each one of you to live in when you're married? I could build the synagogue in the center. We could all live on this island together. A family estate."

Leah and I look at each other. Ma's right. Father is crazy, a crazy dreamer.

He finds a soft grassy spot under a tree, and Leah and I spread the blanket. We sit in a circle and pass the sandwiches around.

Everyone has seconds and thirds. Then we pass out cookies. It's funny seeing Father bite into a chocolate-chip cookie so seriously, the same way he eats everything else. Then he starts the blessing, and we all say it with him. He closes his eyes and sways as he says the words. The branches above sway with him, and the brown water in the lake moves in the breeze. No one complains of the cold. Suddenly the ducks swim into view, and Sarah jumps up.

Father stands, brushes grass and crumbs off his knee-length pants, and straightens his coat. Ma hates these George Washington pants that tie just below the knee. Short pants, she calls them. Her father and brothers don't wear them; almost no one wears them.

"He looked so good when I first met him," she says. "A mensch in a nice wool suit, long pants, and a long jacket. But your father has to be a rebbele."

Father puts his hand on Sarah's head and smiles. "Don't stay too much longer," he says. "Mama wouldn't want you out here late."

"A good evening," he says in Yiddish, and we answer together.

We watch him walk across the bridge and turn left toward Ellish, toward Luria's synagogue, because during the week there's no minyan at ours. His arms are behind his back. He doesn't look like someone who's just been sitting cross-legged, eating salami sandwiches and talking about goats. He looks like an important man, a Chassid doing important godly things.

"It's good for you girls to practice keeping house," Father says the next day. "You'll need to do it soon enough for your own families."

I don't know if I want a family. I'd rather go to the store and buy sandwiches, like Julie. I don't want to cook. I don't know if I want babies. That's how you look good after you're married. Julie couldn't come today, so Tom drove to the store and brought back sandwiches for himself and Gil. They sat on our front stairs and ate. Tom drank Budweiser, and his knees stuck out over the steps. I took my sandwich outside on a plate and sat on the stairs with him and Gil, eating. It was sunny out, and Tom wore shorts, and the dark hair on his legs moving in the cold wind gave me goose bumps. He smiled, and I smiled back. We didn't say anything. I wanted him to touch me. I wondered how it would be, him touching me. On his T-shirt was a picture of a man smoking; it said "Monsieur ZigZag," and I wanted to ask who that was.

CHAPTER THREE

MA ARRIVES HOME in a taxi at one-thirty on Friday, when
Leah is just out of the shower, late as usual, her hair wet and
tangled. We run out to help. I carry the baby in a bundle of
blankets, and Leah holds Ma's arm as she steps out of the car
slowly, holding on to the door, afraid of falling. Her face is pale,
and she looks tired. She's wearing the same old blue maternity
dress, only her stomach doesn't stretch the fabric anymore.

"You should've asked me for a clean dress," I say. "I would
have sent one of your regular dresses with Father."

"Nothing would fit yet. I have to lose another fifteen pounds
before I can even think of getting into anything." She turns to
Leah. "You're hair's still wet. You'll get sick out in the cold with
wet hair."

Ma puts her arms out for the baby. I say, "I'll carry her in. It's
slippery."

She nods and waits for me to walk ahead of her, where she can
see me. I walk carefully, holding the baby tight, thinking that

even if I fall, I won't let her go, I will fall with her still safe in my arms. She's so bundled I can hardly see her face. Her eyes are closed tight, and her skin is reddish-brown. She's sucking her index finger, like Father said. David holds the door wide open, and I walk straight into Ma's room, to Aaron's crib, ready for a newborn, the mattress raised high and covered with a clean pink baby sheet. I put her down right in the middle, and she doesn't seem to know the difference, Ma's arms, mine, or the crib. I leave her there and hurry out to the front door. I don't want to miss Ma's face when she sees the new room.

She's walking up the steps slowly, as if in pain, and halfway up she stops and smiles, realizes what's different. I move away to let her in. Leah and I tried to make the room look as finished as possible. The floors are still plywood and the walls have only an undercoat of paint, but we swept, and in the center of the room we put a white pressed cloth on a milk crate, and the bowl of plastic fruit on top. Sarah and Levi colored Welcome-Home signs for the walls. All eyes are on Ma's face, but I watch Father watching Ma.

"This is beautifully big," she says softly. "And bright. Four big windows." She steps into the center and turns a full circle. "I wonder, what color should the walls be?"

"I left the walls for you," Father says. "I knew you'd want to choose a special color."

Sarah pulls at Ma's dress for attention. "That's how I became itchy. There was insulation here and I sat on it. I told you by mistake. I almost gave the surprise away."

Ma laughs and puts her hand on Sarah's head. "When did you have time to do this?" she asks. "It will be a beautiful dining room, always ready for guests."

The step that will always show that this room is really a porch and not part of the house doesn't seem to bother Ma. Or she just doesn't mention it. We follow her into the small bedroom and crowd around the crib. Ma unwraps the baby's layers, rolling her this way and that as if she were a doll. She sleeps through all of it.

"She's tired after Dr. Lewin's checkup," Ma says. "He gave her some extra shots. She's been getting so many shots, poor thing." Ma lifts her tiny red foot to show us. There's a round Band-Aid on her heel.

"Why on her foot?" I ask.

"The nurses say that's the best place for babies. Dr. Lewin started immunizations early. He says you have to with schoolchildren in the house."

When Ma gets to the bottom of all the layers, she says, "Close the door. There's a draft."

She unwraps the last blanket, and there's the baby, long and skinny, in an undershirt and a diaper. Ma removes the wet diaper and asks Leah to reach into her bag for a fresh one.

"She's teeny-tiny," Sarah says.

"Yes. She lost a few pounds since birth," Ma says. She sprinkles some Ammens powder on the diaper before she pins it closed, and the room smells like a newborn.

"Her name will be Esther Chaya," Ma says even though you shouldn't tell before it's announced in the synagogue.

The baby looks like an Esther, I think. Not so much a Chaya. But Ma's grandmother was named Esther Chaya. I decide to call her just Esther. Queen Esther of Persia. She has very black hair and eyes. Dark, smooth skin and soft, chubby legs. Leah and I want to start stretching her bones early. If we put her legs in a split several times a day, we think she can be double jointed like a ballet dancer.

"Now I have to feed her," Ma says. "Rachel, the room looks very nice. The beds, my favorite linens. Thank you." She reaches for my head and kisses me, leaving the warmth of her moist lips on my forehead. She loves white spotless linens.

We all leave the room, except for Father. He gets to watch Ma feed the baby. I wonder if he looks at her breasts while she's feeding. I saw them once for a second. She was getting dressed, and the door wasn't closed. She said, "Next time knock before you enter."

Ma's nipples looked funny, and her breasts were long and stretched.

I hope, please God, my breasts don't grow that way.

For the baby's kiddish, people come and Father doesn't have to go looking for minyan. David says people come for Ma's cake and that we should give a kiddish every Shabbat, like the small shtiblech in Williamsburg. Father nods.

Ma says, "Over my dead body. Aren't you ashamed? You should be ashamed, deeply down your throat. People should come for better reasons, not cake."

"People are people," Father says. "You want them to come, you give them cake."

"What about the money and the work?" Ma says. "Even if you don't care that I kill myself with work, where will you get the money? Out of my underpants? The kolel check you get every month isn't enough for a pair of newlyweds, never mind a family of nine. With those few dollars you want to start giving kiddish. Then you'll want that new synagogue. Bad enough you waste hours and hours writing, bent over the table scribbling. And for what? Pennies. That's all that will ever come of it. I'm warning you. You raise a hammer for that new synagogue you're planning, and I'll leave you."

She's always threatening. Her voice gets higher, and she looks at me and at David and says, "You are my witnesses. Don't say I didn't warn you."

Maybe it shows how sorry we feel for Father, because Ma turns on us.

"I will leave all of you," she says, looking at me as if it's my fault Father wants to build a synagogue, as if it was my idea.

Sarah is about to cry, hearing Ma talk about leaving. "Me too?" she asks.

"Yes. You can all stay with your father. I'll take the baby, get on an airplane, and go live with my old mother and father in Jerusalem. There I can be poor and happy instead of poor, alone, and miserable."

"Sha," Father says. "Don't talk about money on Shabbat. God will provide."

"God will provide," Ma says. "Like he has provided until now."

Father starts to sing and prods David, reminding him to sing along. Ma gets up and shoves her chair back with her leg; it falls. She leaves it there on its side on the floor and goes to her room. Levi and Sarah watch with their mouths open, their eyes wide. Leah and I start humming along with Father, first softly, then louder.

David looks at us and says, "Sha. No girls singing."

I look at Leah; we look into each other's eyes, daring each other, singing louder and louder. Father pretends not to hear us.

"It's a sin," Levi says, and he and David cover their ears.

We raise our voices higher and sing at the top of our lungs. Father stops singing and slams his hand down on the table. The plates and glasses jump and rattle, then there's silence. We all look at the candelabra, which is no longer in the center of the tray.

Levi's eyes are shiny, and Sarah lets two fat tears roll down her cheeks.

I get up hard, pushing my chair back noisily, not daring to throw it down the way Ma did. I pick up plates, forks, and knives and carry them into the kitchen. Leah follows.

Nothing ever changes. A new baby, a whole new room, a week in the hospital, and still things are the same.

CHAPTER FOUR

THE STOREFRONT WINDOW of the thrift shop is full of old clothes, but at the door there's a wooden bookcase lined with Barbara Cartlands. I read the back cover and the first few paragraphs of *The Unpredictable Bride*, and I don't want to stop. I want to finish the whole book standing here, so I can buy others. I want to buy ten of these books, they're so short and quick. I haven't had a fat book to read since school ended. Miss Dinkels said to get a library card this summer. She said I could have the librarian call home to confirm my address, or I could ask my dad for an Orange & Rockland bill. She didn't understand what I was laughing at, picturing myself calling Father "Dad" and imagining what he would say about a library card.

She said, "When you have the card, call me, and I'll give you a summer reading list."

When Father hears me speaking English, he says, "The Jews survived in Egypt because of three things. They didn't change their names, they didn't change their clothes, and they didn't change their language. Could we depend on you for our survival?"

Leah's standing beside me, reading. I say, "Let's go to the library after."

"You're crazy," she says. "Half of Monhegan is there on a Friday. Everyone goes to the library before Shabbat."

She's right. Someone will see us, the rabbi's daughters, at the library, and it will get back to Ma. In this town, everything gets back to Ma.

There's a Victoria Holt book on the shelf. On the cover, a woman with long pale hair, wearing a sheer white nightgown, runs from a castle. If we buy this book, we can have only one more, because it's bigger and fatter than the others. I decide to buy it, and Leah chooses *The Unpredictable Bride.* Just thinking about the title gets me excited.

The orange-haired lady at the counter looks at us, and her eyes go up and down, from our faces to our shoes. My face is red; I can feel it. She's seen us before—we've been coming here often enough this summer—still she looks us up and down every time, as if to let us know how strange we look wearing dark tights and long sleeves on a hot day in July. Leah does what she said she would do this time: she stares back. Her eyes move up and down the woman's body, stopping at her hair.

"So she'll know how it feels," Leah says. "Give her a taste of her own medicine."

The girls who hang out on Main Street wear shorts and tube tops. On the jitney bus, we watch them smoke cigarettes and comb their long straight hair. They carry pink plastic combs in the back pockets of their cut-off jeans. Leah thinks it's funny that hair is the only part of themselves they worry about keeping neat.

"They rip their jeans on purpose," I say.

I hold my dollar out to the saleslady, and she pulls it from my hand without looking at it; she's looking at Leah, her face angry. When she hands me the change, she pours it into my palm, careful not to touch me, as if whatever it is I am is catching. Leah and I walk out, feeling her eyes on our backs, but the books are already paid for, she can't take them back, and I can look forward to a long night of reading. When we're finished with our first books, we'll switch. In the morning, when Leah's still sleeping and everyone's in synagogue, I'll stay in bed, reading.

We walk to Shop-Rite with our list of groceries. Leah wheels a shopping cart around, down one aisle and up the next one, quickly reading the items on the list. Tomatoes, lettuce, peppers. It's always mostly fruit and vegetables, and things like flour, cocoa, sugar, all uncooked and kosher. This store is filled with things we can't eat. We walk the candy aisle twice, and Leah picks up a bag of marshmallows for squeezing. She loves the way they squeeze. She looks for the kosher sign on the bag, a small U inside an O, but there isn't one, and gelatin is listed as one of the ingredients.

Leah says, "They don't look like they have pig in them. They're so white and light and fluffy."

"Just because it has pig doesn't mean it has to be heavy and ugly. Pig meat is probably delicious. It looks a little like salami."

"These look so good," Leah says. She's poking at the bag so hard it's tearing.

"So taste it."

She looks at me to see if I'm joking and puts the marshmallows back, pulling her hand away quickly as if one more minute and she'd lose control, eat the whole bag. We continue hurrying from aisle to aisle so we can get to Shoppers Paradise, to the clothing department. I take the food coupons out of my purse at the last minute, pay quickly, and hope not everyone in the store sees. If only Ma would use these coupons when she has to pay bills or when she sends Father to the store. He's not ashamed of anything.

———

Leah finds a shirt to match the new skirt she's wearing. It's pale orange, blue, and white, and the fabric is slippery and shiny. I say I love it, that I'll buy it for her, and still she hesitates, worrying about what Ma will say. I talk her into it. She always needs talking into. She says I always need talking out of.

In the shoe department, I try on a pair of blue denim platform sandals. They have red cherries embroidered on the front, and they're only $7.95. I hop to the mirror in baby steps, because the sandals are connected by a string. Leah shakes her head warningly.

"I want them," I tell her. "They make me tall."

I look up and she's still shaking her head, her eyes on mine in the mirror. "You never know when to stop. You have no limits."

"I won't show them to her right away. I'll wait until she's in a good mood."

In the bra section, the saleslady says, "Can I help you, honey?" Her voice is so loud she may as well be on the PA system.

I don't know how to explain that I want a normal bra, not the pointy one Ma bought in Williamsburg. I want one of these soft and flat ones with thin straps and a pink flower in the center, but I don't know what size.

The lady looks at me, at my body, and picks one out. It's $6.99, too much, but it's pretty. Ma will say it's junk because it's polyester instead of cotton, and she already spent money on a good bra for me. She says it's not as if I need to wear one every day, but I want to, everyone in my class does, and one bra isn't enough; it's like never changing underwear. Washing it every night by hand isn't good enough either. The fabric turns gray, Ma says. She says it's fine to wear a dress or jumper twice, as long as we change our underwear. When we suggest hanging the dress back in the closet for another day instead of wearing it two days in a row, she says, "You don't want to wear the same thing twice, but you want to hang dirty clothes in the closet?"

"Leah bought a beautiful blouse for her new skirt," I announce when we walk into the house. The blouse is safe: long sleeves, the right colors. It's always good to mention the safe things right away, like you have nothing to hide.

Ma says, "Show me later."

After candle lighting, she half sits, half lies on the daybed in the boys' room. She asks what we bought, and Leah brings out her blouse and shows how it matches her skirt. Ma feels the fabric and asks if it's washable. I walk in, wearing the sandals. Under my dress is my new soft bra, and Ma doesn't know.

She sees the sandals and says, "You'll break your legs walking in them."

I lie and say that Kaley Weisner has a pair exactly like them, and I show Ma I can walk.

Leah says they're like stilts, and Ma laughs. "They'll last a day and a Wednesday. How much were they?"

"Only $5.99," I say, not looking at Leah.

"They're not even worth that much," she says and returns to feeling the fabric of Leah's blouse. She unbuttons it and looks inside at the seams. "They leave nothing to let out in bought clothes."

The clothes Ma sews always have two-inch seams. "So you can get your money's worth," she says. I've tried to explain that by the time you've grown so much the seams need letting out, you don't want to wear that old thing, that by then it's no longer stylish.

"Stylish?" Ma said. "Since when does a twelve-year-old know what's stylish?"

Hanging in her closet are dresses that are more than ten years old. A navy-and-white knit suit, the skirt straight and just below the knees. The black wool suit from Abraham & Straus, bought for becoming a U.S. citizen. Ma studied hard, she knew the names of all the presidents and all the states, and still she was nervous.

She and Father went together, dressed in black, Father tall in his black hat and Ma in her green silk turban. David and I became citizens by naturalization, through Ma and Father. The others were born American.

When I tell Ma to wear that suit to synagogue, she laughs. "I couldn't if I wanted to. That skirt would fit my little finger."

The Victoria Holt book is so good. Someone is trying to kill Lilliana. Dorian comes home and Lilliana is missing. He questions the servants. The stableboy says she took a horse and rode off that way. He points to the cliffs. Dorian realizes how much he loves Lilliana and doesn't want to lose her. He shouts her name, and his voice echoes through the mountains. Lilliana hears him, but she's lying in a heap on the rocks. Her horse ran off, frightened by the ghost who's trying to kill her. She thinks she's going to die, but she's happy. Dorian loves her, he's looking for her. By the time he finds her, Lilliana has fainted. He picks her up in his strong arms and takes her home, holding her, talking to her. He carries her to his room, not hers. I wonder if a man will carry me in his arms someday.

Ma comes in to see if I'm up. She's wearing her new cotton dress, green like her eyes.

"How do I look?" she asks, turning sideways in front of the mirror behind our door.

Chulentish, I think, like the heavy bean chulent we eat for lunch. It's her first waisted dress since the baby, still you'd never know she's nine pounds thinner.

"OK," I say. "It's summery."

She straightens the skirt, runs her hands down to smooth the sides, and sucks her stomach in. "It will look better after I lose a few more pounds," she says.

I am sorry for her and not. Every time she loses enough, just when she's beginning to look good, she gets pregnant again.

She smiles, still looking at herself in the mirror. "My daughters want me to look good. They're ashamed of their fat mother."

The book is under my pillow and I have only five pages to go, but just as I start to pull it out, Ma sticks her head back in. My heart leaps from its place in my chest and drops down to my toes. This, I think, is what dying feels like.

"The hard-boiled eggs are in the fridge. Make deviled eggs for lunch. The children love them," she says and pulls the door shut softly behind her. But the beating in my chest won't quiet down, and I lie back and breathe deep, following the sound of her steps all the way out into the small women's section in the synagogue, where her index finger will follow the cantor, word for word, in her prayer book.

I finish Lilliana's story and get dressed. My eyes are tired and my head feels heavy, the way it always does after a long night of reading. I wash my face with cold water. The Cartland book will wait until after lunch; I want to think about Lilliana and Dorian while I make the beds, set the table, and peel the eggs. I found a recipe for deviled eggs on the label of a mayonnaise jar, and everyone loved it. Ma calls the recipe American because instead of olive oil and scallions, there's ketchup, mustard, and mayonnaise.

When Leah wakes up, I tell her about the book.

She says, "Don't tell me, just hand it over."

She doesn't like to hear about a story before she reads it. I do. I read the last page first so I'm not hurrying to get to the end. My lips move when I'm at a good part, and Leah always laughs. "That's why it takes you so long to finish."

She reads with her eyes, a whole line at a time. But what's the good of finishing quickly, I think. Then you have nothing left.

"If only we could go to the library," I say.

Leah shakes her head. "Then go already."

We decide to wait until Ma's not home, until the day she goes to New York City to shop. She goes every year, midsummer, when things are on sale. Leah will stay home to answer the phone. She'll say, Yes, I am Mrs. Benjamin; yes, we live in Ashley; and I'll be the owner of a library card. I will be allowed to take out three books that day, then six every time after.

Ma finally goes to the city on a Wednesday, which is lucky because there are fewer people at the library midweek. I walk to Blueberry Hill and wait for the jitney bus. It takes forever to come, and I think the whole world is looking at me and knows exactly where I'm going. Every car worries me. On the bus, I can't decide whether to get off in front of the library or a block away.

I walk up the four steps, first slowly, then quickly, and push open the heavy door. It's cool and quiet inside, like a doctor's office, but with the smell of books instead of medicine. I walk among the shelves for a few minutes, just looking, not touching. At the front desk, I ask for an application form, and the librarian gives me a tiny pencil for filling in the boxes.

She speaks softly. "Why don't you go and look for the books you want while I make the call and prepare your card."

The bookshelves circle the large room; in the center, there are tables. I'm afraid to sit there reading, afraid someone will see me. I

stand between the tall shelves and reread parts of *Little Women*. I
see books Miss Dinkels brought to school. *Johnny Tremain*. *Jane
Eyre*. I picture Miss Dinkels here, walking from A to Z. There are
so many books; I wonder how she decides. She's not afraid of
being seen. She walks in with a big shopping bag and takes out as
many books as she can carry.

It's quiet in this place; the sound of my shoes on the shiny
wood floor is the only noise. I tiptoe. The librarian's wearing soft
rubber soles, and I don't hear her when she comes up behind me.

"Honey, the phone is busy. Do you have any proof of address
with you? A school ID?"

I shake my head.

"I'll try again," she says.

What's Leah doing on the phone, blabbing, with me here
waiting? There's a public phone on the stairs. Should I call? I
wonder. I can do an emergency interrupt if it's busy and get her to
hang up. I find a dime in my purse and dial.

"Hallo." Father's voice comes out slowly, the way he always
answers, and my throat gets stuck; I can't swallow. I hang up
quickly. He never comes into the house in the middle of the day.
He should be in the synagogue, writing. Someone else comes up
to use the phone, and I step away. Should I tell the librarian to
forget it? She'll think I'm crazy. I go downstairs, where the children's books are. It's noisier and brighter, and the tables are small,
like kindergarten tables. Nancy Drew books are on the shelf in a
row. I pull one off the shelf and try to read a page. My hands are
shaking and the words waver. I have to put the book down. Father's in the house, near the telephone. But maybe he won't answer, maybe Leah will pick up in the kitchen. I sit and try again to
read, but can't. When I stand up, I feel dizzy.

I finally go up the steps, and the librarian walks toward me.
Her face tells me everything. She says, "You've upset your father.

He says you came here without permission and that you should take the bus home right away."

If I tell her the truth, I wonder, will she help me? Adopt me? I look into her eyes, hoping. She looks into mine and says, "You should inform someone of where you're going before you leave home."

Father told her I came without permission. He didn't say why. He didn't say that he would never give me permission to come here. He didn't explain that he's a Chassidic rabbi, who doesn't allow his children to go to the library. If she knew, she might feel sorry for me, she might be on my side. I think Father knows this.

I leave the library slowly. There is no reason to hurry now. If I could concentrate, I would go downstairs and sit at a table. I could read and read, and hide in the bathroom when they're turning off the lights. I could stay all night, alone in the library, reading. But Father knows where I am, and he'll tell Ma.

My head burns like a fever. I'm so angry at Leah I want to tear her hair out. She promised to do this right. She said I could depend on her.

Now that I don't care how long the jitney bus takes, it's fast. I'm the only passenger for most of the ride. I say hi to the bus driver when I get on, and he doesn't answer. He sees us all the time, but he's always unfriendly. Leah says to stop trying. She makes faces and sticks her tongue out at him in his rearview mirror. When I get off the bus, his eyes are on my back. I can feel his hate, his impatience; his hand is on the lever, the hand that wants to close the door before I am completely through it. If I looked like the blond girl who works at McDonald's, he'd take his hand off the knob and wave.

———

Zeldy and Leah are sitting on the front steps. They stop talking when they see me, and I step around them, not saying a word. Father meets me in the hallway and says, "Come with me."

I follow his long black back through the house and into the synagogue. I feel Leah's eyes following me.

Father sits in a chair at the head of the table, and I sit at the end of the bench, the length of the table between us. In front of him are pages and pages of the book he's writing. What made him stop, I wonder, what made him suddenly get up and be there to pick up the phone when the librarian called? Was it some voice, some mystical force?

I'm afraid. He never raises his voice or hits me; I don't know what to expect. In his hand he holds the first book of Isaiah. He opens the book and reads, his voice hard, harder than I've ever heard it. It is the prophet's warning to the people of Judea. The words speak of destruction, pestilence, and plague. They speak of the sin of assimilation, of trying to be like other nations, of wanting to be liked by them, and of never succeeding.

"A Jew," Father says, looking up at me, translating for me, "is never liked by other nations. A Jew reads only Jewish books and must remain separate."

I can't wear a McDonald's uniform and expect the bus driver to like me. I am a Jew and will remain hated.

He reads on, and the words ring out, phrase after phrase. If you stop thinking about what they mean and just listen to the sounds, it's a poem. A beautiful, cruel poem.

Father says, "The Jews in Germany thought they could be good Germans first, Yuden second. And what happened? Six million killed by Hitler, may his name forever be erased."

I am guilty, an assimilated American Jew.

Father closes the book and sways. As if he's studying. "There

are so many good Yiddish books, why read books written by someone you don't know, some evil, dirty mind?"

"They're different," I say. "They talk about regular life."

"Not your life," he says. "I don't want you to read about
goyim. I'll buy any Yiddish books you want." He pauses, and I get
out of my chair. Even when he's angry, Father doesn't raise his
voice. He remains controlled, calm. Still, with his voice hard like
this, he's different, not the father I know.

"I'm not finished yet," he says. "I don't want this ever to
happen again. Take this as a last warning. If I catch you reading
goyishe books, you will stop going to school."

I sit there not saying anything, afraid to move. Stop going to
school? Aren't there rules about parents sending children to
school?

He looks at me. "Now I'm finished. Now you can go."

In the synagogue, on every wall, are stacks and stacks of
books. There are books from Father's father and grandfather.
Books shipped out of Europe just in time. Hebrew books come in
sets: five books of the Torah, thirty-four books of Prophets and
Writings, sixty books of the Talmud. They have their own order,
not alphabetical. There are so many books in this small room:
prayer books stacked on the tables, books for men and boys to
study. If I were a boy, studying hard like David, would I still want
to read library books?

I go to my room and lie down. I am so angry I can't sit or
stand. It's over, but I'm still shaking.

Leah comes in. "I didn't know he was in the house. For some
reason, he went into his room and plugged the phone in."

"I don't want to talk to you ever again. Leave me alone."

"What could I have done?"

"You could've kept better watch and seen him coming in.

Where were you—sitting outside talking to nosy Zeldy Shulman? You should have stayed right by the phone. Then you would've heard him come in. You could've said you're expecting a call from a friend, so he wouldn't pick up."

Leah stops to think about it. "That would've made him suspicious."

"Maybe, maybe not. This is worse. What did you tell him when he asked you whether you knew where I went? That you had no idea, right?"

Leah doesn't answer, and I know I guessed correctly.

"You were sitting outside, weren't you? Blabbing."

Again she doesn't answer, and I know Zeldy Shulman knows about the library—Zeldy, who acts as if she's one of us just because she's young and newly married and not yet a mother. But when she talks to Ma, she repeats everything we say. Leah probably told Zeldy she had nothing to do with the library, that it was my idea, that I am the bad one, the shiksa.

"I don't want to talk to you," I say.

"Think whatever you want, but it's not my fault," Leah says. "You couldn't have done any better."

Before she even arrives home, Ma hears about my going to the library. As soon as she walks into the house, I know she knows, because she looks at me as if she wants to spit in my face. She says, "Don't do me any favors with the dishes; not with hands that touch dirty books."

She talks only to Leah, asking questions about what Aaron and Esther ate, how things went, if anyone called. It's like I'm not there, not the oldest in the family, not the one who does all the work. How quickly the good things you do are forgotten. There is always someone else to fill in and help out.

Days later, Ma's still talking about the library. She won't let anyone forget. I go to work early, saying Mrs. Glickman needs me. I get there before the kids are home from day camp, and walk down the long carpeted hallway to the large master bedroom. The plush pink carpeting, the walls papered with flowers to match the beds, the soft wide mattresses feel like a sin. Mrs. Glickman's high-heeled sandals, in every color, are everywhere. I put them on and walk in front of the mirror, and the heels catch on the carpet.

As soon as I get back home, Ma starts again. I wonder if she talks when I'm away too. The thing about Ma is she can talk about the same thing for a month. She says, "Mrs. Beck called today to say how shocked she is, the rabbi's daughter at the library."

Father looks down, not saying anything. That doesn't stop Ma. She enjoys making me uncomfortable in front of him, like she's making me pay for my sins. She continues. "I didn't know what to say. What do you say to someone when unfortunately it's true and you're burning with shame? Your own daughter at the library, reading trafe books." She stops and looks around from one of us to the next, and I do what Father does and look down.

Ma continues, even louder now. "I had to swallow it, and it hurt going down. My eldest daughter. This is the example she sets for the younger ones. This is the kind of name she's giving the family."

Father says, "Enough already. What's done is done. I don't want to hear about it anymore."

That doesn't stop Ma. She says, "Look what you're doing to us. Look at your father; his beard is going gray. All because of your sins." She turns on Father. "It's all your fault. You've been too lenient, letting them read too much. I didn't finish the fourth grade, that's how my parents raised me."

Father looks up. "I told you I don't want to hear another word about it. Not now or ever. Understood?"

Father looks down, and Ma silently wrings her hands and bites her lip, her face red. She's acting for the others, showing them how terrible I am and what I've done to Father, when it is really her own fault for dragging this thing out forever. I want to hit her, she makes me so angry. I want to go around and slap everyone in this house, loud and hard enough that the shape of my hand remains on their cheeks awhile. I want to start with Leah, who sits there so blamelessly. I could get up now and walk around the room and slap every one of them, starting with Leah, Ma, and Father.

I hear Ma murmuring late at night. I hear my name and burn, knowing they are talking about me. I don't hear the words, but I think Father would say that talking about it so much can only make things worse, and I lie there feeling good. I can blame Ma, say she talked too much and now it's too late. I am rotten through and through. A bad apple. Ma responds with a murmur, and it sounds like she's agreeing. In bed is the one place she listens to him. In bed she's soft.

In front of Father, Ma doesn't mention the library again, or any more phone calls, which makes me wonder about them in the first place. Ma doesn't talk to me, and I'm not talking to Leah. There's silence around me. I can go on not talking to either one of them, or to anyone, for the rest of my life. But they're breaking down, trying to break me down. Leah talks to me as if nothing happened. She comes and tells me stories, hoping I'll forget. Ma talks to me through Leah. In a loud voice, she says, "Tell Rachel to clean the stove tonight," or "Tell Rachel to change all the linens." On purpose I don't change the linens. If she won't talk to me, she can't tell me what to do. I'm not the one who will suffer from her silence.

The women in Ashley look at me the way you look at a sinner. So stone me, I think, walking past them, not looking their way. Afternoons, I don't sit with them under a tree, playing Scrabble the way I used to, the way Leah and Ma still do. Monday, Wednesday, and Thursday I work for Mrs. Glickman as a mother's helper. Other days, I swim in Ashley's pool, which is only half full of water. Everything in Ashley is halfway this summer. Only half the bungalows were rented, and the casino wasn't opened; the grass around only the rented bungalows is mowed; the pool hasn't been repainted and the cement is crumbling. Everyone is saying this is the last season, that Ashley's being sold to builders.

I can't wait to see these families load their vans and cars with boxes, bicycles, Port-a-Cribs, and children. Moving in is always a slow trickle, one or two families a day. But every year, the day after Labor Day, Ashley empties out. The women come to our door to say good-bye. They bring leftover flour, sugar, noodles. Ma says, "I just bought a five-pound bag of this." Still she takes it. I listen to hear if she ever says, This is exactly what I need, I just ran out.

One day, I will have my own bookcase. On my shelves I'll have at least one book for every letter of the alphabet, with room for more. They'll be my books. I'll build a bookcase like Father built; it takes up a whole wall in our new dining room. I helped with the trim. I hammered small finishing nails into the wood scalloping on the edge of each shelf and into the carved strips of wood on the sides. In my bookcase, every book will have its place, like Father's books, and if I take one out, I'll put it back where it came from.

Next Saturday, when everyone is in the synagogue and Leah's still asleep, I'll go into Father's study and find an Orange & Rockland bill as proof of residence. He keeps all documents and bills in an old, heavy credenza. He won't miss a bill that's already paid, and I'll have a library card. With an Orange & Rockland bill, the librarian won't have to call home. This is how I should have done it from the beginning, without Leah. Anytime you can find a way of doing something without relying on others, that's the way to do it. Alone, there's no danger.

It's a sin to touch office things on Shabbat, but it's the only time I can do it. I don't know which is worse, going to the library or stealing and breaking the law of Shabbat, but I know what the prophet's talking about when he says one sin begets another.

CHAPTER FIVE

I'M FASTING THIS year. I'm almost thirteen, so there's no question about it: girls start at twelve, boys at thirteen. In school, we learn a lot about the prayers and the three steps to repentance. First you have to admit your guilt.

I admit I've sinned. Mostly with Elke. We take turns. We lock the door to her room, and Elke takes off her shirt, lies down on the bed, and closes her eyes. I tickle her breasts and nipples, and they become hard and pointy. Then I slowly move down to her stomach. Sometimes I use a feather from her pillow, but mostly just my fingers. I go back and forth, a little farther each time. I know how good it feels this way. Slowly, lightly. Once, I pulled her panties away from her body, and Elke started breathing so quickly we got scared and stopped.

It's not very hard to admit your sins when you're just admitting them to yourself. I don't understand the big deal about admission, as long as you don't have to tell someone else, your mother or father. It's really more like remembering, making a list of all the sins you've committed during the year. A year is a long time. I've stolen. Books mostly. I stole *Huckleberry Finn* from Waldbaum's, and it was so good I went back and stole *Tom Sawyer*. I wanted the set, matching. This is how Huck would have gotten it.

I also ate candy at Waldbaum's, non-kosher candy, right out of a small hole in the bag. Most of the time I didn't even have to tear the bag; the hole was already there, the candy spilling. Mounds. Raisinets. If I ran away like Huck, I wouldn't be hungry. I could walk the aisles of Waldbaum's or Shop-Rite. I see housewives eat grapes in the fruit aisle, unwashed grapes. They make believe they're just tasting, but they eat a whole branch.

The next step is regretting. This is hard. I don't feel sorry enough about anything. I'd probably do it all again. I ask Elke whether she's sorry.

"Of course," she says. "It's before Yom Kippur. You have to repent. I am."

"How?"

"No tickling this month," she says.

"Yom Kippur is not just for a month," I say. "You should say no tickling, period."

"You have to start somewhere," Elke says. "It says so in the Kitzur."

Then there's promising. You have to promise not to sin again, or you haven't truly repented. Unkept promises are greater sins than sins already committed. There's a special prayer for broken promises on Kol Nidre night. I'd rather not promise. I know that I will want Elke tickling me. Somehow she always ends up owing. Last time, I missed my turn. Sometimes at night, under my covers, I do it to myself. I go up and down my stomach. But it's better having someone else do it: you don't know where her fingers will go next.

I think Elke is just making believe, saying she's sorry and promising not to do it again. I know that in a few weeks she'll be ready. But maybe she's right. Maybe you just have to start to repent, make the effort to stop sinning, and then God helps you. He can keep temptation from coming your way, he can hold Satan back.

The time to follow through with the steps of repentance is between Rosh Hashanah and Yom Kippur, the ten days of atonement. On Rosh Hashanah, God writes your fate, and on Yom Kippur, he seals it. You have to try and get to him in between.

During these ten days, Father gets up early for special prayers at the synagogue. The last day, the morning before Yom Kippur, I say I want to go with him. He puts his warm hand on my head the way he did when I was little, and in his heart I know I am forgiven. He says he'll wake me. I don't tell Elke about it; I want to do this by myself, perfectly. I want to repent for good, not just for a month.

The air is fresh and sharp at 5 A.M., and the sky is dark. I am the only one in the women's section, but the men's section is crowded; there are more than twenty people. I stand near the window, look out, and chant silently with Father, who's leading the service. The men in this synagogue are workers; they asked for an early, quick minyan so they can get to work in time. They're here to get it over with.

"A minyan of good-for-nothings," Ma says. "That's what you're leading."

"Better than not praying at all," Father says. "Think of the good I'm doing. I'm making prayer possible for everyone. In my small synagogue, prayer is possible for workers, not just scholars. The Baal Shem would have supported this: this is the true meaning of Chassidism."

Father faces the ark in front of the synagogue and sways. His voice chants, begs. From the back, his body draped in a tallis, he looks mummified in soft cream-colored wool, the fringe of the tallis swaying with him. I stand near the window in the women's section and watch the sun rise slowly, then quickly. The sky goes from midnight blue to purple to pink to holy. Everything in this world happens in steps.

After prayers, Father comes in to see me. "Rachel. How do you feel? Are you tired?"

"No. I'm fine."

"I was having a hard time with that tune." He hums it and gets stuck again, the way he did during the service. I start him off again and sing it through past where he keeps getting stuck. He nods and hums. He's got it now. He smiles and puts his arm on my shoulder and kisses my forehead. He says, "If you were a boy, I'd keep you near me during services. You could help me."

I don't know how to answer this. I'm a girl. Should I wish I were a boy?

He reaches over and kisses me again. A hot, breathy, garlicky kiss. He likes kissing. Ma makes fun of him. She says it's Romanian. Lickers and kissers, she calls them. Brown nosers. I try to avoid him when he's in a kissing mood.

I wonder how Ma can stand him in bed with her. I can't imagine them in bed together.

Elke said, "Husband and wife kiss when they're in bed. First they kiss, and then they start the other thing."

I didn't believe her at first. I told her it sounds like the man's peeing. I told her I read a lot of books, and this is never mentioned.

She said, "They're just stories. What I'm telling you is true. That's how you were born. It starts with kissing. My cousin told me this a long time ago. Then they touch each other everywhere. Then they do it."

I told her I know for sure Ma doesn't like kissing. I can remember only a few kisses from her. She kisses the babies a lot, then she stops.

Elke said, "Your mother must like it. There are seven of you."

On Yom Kippur, Elke and I sit next to each other, right behind our mothers. We're praying in the Viznitzer synagogue this year. No one wants to pray in a small shtibel on the High Holidays. Not even Father. He closes his synagogue and takes David with him to Williamsburg to pray with the Satmar Rebbe. They sleep on a bench in the Satmar synagogue.

When the cantor skips a few pages forward or back, Elke and I look over our mothers' shoulders to find the place. This is the first time I'm in the synagogue all day.

Last year, Father said, "You're so close to twelve, you should try to fast."

But I was thirsty as soon as we got home from Kol Nidre. Two hours before, I'd eaten so much my stomach was bursting.

This year, it's easier. Last night, after Kol Nidre, I was fine. I didn't even want a drink of water. Now my stomach is beginning to growl. Elke's too. We laugh when we hear each other.

I hum along with the cantor. The Hebrew print tells me who wrote the poetry and when. There are liturgical prayers and songs from the ninth and tenth centuries, and when I figure out how many hundreds of years that is, it adds up to a long time ago. At the bottom of the page, there are stories about the prayers. David, Leah, and I rate prayer books, Haggadahs, and megillahs by the number of stories in them, and by now Father knows which ones to buy. I thumb through the book to see how many pages are left.

At noon, Ma turns around and says, "Why don't you and Elke go home and take a nap?"

But we don't want to. We're proud of fasting and sitting in the synagogue all day.

Ma says, "It's a long day."

At four-thirty, Elke puts out four fingers to show me that there are only four hours left.

Ma sees her and smiles. "The last hours are the longest," she says. "Go home and take a nap. It will go faster that way."

Mrs. Sklar nods. She doesn't say much on Yom Kippur. Or ever, really. I watch her during prayers. She doesn't even cry. But she must feel like crying, I think. Her life has been awful from the beginning. Watching her father and brothers getting shot. Working in a concentration camp. Living in an orphanage.

Elke and I go out. It feels good to breathe fresh air, and we walk up and down the block in front of the synagogue before going home. Our legs are wobbly, and we laugh about it. We talk about what we will eat tonight. That's what fasting does to you. You spend most of the day thinking about food. I plan on a tall glass of hot milk with a teaspoon of instant Sanka in it, the only way Ma lets us drink coffee, and a big slice of cinnamon babka. Elke wants a chocolate bar first; she eats a lot of chocolate. Ma says that's why her front teeth are rotting.

"After dessert," Elke says, "I will eat chicken soup with pieces of chicken floating in it."

I never liked chicken soup, but right now even that sounds good.

Elke is a half year older than I am, and this is her second time. She is a veteran faster. She says, "You'll see. After fasting, you eat just one thing and you're so full you can't move. Then the next morning, you wake up starving."

I can't imagine ever feeling full again.

Outside, kids are trading snacks; we watch a chocolate-chip cookie go for a lollipop, popcorn for a pretzel. Children under twelve get snack bags, so their mothers don't have to handle food during the fast. Sarah is in charge of Esther and Aaron this year, but she's playing jump rope with her friends.

"You better keep an eye on them," I tell her. She nods and jumps in to take her turn. She's almost seven now, old enough to do things. At her age, Leah and I were keeping house and taking care of newborns. But she's spoiled. Ma says it's because she has older sisters.

Leah's baby-sitting for the Daskals this year. I always turned down baby-sitting jobs on Yom Kippur, even though they pay well. Leah wanted the money.

Elke and I go home and sit on the daybed in the boys' room. When I lean back, I feel dizzy. Something's stuck under the bolster, and I pull it out. It's a brown lunch bag. I look in. Pretzels. Elke leans over and looks in, then puts her hand out. I put a pretzel into it, and she takes it. I take one for myself. We say the blessing and bite down together. I think how strange it is, saying a blessing before sinning. You get so used to it, it's automatic, you say the words without thinking. But that's not how righteous people say them. They concentrate every time.

Before she's finished with her first pretzel, Elke puts her hand out for another. We finish the bag quickly and go into the kitchen for more. My mouth is dry. Elke keeps watch while I jump up on the counter and get down the canister. Ma keeps snacks on the highest shelves, so we're all good at jumping up and down one-handed. In my room, we lean back on my bed, close our eyes, and chew. My mouth gets too warm. Too many pretzels always make me feel funny, but today it's worse. It's the only thing in my stomach.

The sun is low in the sky, it's not as bright as before, but I can't sleep. I want Elke to touch me.

She says, "Not on Yom Kippur. I told you, not this whole month."

I don't see what difference it makes. She's done a lot worse, eating. She doesn't answer. I wish I didn't always want to be touched. Every morning, when I first wake up, it's like there's something inside me. I'm growing hair under my arms and on my legs. Like Faivel when the dybbuk possessed his body. His voice changed, and his arms and legs became hairy.

Elke's saying no bothers me so much that I decide right then I will never do it with her again. I am so certain now, it's like I've repented. I will be the one to refuse. And I decide not to tell her until she asks for it. I want to say no.

She sits up and starts putting on her sneakers. I watch her. She's stubbornly silent; she won't talk. I look at my watch. We've been away for only an hour. Three more to go. I tie my laces. Elke watches and waits; she doesn't say anything. We walk back. At the door, we check each other's teeth for crumbs.

The brown stairwell is dark and smells like people. Hundreds of people. And when we get to the top of the stairs and open the door to the women's section, they're all there, the rounded backs of hundreds of women, their white-kerchiefed heads bent over their prayer books.

"So soon?" Ma says when we come in. If she knew what we'd done in this short time, she wouldn't think it so soon. It was long enough to commit a sin. Eating on Yom Kippur, my teacher said, separates you from your nation, cuts you off.

Elke bends her head over her prayer book and doesn't look up even once. I'm feeling stuffed, and I worry that I won't seem hungry enough when we get home. It wasn't even worth it. Not for plain old pretzels. I have a headache now. And I don't like Elke sitting there, acting as if it's my fault. I blame Ma for sending us home. Then I blame Elke for putting her hand out. Then I blame myself. I ate last year too. Elke has at least fasted once.

These prayers are going on and on. I'm tired of praying so much. The minute hand on my watch is so slow. I silently count to sixty and check if it's moved. I can't wait for the sun to set, for it to be completely dark outside. I want the dark, the night, to hide in. Sitting in one place for so many hours, praying, and then wasting it all makes no sense. I have no right to pray. I shouldn't bother praying. But we're still twenty pages away from the shofar. I wait for the sound, a sound like a lost sheep, a sad bleat. Everything having to do with Rosh Hashanah and Yom Kippur is sad and holy. Holy is sad. After this full day of prayers, at the last minute, just before God closes his books and seals all our fates, the cantor blows the shofar. The sound rises and keeps open the closing doors of heaven for one more minute. I try to think of a special message to send through. I didn't mean to eat. I didn't mean to break my fast. What *did* I mean?

I'm not turning pages; I leave them unturned for a while, just so I can turn five pages at once, feel as if we're making progress. I look up over Ma's shoulder. We're almost there; another two pages. It's dark enough outside; the stars are starting to shine. We won't have to wait for sundown; it will be here before we're done.

Finally, feet shuffling, everyone stands. The whispering begins. Then there's silence. I can almost hear the rebbe taking his
shofar out of his pocket, lifting it up to his lips, puffing up his
mouth.

On his first try, no sound comes out. The second time, we
hear the sound of spit going through the horn. People shift their
feet, then fall silent again. We're all standing, concentrating, waiting, trying to send strength to the rebbe, collecting it and giving it
to him. He must be tired, weakened by his fast and by leading the
service. He always stands through the entire service. His legs must
be weak and his mouth dry, after all the reading and chanting.

Suddenly the sound comes out smooth and strong, a long
blast, three short blasts, a series of short broken blasts, and one
extra-long one. The men sing. Yom Kippur is over. Ma wraps her
white shawl around her shoulders and closes her prayer book. We
start filing out of the synagogue. People stop to wish each other a
happy and healthy New Year. There's a long line in the stairwell.

We walk home in the dark hurriedly, saying little. Everywhere, women and men dressed in white, like angels, are hurrying
home from synagogues. People smile to each other, nod their good
wishes. The whole world is white and pure right now, cleansed,
fully repented. But I'm already dirty. I'm starting the year off
impure.

On our way out, Elke said, "For the rest of my life, I will fast
every single fast, even the little ones no one bothers with."

I don't believe her. She always repents so quickly.

When we get home, Ma pours a quart of milk into the saucepan.
She says, "Sit down and rest. Leah will set the table tonight."

I love her special attention. I want more. If I told her I ate on
Yom Kippur, she would change quickly. She hasn't been good to

me since the library. Maybe she thinks my fasting was enough repentance.

"What about you?" I say, feeling false. "You were fasting too."

"It's your first time," she says. "It's harder the first time."

She pours the hot milk into a tall glass, and I watch the teaspoon of coffee dissolve in the bottom. She stirs the milk with a spoon and hands me the glass. I take it and sit on the chair she pushes up. I sit there right in the middle of the kitchen, as if I would collapse of hunger if I took another step to the table. I sit on the edge and drink slowly. The milk burns down to my stomach. Things look different from the middle of the room. I watch Ma's hurried, perfect movements at the counter. She pauses to sip from her glass. Her special attention makes my having eaten feel like a crime, a sin against her. I want to put her in my chair and do all the work, I want to change places with her; she's the one who's hungry, who fasted all day.

She starts to put a slice of babka on a separate plate for me. "I'll wait till everyone else arrives. I'll eat with the others," I say.

She smiles. "You're learning to like the empty pure feeling," she says. "You're beginning to understand the idea of fasting."

She doesn't suspect a thing. She wouldn't dream that I'd eat three hours away from the end. No one would.

Leah arrives home. "The kids were brats," she says. "Like they wanted to make me work harder for the money. I'm never baby-sitting on Yom Kippur again."

Ma doesn't say anything, but she doesn't need to. Her standing there says, I told you so.

"You were right," Leah says. "I shouldn't have worked on Yom Kippur." She straightens the three twenty-dollar bills on the table.

"What will you spend it on?" I ask.

"I don't know. I think I'll save it for a while."

Ma offers Leah a glass of milk and coffee. She takes a long sip and looks at me. "Are you starving?"

I nod and feel my face turn red. I look down and sip. What would she say if I told her I'd eaten?

Even though I swore I'd never tell Leah a thing, I can't help it. When we're both in bed, I try holding back, try to stop thinking about those pretzels, and I just lie there, knowing I will never sleep unless I tell. I have to.

"You what?" Leah says right out loud.

"Shhh. What do you want to do, announce it?"

She sits up and stares at me, like she doesn't know me or something. I tell her about finding the bag and eating what was in it. She doesn't say anything, just sits there shaking her head. I can see the whites of her eyes in the dark.

"Say something. Don't just sit there," I say.

"You're possessed," she says. "You have a dybbuk inside you."

"A dybbuk? You mean like Faivel?" I laugh.

"I'm serious. You couldn't wait three more hours? On Yom Kippur?"

"There's no such thing as a dybbuk," I say.

"How do you know? Zeldy said you're strange, that something is different about you."

I get up, turn on the light, and look into the mirror. I stand right up near the glass and stare. Faivel's neck and face bulges and turns red and ugly when the dybbuk takes over. A strange deep voice speaks. But it is only my face looking back at me: gray skin, thick lips, wide eyes. Then my eyes stretch thin, and I laugh. I can't be serious when I see myself in the mirror.

I tell Leah, "I'll have to catch myself when the dybbuk starts up. Right at the moment when it tells me to do things. Like the minute before I ate."

Leah says, "You think it's a joke. I'm serious. You have to exorcise it. You will have to go to a rabbi. I can't believe you couldn't wait three more hours."

"I couldn't help it. I don't know what happened."

Leah looks at me. "The dybbuk."

She lies back on her pillow and stops talking. She just keeps looking at me, like she's afraid of me. Then she whispers.

"We can't go to a rabbi. We'll have to get David to help us. He knows the Faivel story."

Dybbuk stories always end at the rabbi's house, with a miracle. The rabbi talks to Faivel's dybbuk, scares it, starves it, prays, and the dybbuk leaves his body with a screech that's heard to the ends of the earth. Then the rabbi puts garlic around Faivel's neck to keep evil spirits away.

In the morning, I'm careful about washing my hands before I get out of bed, the way Father taught us. I lean over the edge and do it slowly and thoroughly. Negel vasser to rinse off the remaining demons of the night.

"If you wake up early and look at the floor," Father said, "you'll see the demons' webbed footsteps in the dust by your bed."

I've never seen them. You need a dustier house, I think.

Ma believes. If someone cuts a finger during the day, or spills something or drops a plate, she says, "Go wash negel vasser again."

Maybe if you believe in something it becomes true.

Father wants Lazar Pal to read parts of his book before he pays Gross Bros. to publish it, and Gita and Ma decide to make a visit of it. They will sit in the kitchen, sipping tea or coffee, whispering and laughing. The men will be at the dining room table, the handwritten pages, narrow slanting Hebrew, in front of them.

David waits for Ma to leave and then raids the freezer. He cuts slivers off the frozen quarters of cake. He loves cake.

"I have to even them all out so Ma can't tell," he says.

Leah and I laugh. He always finds a reason to do what he wants to do.

"Ma will know because your pants will pop. She'll have to let them out again," I say.

But he doesn't care about his weight, even though we call him Fatso.

"We want your help with something," Leah says. "But you have to swear not to ever tell."

"You're not allowed to swear," David says. "We can shake hands on it. A handshake is a contract."

I don't trust him. "Then promise. It's only if you don't plan to keep a promise that you have to worry about it being a sin. Promise you won't ever tell."

"I promise," he says.

"You promise what?" Leah says. "Say the whole thing."

David stands up and says, "I promise never to tell whatever it is you're going to tell me."

We take him into our room, close the door, and tell him about my dybbuk. We don't say anything about my eating on Yom Kippur; we agreed it's better not to. We talk about the library, and he nods impatiently. He already knows about it. He knows about stealing candy; he does it too. What he wants to know is how I manage to get a whole book out of the store without getting caught.

"We have to exorcise her dybbuk," Leah says.

"OK," he says. "But I have to be the rabbi. I'm a boy."

"Why do you think we asked you?" Leah says.

"Then let's do it quickly," I say, "before Ma gets home."

Leah gets wine and the kiddish cup from the cabinet, a candle, a feather, a needle and thread, and garlic. David brings Father's old gartl and a book of psalms. I lock the door to our room.

David laughs, then says, "Lie down on the floor, on your back."

"Faivel sat," I say. I don't like him bossing me. I'm a year older than he is, and I almost regret telling him, telling anyone. But it is impossible to exorcise your own dybbuk.

"Then kneel here in this corner." He laughs again. "This is fun."

"Fun for you," I say.

"Not on your knees. That's idol worshiping," Leah says.

"It doesn't matter," David says impatiently. "If she's possessed, it's not her fault. It's the dybbuk's sin."

He starts reading the first psalm. Leah interrupts. "Does the dybbuk understand Hebrew?"

"It will scare him more if he doesn't understand. What language do you think the rabbi used for Faivel's dybbuk?"

We're all calling the dybbuk a he. It *is* a he, I think.

David reads. "How good is the person who does not walk with the ideas of evil, or stand with sinners, or sit with pranksters. Because if it is God he wants, he engages with and reaches for Him day and night. God knows the ways of the righteous and destroys evil."

He stops reading and tickles the back of my neck with the feather, and I get chills going up and down my spine, like from Elke's fingers. He doubles and triples the long, shiny gartl and swings it over my head like he's hitting me. I duck.

He reads another paragraph and stops to light the candle with a match.

He rubs the warm ash from the match on my forehead and chin. Then he moves my hair away from my neck and drips candle wax on me.

"Ouch. Are you crazy?"

"That was the dybbuk screaming," he says. He wraps the gartl around my waist, and he and Leah pull tight to squeeze the dybbuk up and out through my throat. They move the gartl to my neck, and they pull so hard I can't breathe. I make sounds like I'm choking, like Faivel's dybbuk made. My head feels red. They let go, and David rubs the wax off my skin and shapes it into a ball. Then he turns a page and continues reciting in a monotone. Leah opens the window, and David tosses the wax ball out.

"There goes your dybbuk," he says.

There's no loud screech.

Leah pours wine into the kiddish cup, and we say the blessing together and sip. The leftover wine is rubbed on my forehead and on the red burn from the hot wax. Leah pierces a clove of garlic with the threaded needle, wets her fingers in her mouth the way Ma does, and ties the two ends in a knot. David slips it over my head.

I wonder why dybbuks hate garlic and if this is why Father eats it. Mornings, he slices several cloves and puts it on his buttered bread like jam. He always offers a bite and quotes the Rambam, saying garlic is good for a hundred things.

I walk around feeling no different, except for the burn on my neck, which hurts. I wonder about dybbuk stories, about why Father doesn't say they're nonsense. When we talk about them, he just smiles.

CHAPTER SIX

————————

BRIGHT-ORANGE LIGHT COMES in from the back windows one night after dinner, and when we look out, all of Ashley is lit up. The bungalows are on fire, and Father's in Canada, getting his driver's license. He failed three times here, so he's taking it there, where the roads and drivers are more civilized, he says.

David loosens the staples of the winterizing plastic to look out the window. "Fire trucks," he says. "Four fire trucks."

I lift the plastic off the other corner. There are police cars too. We turn off all the lights to see better, and the room remains bright.

"Your father," Ma says, "is never home when you need him."

"You have nothing to worry about. The police are here," I say.

"Since when are the police nothing to worry about?" Ma says. "Goyim. In America, the children learn to trust goyim."

"Kristallnacht," Levi says, which is what we are all thinking now that Ma has brought it up.

I open the window, and the crackling sound of wood burning comes in. A red flame shoots up, and from the window in the girls' room, Leah announces, "That's Feferkorn's bungalow. Or was."

The smoke is so thick it burns our eyes. "Close all the windows," Ma says. "The house is filling with smoke."

No one listens to her.

"Call the fire department," Sarah says. "Quick. Call."

"They're here, you fool," Levi says. "Don't you see the trucks?"

The fire spreads, more bungalows light up, and the air blowing in on this cold November night is warm. Black ash floats and gets caught on the hair of our arms and in our eyelashes.

"It smells good," David says. "Like a matzo oven."

I inhale the smell of wood burning and can almost taste fresh Passover matzo.

"My white cloths are turning black. Close those windows. I wish your father would call."

"Everyone said this was the last season for Ashley as a colony," I say. "Yosel Kleinman is probably paying the fire department to do this."

"He should have called to tell us about it," Ma says. "He's no mensch, that ganef."

"What if he forgot to tell them about our other bungalow and they burn it down because it's dark and empty?" David says. "They won't know we own it."

"What if they burn us down in the middle of the night, when all the lights are out?" Leah says, trying to outdo him.

We look at each other. There's fear behind the talk. Ma's as afraid as we are, and afraid she doesn't look like a mother.

"I am going out to see what's happening," I announce. "I'll talk to the firemen and show them where we live."

"Not alone," Ma says. "A girl alone. Take David with you. And come back quickly."

David and I put on our coats and walk up Ashley Hill slowly. The smoke burns my eyes.

"You think we should tell them where we live?" David asks. "It could be worse. They could burn us down on purpose."

"You sound like Ma. They're official. They're the government."

From the bottom of the hill, I make out the shapes of firemen in their black shiny coats and hats. They look like dark angels moving in the night. The Bergers' bungalow is on fire when we get there.

David says, "They're burning all of Ashley down. Look, there's Kleinman. He's talking to that fireman."

"Good. When he sees us, he'll remember that we live here, that he can't burn the whole place down."

"He should've asked us first," David says. "Ashley is as much ours as his. We live here. We're the only ones here all winter."

"He's probably paying a lot of money for this," I say. "He's spending money to burn the place down."

I suddenly want to report this fire. I want to call the fire department, like Sarah. Firemen lighting fires is illegal. They're supposed to put them out. But who do you report to when the police are doing wrong?

"What do you think Father will say?" David asks.

"He'll be happy when new houses are built and people move in. He'll have minyan."

"He won't," David says. "Kleinman is a Viznitzer and he'll sell to Viznitzer, who will move here because they want to pray with the Viznitzer Rebbe, not Father. No one wants to pray in a small shtibel. Especially Father's. They laugh at his shtibel. They say they'll buy him out. They want to turn all of Ashley into a Viznitz shtetl."

"They say this in front of you?"

David nods. "At least Ma will be happy. She'll have neighbors all year round. She'll like living in a Chassidic community. She likes Williamsburg."

"Ma won't be happy until she moves back to Jerusalem," I say.

"Then let's tell Kleinman to stop this right now. It isn't doing us any good; we don't want this."

We laugh nervously. We're standing at the back of a fire truck, and Kleinman and the chief, in a red hat, are standing in front of the truck, talking. Kleinman spreads wide his arms, embracing Ashley like an owner. When he points to our bungalow, he scares me.

We watch the firemen move to the next bungalow. They hose down the ground around it with water and then put fire to the wood. Everyone stands back and watches the flames begin, first slow, then leaping fast. There is the sound of glass breaking. My eyes burn. The bungalow is there, and then it's not, and where people once lived, there's nothing. This place, the Gelbs' one summer, the Roths' the next, then the Schweitzers', is gone, is now an empty lot.

I am suddenly angry. We own this place more than Kleinman does. We live here, we know every bungalow, every tree. I can walk around here in my sleep. It isn't money that makes ownership. It's being here, living in and knowing a place. We should have been asked. We have rights. Ashley has rights. It was here first, before us and before Kleinman. Every tree belongs here, has been here longer than we have. The hundred-year-old evergreens and the crazy crab apple trees. There should be laws against burning, destroying. Ashley was built as a summer bungalow colony, and that's how it should stay.

A fireman walks over to where David and I are standing. He

pulls his black gloves off and leans against the fire truck. "Pretty, ain't it," he says.

"No," I say. "We live here. We liked it before."

The man looks at me, surprised. "Where do you live?"

David points out our bungalows.

"Well, we're not touching them. We're doing only this section. About twenty bungalows."

Kleinman sees us but doesn't say anything. We don't matter. We're the children of a man who doesn't matter.

Ma tells Levi, Sarah, and Aaron to close their eyes and go to sleep already. It's late for them, it's after nine. But even with the lights out and the door shut, their room is too bright to sleep in. "A vachnacht," Ma says. "You'll be sorry when you have to get up in the morning."

"Ashley doesn't get burned down every night," I tell Ma. "Let them watch."

"For how long? At eight, I said till nine. Now it's nine-thirty."

They finally fall asleep, all in one bed, and Leah and I have to separate them. In our room, it's bright enough to read without a light on, but I just sit at the window and watch one bungalow after another light up and burn to nothing. Flames are short-lived; they live quickly, briefly, changing second by second. Blue in the middle, white around blue, and red at the edges. I stare into them, not blinking, watching how they take everything with them, how they leave nothing.

———

Father comes home with a Canadian license and a black Chrysler New Yorker made in 1959. It's a year older than me.

"What were you so worried about?" he says. "They can't do anything to us. We own our bungalows and the land around it. We also own part of the lake. There's nothing they can do about that."

"Easy for you to talk," Ma says. "You weren't the one watching the fire from your own windows, at night, alone with a houseful of little children."

Father says, "This will be good for us. The value of our properties will go up. Ashley will become an important Jewish neighborhood."

"A Viznitzer neighborhood," David says.

"There'll be some Viznitzer," Father says. "There will also be Gerer and Karliner and Lubavitch Chassidim. Maybe some Litvishe families. Why only Viznitzer?"

"They laugh at you and say they'll buy you out," I say.

"Who? A few pruste yingen who have nothing better to do. No one pays attention to them. What does it matter what they say? Let them talk. The rebbe and I are good friends; we always were. Whenever he sees me there, he greets me, he calls me up for an aliyeh. And once a year, we spend an hour together talking in his shtibel. Who else has that honor?"

CHAPTER SEVEN

—————

DAVID COMES HOME from school one day, and right away Ma makes him empty his pockets. They're stuffed with Wrigley's spearmint gum and a box of Good & Plenty. Chazir trafe, Ma says, because Wrigley's has gelatin.

I am not the only sinner in this family.

Ma yells, "Eleven and a half years' work, and this is my reward. A sheygetz in my house. Imagine how ashamed I was when Mrs. Schweitzer called to say her Avi saw you buying trafe candy. A bar mitzvah boy. Wait till your father comes home. What will he say? Your poor father. Out on the road, peddling his book from one place to another, and at home his eldest son stuffs himself with chazir."

Father is in Montreal, selling the book that took ten years to write. He borrowed money to print fifteen hundred copies, and now he's visiting yeshivas and synagogues all over, bringing his mystical writings to the world. Young men are advised not to study cabala until forty; there are stories about some who went crazy and stopped believing in God. Father started at thirty.

The book sells for eighteen dollars—eighteen for the letters *chai*—but people are sending thirty-six, fifty-four, seventy-two: double, triple, quadruple life. The money arrives by mail, and Leah and I stuff the books into mailers.

"My secretaries," Father says.

After Canada, he plans to go to Uruguay. There are yeshivas all over the world, some too small to make the trip worthwhile, but Father says, "You never know. You never know where a man must go in his life."

Even when he's home, he's out selling. Now that he's driving, he's always on the road. For lunch, Ma packs a box of whole wheat crackers, a pint of cottage cheese, and scallions. Then she worries all day until she sees him again, home safe. Every morning she reminds him to call when he gets there and again before he leaves. Even if it's only Brooklyn, Ma wants two calls a day. And when the phone doesn't ring, she sits on a chair, not moving, imagining Father in a car accident, in the hospital, dead. When he stays overnight, she worries about where he's sleeping. If there isn't a friend from the old days in Romania or from yeshiva in Israel, Father sleeps in synagogues. He arrives home looking thin and tired. But he likes traveling. Watching him talk about whom he met, what they said, what he learned, anyone would know he loves it. That's what Ma doesn't understand. That her husband is following the way of the wandering Baal Shem, that he's in search of new experiences like Reb Bunam of Pshiskhe. This was the life of the founders of Chassidism, and Father wants to be their disciple. Like the founders, he moved far away, to America, to forsaken Ashley, to start a new community. But somehow he settled near Viznitz, somehow he didn't travel far enough away; maybe he didn't entirely want to.

———

Ma says, "Someone has to teach you. With no father in the house, the son grows up a sheygetz."

David just stands there grinning, and Ma gets angrier. She slaps him, and her handprint, every finger, shows red on David's pale face. Still he grins, defiant. But it's only a cover. He's trying not to cry, and I know exactly how it feels, Ma going on and on. I want to hug him, make him stop grinning, tell him not to hold back, not to show off for us. I know he's sorry, but Ma doesn't see that; she just sees the grin.

"I'll give you something to laugh at," she says. She pushes him out the back door, into the hallway and the entrance to the synagogue. "Get a taste of your father's life. Hunger for a night. Sleep on hard benches. That'll teach you."

If I stick my head out the window in my room, I can see into the synagogue. David is sitting there on a bench, doing what I think is his homework. He sees me, waves, opens a window and shouts across. I make room for Leah, and we shout back and forth, the volume on a tape of the London Jewish boys' choir turned up so Ma doesn't hear us. We decide to string a clothesline between us. We can use it to send messages later tonight, when everyone is in bed. Ma's on the phone with Gita Pal, and it's easy to sneak past her with the roll of twine from the laundry room.

At first David doesn't understand what we're trying to do. "It's simple enough," he says, "to climb out your window."

"Not after dark, when it's cold out and we're in our night-gowns," I explain.

"It will be more fun this way," Leah says.

He isn't excited; he'd rather be inside with us. We start the line anyway. I hold tight on the loose end, and Leah tosses the roll to David. He stands on the bench and leans out one window, stretches and catches the twine, wraps it around the sash and out the other window, and throws the roll back.

We miss, and the twine falls on the ground outside our window. Leah climbs out to get it.

I hear Ma's steps. Shhh, I say. Leah hides.

Ma walks in, turns off the music, and closes the window. "I said not to talk to him. Don't you have homework?"

She doesn't wait for an answer.

I signal to David to wait a few minutes. Ma's setting up the sewing machine in the hallway, and I wait for the whir.

Leah hands me both ends of the twine. I tie them around the hook that holds our curtain and help her climb in. Then I scribble our first note: "Testing, testing, 1-2-3." I clip it to the line and pull. David draws it toward him from his end, and the note arrives quickly. He writes on the back of the piece of paper, clips it on, and we draw it back toward us.

"Send food," it says.

I have a small bag of popcorn left over from recess and I clip it to the rope and send it off.

"The Berlin airlift," Leah says.

We watch David eat the popcorn quickly. "More," he writes on a large piece of paper and holds it up for us to read.

"He doesn't appreciate our airlift," Leah says.

"He will if it gets him food."

I walk into the kitchen and open the fridge.

"What are you looking for?" Ma asks from the hallway.

"A snack."

"Since when are there snacks in the refrigerator?" she asks.

"I want a peanut butter and jelly sandwich."

"Don't reach for the crust," she says.

We all like the crust better than the soft part of a rye. Once a month, Ma orders a case of two-pound loaves of sliced rye from Frank's Bakery. The bread arrives warm and soft, just out of the oven, and we gather at the kitchen table for a snack of buttered ends. Ma lets us have only the ends at the tops of the bags, the rest goes into the extra freezer, so there are always the bottom ones to dig for when she's not home.

I take two large slices, toast them, make the sandwich, and bring it to my room in a Baggie. Ma doesn't look up, as if on purpose.

David's sitting with his head down on the table, and he doesn't see me right away. When he hears the rope, he gets up to see what's coming.

We watch him eat; he's taking big bites out of the bread. "Dessert," he writes in big letters on a piece of paper before he's done with the sandwich. We laugh.

This time, Leah goes out, and she comes back very quickly with a piece of chocolate.

"Where did you get that?"

"From Ma's room. Under her pillow. She has another whole one there."

There are six squares altogether. We keep two for ourselves and send the rest over, four squares for David, more than Ma ever gives anyone. She says she buys it because chocolate gives a nursing mother milk.

David just sits there eating, watching us pull the rope. He doesn't know what's coming. When it gets to him, he puts his sandwich down on the table and takes the Baggie off the line. For a minute we don't see his face. Then he holds up another sheet of paper. "More," it says.

"Now he's being a pig," Leah says.

We watch him sit on the table, facing us, biting into his sandwich. His jaws go up and down quickly.

"He's in a hurry to get to the chocolate," I say.

We tire of watching him, and although I feel bad leaving him all alone with his sandwich, I have to sit down to eat chocolate. Good dark chocolate should always be eaten sitting down, so you can concentrate.

Sarah knocks at our door, and we hide the wrapper. She learned to knock before entering. It took a while.

"We need privacy somewhere," I argued. "Besides, she talks so much; she doesn't stop." Ma advised Sarah to knock.

"Elke's on the phone," she says, looking from me to Leah, trying to figure out what's going on.

The phone is in the kitchen. I take the receiver into the laundry room and jam the door closed on the cord. Ma complains that the cord is tearing because we all do this, even Sarah, who's always trying to be like us. This is the only way to have a private conversation in our house. I start telling Elke about our clothesline, when I hear the sound of a page turning, and there's Levi, sitting in his reading spot on top of the old refrigerator, where no one interrupts him. He looks down at me and smiles. He was here first.

"I can't talk now, Elke."

"I'll do all the talking. Listen. If I sleep over, I could bring all sorts of snacks. We have chocolate and potato chips and licorice. We could stay up all night."

"My mother's not in a good mood. She won't let you."

Elke doesn't have a sister or brother, and she gets bored. Her parents let her do everything; they're not even around most of the time. I like going to her house to study or play, because it's quiet. She wants to come here because it's not. The only rule in her house is that you have to whisper all the time. Mrs. Sklar stays in her room, mostly. She's always lying in her high, fat bed. I try to imagine her climbing into bed. She's short and round, her arms and legs are always puffy, and her eyes look crossed. When I asked

Elke what happened, she said her mother's head was shaved. That all the women had their heads shaved.

Ma says, "Mrs. Sklar's father and brothers were shot in front of her. That's enough to make anyone go cross-eyed."

It's late and we're already in bed when the phone rings, and I can tell it's Father. When he's far away, Ma makes this soft murmuring sound, like she's about to cry. Leah and I listen to hear if she tells him about David, but the clothesline starts to creak and we get up to pull in a note.

"I'm cold. Send a pillow and blanket," it says.

We start laughing and quickly hide our heads in our pillows. Ma warns us with a hiss from her room. Every light in the synagogue is on, and we can see David clearly. He's huddled up in his jacket and lying on his back on the table, a holy place, a place for books. He should be sleeping on a bench, like people in stories.

Ma comes into our room, her white nightgown flapping, her voice angry and whispering. She sees the open window, sees the twine, and sees David on the table. She steps up to the window and pulls the line, testing it, and laughs, forgetting herself.

"You did this all today?" she asks. "I can use it to hang up wet laundry."

She looks at David. "What does he want?" she asks.

Leah hands her the note. "He's cold."

Ma walks out of our room, not saying anything. We try to signal David, but our room is dark. We see him but he can't see us, and before we can write and send a note, Ma's at the back door, calling him in a loud, hoarse whisper we can hear all the way from our room. I get out of bed and follow her. David stands at the back door, crying. He's not grinning anymore, he's crying, and he seems younger. Cold can turn anyone into a baby.

"Are you hungry?" Ma asks.

He shakes his head left to right, and tears roll down his round cheeks. "Then into pajamas quickly," Ma says. "And not a word."

She sees me standing in the hallway and says, "Enough already. You'll wake the others, and soon we'll have another vachnacht."

Ma closes and locks the back door and walks to the front door to make sure it's locked. When Father's home, the doors remain unlocked and no one thinks about it. But alone, Ma's afraid. I wait for her to get back to her room, into bed, but she goes into the kitchen and I hear her open the refrigerator door, clank a pot down on the stove. I hear the hiss of the stove when it catches. I go into the kitchen to be with her. She's warming a glass of milk for David.

I stand at the door to the kitchen in my blue print nightgown trimmed with white eyelet, the one Leah says looks like a Laura Ashley. Ma sees me and smiles. I step closer, lean over the stove, and watch the milk move in circles with the heat. Ma's on the other side of the stove, by the sink, her arms around her body for warmth. It's crisp cool outside, early March. We both stare into the fire.

"A watched pot," Ma says and stops, smiles, not finishing the sentence, not really minding how long the milk takes to boil.

"You'll be tired in the morning," she says, looking at me. "At your age you still need eight hours of sleep. You shouldn't read so late. Levi too. He reads late at night in the dark. You're ruining your eyes, and you'll need glasses. A girl in glasses."

My breath gets stuck in my throat. She knows we read.

She smiles. "What did you think? That I didn't know? A mother knows everything. I hear the pages turn."

She sticks her pinkie in the milk to see if it's warm enough, grasps the hot saucepan with her bare hand, and pours into a glass.

I wonder how much she knows. She wouldn't be smiling if she knew about the library books. With Ma, so much depends on her mood. Tonight she's soft and giving. Maybe because she spoke to Father. Tonight she's in a good mood after Father. When he's home, she's mostly angry at him for being away so much, for leaving her all alone, and for planning to build a new synagogue. She can't argue too much about his traveling, because the book is bringing in money. Father's already planning a second printing.

She carries the glass out and I follow her to David's bed and she lets me. Leah's in there with him.

Ma hands David the glass and says, "Drink it and then, all three of you, go to sleep. Good night."

She walks across the hallway to her room, leaving us there to talk. At the door, she stops to kiss the mezuzah with her fingertips. The light from the lamp in her room glows through her thin nightgown, and I can see the outline of her legs, her white underwear. She moves her arm, and for a second I see the shape of her body, the curving under her arms.

David's already in his pajamas. He drinks in small sips, not stopping to say anything. He hands me the empty glass and pulls the covers over his head. He doesn't want to talk.

I have a hard time falling asleep, thinking about David in trouble, about me liking him in trouble, and I remain wide awake feeling mean, feeling as if I'd wished it. I try to think myself away from this feeling, and suddenly I remember what Ma said in the kitchen. I tell Leah.

She grumbles, "That's all? I was just starting to fall asleep."

CHAPTER EIGHT

SARAH COMES OUT and chants, "We're going away. We're going away."

She's gotten into chanting lately. It used to be she just talked all the time. She talked so much Ma called her a talking machine. Now she chants.

"We're going to Sea Gate. Ma says we're going to Sea Gate. In Father's car."

I am sitting on the brick flower box at our front door. We've long since given up growing anything in there; it's just a hard bench with dirt in the center. On special days, Ma sticks pink plastic flowers in the dirt. She bought them for David's bar mitzvah.

"Ma says to get ready, to start packing," Sarah continues breathlessly.

Family trips. With our luck, the radiator will spring a leak or we'll run out of gas. That's what happened on the Tappan Zee the last time we tried to go somewhere. Father had to walk across the bridge to a gas station and bring back a gallon of gasoline.

Ma comes to the door, wiping her hands on her terry-cloth apron. "How about it? We're thinking of going to Sea Gate for a few days. Father wants to see the Satmar Rebbe. We can go to the ocean. The children will love it. I've never been to the ocean in America."

Aaron and Esther come up behind Ma. Esther pulls her finger out of her mouth just long enough to lisp, "Sea Gate."

Sea Gate. The gate to the sea. I would love to swim in salty water. The Bobbsey Twins went to a place called Nantucket one summer. If only David and Leah were here; I'd have more fun if they were going too. But David's in yeshiva and Leah's working as a mother's helper in the Kerhonksen girls' camp this summer. Ma convinced Father that it's a good job, that she knows the head counselor, Mrs. Leifer, and that it would be good for Leah to be in camp with other Chassidic girls. I am working at the Glickmans' again this year. If I go to Sea Gate, I'll have to get Elke to substitute. She stayed home to sew this summer. She decided to teach herself how to sew, and every time I see her, she's starting something new. Already she has five new outfits for school.

"What about Levi?" I ask Ma.

"I called. They're letting him out of cheder early. Father's picking him up on the way back from the gas station."

I don't know if I want to go. The car always overheats in the summer. And going will mean being around them the whole time, forty-eight hours of no privacy. Ma's standing at the door, waiting for my answer, my nod. She does not want a no.

"It's a long way," I say. "And with Father driving."

"I should be the one worrying about Father's driving," she says. "But better than sitting home and worrying. And I need you. I can't take care of all the children by myself."

"You'll have Father," I say, knowing this is no answer, knowing how much help he is with children.

Ma doesn't answer. She turns to go back to the kitchen and says, "Then we won't go."

Sarah stops chanting. "You're so mean. Say you'll come, pleeeease."

Esther stands at the door with her big brown eyes. She sucks her finger and curls her hair at the same time.

"Say yes, yes, yes," Aaron says. His green eyes dance.

"OK, maybe."

Sarah doesn't wait to hear more. Already she's in the kitchen, telling Ma, who's cradling the phone between her neck and chin and packing cans of sardines, hard-boiled eggs, bread and butter, into a brown Waldbaum's bag. She knew all along I would come. She's already telling Gita Pal that we're going.

She covers the mouthpiece and says, "Start packing. Two sets of clothes for each child."

"What about swim clothes?"

"It's mixed swimming—men and women. Maybe for the younger ones. Pack something for Esther and Aaron."

Already I am sorry I said maybe. Clothes on the beach are unnatural. Father wears a long black coat and hat on the hottest days of summer.

Sarah, Aaron, and Esther pull me along to their rooms, and I let them. Ma washed laundry yesterday, so all their favorite clothes are in the dresser. Sarah's favorite jumper was once mine, and Esther's was once Sarah's. We can all be identified as Benjamins by our clothes. Each piece stays in the family; there's always someone who'll grow into it.

Ma comes in. "Father will be back any moment. Then we can leave."

I go to my room, thinking he'll never get back from the gas station—they'll tell him the car needs work. Or he'll get stuck somewhere. Sea Gate is only two hours away, but it will take us four. Even when a good thing happens in our family, it's never perfect. We're so used to not having things the way they should be that if something's too good, Ma says knock on wood.

Father gets home and says the car is making a noise.

"A new one?" Ma asks.

"No. But I should call Mr. Davis. Maybe he can tell me what the problem is over the telephone." He takes off his hat and looks through all the pieces of paper he keeps tucked inside along the rim. A portable file. Mr. Davis's phone number is scribbled somewhere, and finding it will take a while. Also, Mr. Davis lives in Williamsburg. Father doesn't trust just anyone. He likes a mechanic who speaks Yiddish, a religious mechanic who won't cheat him.

Levi and Sarah start pushing and elbowing each other. Esther puts her finger in her mouth and closes her eyes. Ma acts as if this sort of thing is a complete surprise, as if she never thought it could happen. After every car trip with Father, she swears never again, even though Father says not to swear. Then she forgets. That's why she can still live with him. That's how women live with their husbands.

Mrs. Davis says her husband went to a car auction with a client and that he won't be home till later.

"Perfect," Father says. "We'll stop in Williamsburg. It's on the way."

I wonder how far out of the way it is.

Ma begins bustling. She wipes Levi's face with the tip of her apron, wets her fingertips in her mouth, and curls his locks.

"Nothing works as well as spit," she always says.

She works quickly, going from Levi to Aaron, then to Sarah, whose hair is stick straight and always in her face no matter how much spit is used. Even barrettes don't stay in her hair for long. Esther gets a curl on top of her head; a kokosh, Ma calls it. They each know to stand still for this finishing touch.

We carry the bags out to the car and wait for Father. He finally comes to the door, reaches his hand up to the mezuzah, kisses it, steps out with his right foot for good luck, and locks up behind him. He looks perfectly neat, his black shoes and his European leather briefcase freshly polished. They shine like new. He puts the briefcase on the floor between himself and Ma, folds his coat up above his waist smoothly, and sits in the driver's seat.

The dashboard in the old Chrysler seems designed to make Father slower than he already is. It has buttons instead of the handle other cars use for shifting gears. Father leans forward to push the reverse button, then backs out of the driveway. He does it all so slowly, watching him makes me want to jump out of my skin. With him driving, you feel as if you're standing still all the way to your destination. I try thinking about other things.

We take the New York State Thruway south to the Palisades and the George Washington Bridge, then the FDR Drive forever. I read cigarette ads that have nothing to do with cigarettes. Understandably, I think, because there's nothing you could say about smoking that would stop my nausea as soon as I smell the smoke. Ma and I watch out for cars with wild or anti-Semitic drivers. We can tell when people look at us that way: they stare at Father, at his hat and his locks. They laugh. Ma keeps telling Father to go slow: slowly, slowly, as if we're not crawling already. I tell him when to switch lanes or let someone get ahead. At stoplights, we have to tell him when to start up again, because he's reading from his psalm book. When I say he shouldn't be reading behind the wheel—it makes other drivers angry—he says, "What's the hurry? They should run as fast to do God's will."

The traffic in Brooklyn is heavy, and even with all the windows down, there's no breeze to dry our sweaty faces. My skin is hot and wet like the steamy air, and my legs are glued to the seat. We get off the Brooklyn–Queens Expressway in Williamsburg. It's good timing, Ma says, because everyone has to use the bathroom and we're hungry. In books, people never go to the bathroom.

The streets are quiet. Most Chassidic families are in the Catskills for the summer. We get out on Lee near Hooper, at Jerusalem Falafel, and Father drives to Mr. Davis on Marcy, where a can of oil and a few turns of a few screws under the hood satisfy Father. The noise continues.

Ma orders six half falafel with hot sauce and a whole one to go for Father. He doesn't eat in restaurants, in public. She gives me a dollar and sends me next door to get a quart of milk. Milk is the best way to soothe a tongue burning with hot sauce.

After eating, we walk up Lee to Kauff's Bakery. Everyone has to hold someone's sweaty hand when we walk in the city. I am holding Aaron's, which isn't easy because he is taking hops and jumps on the sidewalk, imitating Sarah, who's playing hopscotch on the squares.

Ma buys a dozen hard rolls for tomorrow and three black-and-white cookies for dessert now. She breaks them in half so everyone gets both colors.

It's almost dark when we finally get to Sea Gate, and the guard at the gate asks whom we are visiting.

"The Satmar Rebbe," Father says.

The man nods and waves us through. We wonder about the gate, which separates Sea Gate from the rest of Brooklyn.

"An excellent thing," Father says. "It makes Sea Gate safe."

The streets are dark with trees, and we can hear and smell the ocean. The hotel is white and large. A sign on the door says "No Vacancy."

Father parks the car and goes in to ask about rooms. It's cool here, and I wish we'd brought sweaters. Ma talks to a woman sitting on a bench.

She says, "Rooms here are booked months in advance. You won't find anything for the night."

Ten minutes later, Father comes out to tell us the same thing. The woman, who introduces herself as Mrs. Itzkowitz, says to try some of the old houses with Room to Let signs. We pile back into the car and drive around in the dark. It's hard to see behind the trees and bushes, and I get out to look for signs. A woman sitting on the porch of her house says, "What are you looking for?"

When I tell her, she gets out of her chair and comes over to the car to look.

"How many children do you have?" she asks and begins to count.

"May her eyes and teeth fall out of her head," Ma says in Yiddish. Everyone knows not to count children, not to cast the evil eye.

The woman's voice gets higher, and it shakes. "You come all this way with five children, and you don't even think to make reservations? What kind of parents are you?"

In a quiet voice, Father asks, "Do you know a place we could stay the night?"

The woman says, "You should have thought of that before you left home."

I know Father's not good at things, but hearing an adult and a stranger question his ability makes me want to cry. Esther is asleep on Ma's lap. Levi and Aaron are leaning on each other, dozing. Sarah's only half awake.

The woman is still shaking her head. "Try Mrs. Blackwell,"

she says. "Twenty-one Jefferson. She once rented rooms. Maybe she'll do it for one night."

We drive around, looking for Jefferson. Ma's angry now. She calls Father a shlepper. In a low voice, not to wake the children, she says, "You call this a vacation?"

At number 21, Ma says, "Rachel, go knock at the door."

"Let Father go," I say. "It's his fault."

She turns to him. "Even your daughter has no respect for you."

Without answering, Father pushes the button that says Neutral, sets the brake, and gets out of the car. Watching his long back stop at the door and then go indoors, I'm sorry I said anything, sorry I gave Ma a chance to use my words to hurt him.

"That's how you talk to a father?" she says. "Is that what they teach you in school?"

They're always blaming my school for everything. As if I couldn't learn this on my own, or from her. "You called him a shlepper," I say.

"I'm his wife, you're his daughter. Remember that."

Father comes back and says to go look. Ma says, "It's not as if we have much choice. Are there beds?"

"Go see for yourself," he says, afraid to decide for us, afraid of what we might say after. He stays in the car, and Mrs. Blackwell takes us up to the attic. There are three large rooms up there, but not enough beds. We'll have to share.

We park the car and unload. I wake Levi and Sarah, and carry Aaron up the stairs. Ma carries Esther, and Father carries the bags. Aaron's getting heavier and heavier these days, and by the top of those narrow stairs, he weighs a ton. Everyone is tired and cold now. In the attic, the mattresses are bare; there are no sheets or blankets anywhere. Ma sends me down to ask Mrs. Blackwell about linens.

She says, "I'll see what I can find and bring it up."

I say I'll wait. I don't want her coming up. Seeing all of us crowding her attic might change her mind about letting us stay. She gives me four white sheets and two towels.

There is a light in the sky that turns and brightens the room every other minute. It's a coast guard light, Father says, and when everyone is in bed, I sit by the dark window and wait for it to come back and light up my face. There's a rhythm going between the ocean and the light: five waves crash to every revolution. It's hypnotic, and I fall in love with this place without having seen it.

Sarah and I share a bed, and during the night it gets so cold we use the folded draperies stacked in a closet as blankets. In the morning, our skin is red and we can't stop scratching.

Ma looks at the draperies and says, "Fiberglass material, that's why."

For breakfast, we each eat a cold hard-boiled egg and a roll. Ma doesn't want to trouble Mrs. Blackwell any more than she has to. We're all still hungry when we leave the big house and go for a walk around Sea Gate.

Ma wheels Esther in the stroller, Aaron and Levi hold on to the sides, and Sarah skips beside me. Our skin is still prickly, and we stop to scratch each other's backs. Father got up early this morning and went to the synagogue. The Satmar Rebbe has a summer house here, and Father's hoping he'll be allowed to see him. He wants to ask the rebbe about building a new synagogue. If the rebbe gives his blessing to go ahead, Ma will have to agree.

The streets are wide and shady, and dark Victorian houses stand tall on both sides of the road. The old slate sidewalk rings under our shoes. Does anyone live near the ocean all year? I look for a school building.

Families flip-flop to the beach, with tubes around their waists and towels over their arms. I want to see the water, but we're dressed all wrong for it: I am wearing a pleated navy skirt, white tights, and a white shirt. We always travel wearing blue and white. Ma wears a blue dress and a matching print kerchief on her head.

We're heading toward the hotel, because Ma wants to see if she knows anyone here. Sea Gate has become a vacation spot for Chassidim ever since the Satmar Rebbe started coming. We walk past his house, and I think it is the ugliest one on the block. It's not old and tall like the others. It's a low, boxy, pale-brick building.

"I don't know why they went to the trouble of getting rid of a beautiful old house to build a new ugly one," Ma says. "They probably thought they were doing something special for the rebbe. No taste. Chassidim have no taste."

Mrs. Itzkowitz is there again in front of the hotel. She asks Ma about last night, and they talk, Mrs. Itzkowitz with an accent like Father's, Romanian. This is what Ma likes best about vacations: she likes meeting and talking to people.

I listen to them for a while and then lose interest, until I notice they are looking at me. Mrs. Itzkowitz's eyes are on my body. She says, "I can always tell when a girl is almost there. It's in the hips. They start showing."

I wait for her to say more, to hear if mine show yet, but she doesn't continue. I look at everyone's hips. At the beach, I know, I can see hips out in the open.

Mrs. Itzkowitz finally goes in to have lunch, and Ma starts to wheel the stroller again. We head toward the ocean. It's warm now that the sun is overhead. It would be nice to jump into cool water.

Getting there takes longer than it should. We walk down several roads and find out you can't just walk in the direction of the ocean; there are fences. You have to go to the gate, where someone checks your seasonal pass or charges three dollars per person. Everything costs. You could hike to the end of the world, and someone would be there to charge you.

Ma says, "Three dollars per person. We'll be throwing eighteen dollars into the water."

I argue. "What else did we come for?"

She says, "You can't go in the water anyway. Men and women together. Naked. You shouldn't even be seeing this."

I don't answer. I'm hot and angry. I'm sorry I came. We may as well have stayed home, if we can't go into the water. After coming all this way, I'll never get near the ocean.

"Let's go eat lunch," Ma says. "Father's probably wondering where we are."

In daylight, Mrs. Blackwell's house doesn't look so tortured and spooky, just large. A dark Victorian house with gables, like the houses on the covers of Victoria Holt books.

Inside, Father's eating a buttered roll with tomatoes and garlic. There's no table; he's sitting cross-legged in front of a cardboard box. He looks perfectly satisfied sitting there, eating raw garlic. With all the garlic he eats, he must be the healthiest human being on earth.

Ma opens two cans of sardines and slices the rest of the large red tomato. She asks where the store is, and Father says, "We'll go there later. There are two aisles filled with kosher food. Chassidim have influence here in Sea Gate. We can buy a good dinner there."

I say it costs three dollars per person to get into the water.

"That's the mind of the goy," Father says, shaking his head. "He wants money for what's not his, for what God created. We will go later in the afternoon, when the sun is lower in the sky.

We'll find a nice quiet spot, where we won't have to pay anything and there will be no nakedness to look at."

I'm not meant to see naked hips.

"What are we going to do until then?" I ask.

Father doesn't answer, and I can see that he and Ma plan to lie down and rest. Aaron is already in bed for his afternoon nap. Esther has to sleep too. It's strange how Ma and Father can go back to bed a few hours after waking. They do it on Saturdays too, after synagogue and lunch. Leah and I are expected to keep everyone quiet. I wonder if they will do it in a strange bed, in someone else's house.

I could walk on the sand, swim in the ocean, look at naked men and women. I have money with me to pay for my ticket. It's quiet in this big house now; Levi and Sarah are playing checkers. This is the best time to sneak away; now or never. It would be easier to do if Leah were here. She could stay and watch Sarah and Levi. If Ma got up, she could say I went out for a walk. I could tell Levi and Sarah that's what I'm doing. Going for a walk. But I don't. I read, for the third time, the Harlequin book I brought along.

The supermarket is at the edge of Sea Gate, near the wire fence that surrounds this whole town. The YMCA is here also, and we stop to see if there's anything to do. The bulletin board lists ceramics classes, judo, ballet. Nothing we can do without belonging already. There's a sign that says the swimming pool is closed until mid-September.

In the store, we buy things we never even look at back home. Ma lets us have chips, hot dogs, sauerkraut, and mustard. For dessert, chocolate-chip cookies. She says we'll get Mrs. Blackwell to boil the package of hot dogs for our dinner. I feel better looking forward to a good dinner. Ma opens the bag of cookies and lets everyone have two for now.

In aisle six, there are fat soft-cover books, but I'm afraid to try anything, with Ma and Father here.

It's four in the afternoon when we come out of the supermarket. "A good time to go bathe in the ocean," Father says. "The sun is low enough; we won't burn red like Polish peasants."

He leads us to the tip of Sea Gate, past a low fence, where we shouldn't be. We walk around the fence and over dunes to get to the water. From here, the lighthouse is in full view. Father and Levi walk farther down, past the dunes, away from us because they're men.

Sarah takes off her shoes and tights, and I help Aaron with his shoes and socks. Ma sits on the sand, with Esther at her side. She doesn't even take off her black stockings; she's worried about someone seeing her. Maybe she's ashamed of her blue swollen veins. I take off my tights, lift my skirt, and wade into the water.

"Be careful. You can get pulled in," she says.

When a wave hits, the hem of my skirt gets wet. I want to dip and splash into the water, all the way, over my head. But I don't have a change of clothes with me. I lift my skirt higher and go in deeper. A wave comes, and the bottom of my underpants gets cold and wet like a warning. The water sways higher and lower, teasing. I take another step and a wave comes, and I have to lift up my skirt to keep it dry. My underpants are wet and heavy, weighted, pulling down to the ocean floor. The water, too, pulls hard, calling, but from the top of the dune, Ma's face disapproves. I have a choice: I have to say yes to one and no to the other. I want to get all wet. Wet, my clothes will stick so hard it will be like going naked. I can peel them off and let myself float away to the middle of the Atlantic. I can swim and swim with nothing on. I wonder what that would feel like, swimming naked. Here, in this big wide ocean, I can stay deep enough in the water, and Ma will never know. Without clothes on, I will be naked Eve in the garden before the sin. Eden is an ocean, a wide blue ocean. I look at the land, at the edge, where the water foams, a curvy surf line. Sarah and Aaron are collecting shells and smooth rocks. I want to stay here forever, come here to our private spot every day, live here. If we lived here, Ma would get used to our going by ourselves to the water. You can't be near an ocean and not get wet at least once a day. If I lived here, I could come alone and swim. When I grow up, I will live here. I wonder why the whole world doesn't want to move to Sea Gate. I will move here alone, without Ma and without Father. Alone and free, without anyone. I want to tell someone, I want to say it out loud, make it come true, but there's only Ma to talk to. I pull myself back to the edge, out of the water, to tell her. Under my skirt, my underpants hang heavy and cold.

"Rachel, you're old enough not to lift your skirt up like that," Ma says. "You're old enough to know better." She's speaking softly, as if the sun has quieted her.

"There's no one here to see me," I say.

"God always sees," she says.

"God sees underneath my clothes too. He sees me naked."

"That has nothing to do with it. You know that." Her voice is harder. "It's a matter of modesty. A girl who can lift her skirt like that is a pruste meude."

I don't say anything about living here.

Father and Levi come back with their hair wet and their clothes dry. They look completely cooled off and comfortable. It is obvious that they removed all their clothes and went in for a good swim. But they're men, and they're not ashamed of their bodies. They are not the sinning Eves we are.

Levi shows me the goose bumps on his skin, and seeing how

refreshed he and Father are, I don't forgive Ma. I watch her dust
the sand off her dress, her pale skin shiny and sandy.

At dinner, we sit in a circle on the floor and eat boiled hot dogs
with plenty of sauerkraut and mustard. Ma passes out seconds,
and Father tells stories about summer visits to the Black Sea. I eat
two hot dogs, and my stomach is quiet. We have only four plastic
cups for drinking. Ma pours orange soda, passes the cups out, and
then takes them back for another round. Sarah, Levi, and Aaron
are falling asleep in their clothes. Ma and I get them into pajamas.
    Father wants to go for a walk, but Ma is too tired. "Take
Rachel," she says.
    We walk, and Father tells me about the Gypsies who camped
out on the farms in Romania. He takes long, smooth strides that
give us enough time to see things. He's elegant in an old European way, walking with his back straight. Older women admire
him. He's carrying a copy of his book, to give to the Satmar
Rebbe.
    "This might be a good time," Father says. "He was too busy
this morning. It shouldn't take long; they only let you stay a few
minutes."
    Father goes in, and I cross the street to sit on a bench. I can
see into the house, even though the curtains are drawn. I see dark
shadows of Chassidic men walking back and forth, across the
room. The only woman in that house is the rebbe's wife. I think
she must be lonely, with only men around. I look at all the windows and wonder which room is hers.
    On the dark street, a group of old people walk by, their arms
linked. People who live here all year are mostly old.
    Father finally comes out. He doesn't see me, and I stay where
I am, watching him. He waits calmly, not worried, confident that I

will show up at any minute. He doesn't get frantic, the way Ma would. I get up and walk over.

He puts his arm on my shoulder. "The rebbe said he heard about my book and looks forward to reading it. He gave me his blessings for the synagogue and a thousand dollars to start pouring a foundation."

"Did you tell him Ma doesn't want a synagogue?" I ask.

Father doesn't answer. He didn't explain that his wife is against it. The rebbe wouldn't have given his blessings if Father explained about Ma. He didn't tell the rebbe that there's no money for it and that Ma threatens to leave, to move back to Israel the day he lays the foundation for a new synagogue.

"A Barditchever synagogue in America," Father says, with a smile on his face. "Not just a small shtibel. I'll start a Barditchever yeshiva, and with God's help it will blossom into a house of study for the finest young scholars. If the Barditchever Rebbe, may his soul rest in peace, wants, it will become a lively new center of Chassidus, the way Barditchev was in Europe before the war."

Father looks at me and continues smiling. "And for my daughters, I will handpick the best of the Barditchever scholars."

"I want to live here in Sea Gate," I tell Father. "You'll have to find someone who agrees to live here."

Father smiles. "If the Satmar Rebbe continues coming here summers, it's possible. Maybe by then there will be a small yeshiva here in Sea Gate."

CHAPTER NINE

———

NOW THAT HE drives, Father likes going places, and for the High Holidays we're trading apartments with a Viznitz family from Williamsburg, so they can be with their rebbe and we can pray with ours.

We load everything into the Chrysler. It's the day before Rosh Hashanah, a cool fall day, perfect weather for going places. It's the kind of weather you expect but don't get for your first day back to school, the kind of day you wait for all the long, hot summer. The cool stirring air whips my hair around and makes me feel strong. In this weather, I can go anywhere, do anything.

David sits tall in the front seat between Ma and Father, a yeshiva boy home for the holidays. He looks like Father, with his black hat and his swinging black peyos.

"Take your hat off," Leah tells him. "You're blocking my view."

As his argument, David looks at Father who's wearing his hat. "But you're in the middle," Leah says. "It's worse in the middle."

Father takes his hat off and hands it to David. "Hold them both in your lap. A Chassid always considers another's comfort first."

David puts his hat in his lap. Things are only right if Father's doing them.

The leaves crunch under the tires backing out of the driveway. Ma says, "Remember, go slow. You promised me you will drive only slowly."

Father says, "We'll have a safe trip because we're traveling to be with the rebbe. The rebbe's holiness will keep us safe."

All week Ma cooked, froze, and jarred. We're bringing along frozen everything: soup, fish, and meat. She packs paper plates, plastic bowls, forks, and spoons. Napkins, tissues, paper towels, foil, Baggies. We use so much paper, it makes you wonder how people did without.

"It's not that we can't buy these things there," she says. "It's a city. But there will be enough to do when we get there, all the last-minute things. We can use a shopping cart like city people."

The rooms in the Williamsburg apartment are lined up in a row: one room leads into the next and the next and the next, like a train; that's why it's called a railroad flat, Father says. You have to walk through every room to get to the last one, where Leah, Sarah, and I will sleep. From our windows you can see the elevated trains. We're on the second floor, almost even with the tracks, and with a long broomstick I could almost touch the moving train. Black metal gates cover all the windows in this apartment. Listening to the sounds of the street, the cars, and the trains, I don't sleep well. I don't know how anyone can sleep in a city. Leah and I lie side by side on our stomachs for a while. I'm on the high-rise bed next to her, and we're both facing the windows. Even in the middle of the night, things are constantly moving. The traffic lights flash green-yellow-red, and our room changes color with it. All the lights inside are off, but it's never completely dark, the way it is at home. Every time a train comes, the room lights up, a blue-orange glow like early morning before the sun rises. The lights move across the walls, over Sarah's sleeping face, then on the floor.

There's a German train in the book I'm reading, and the sounds of the train outside my window mix with the sounds in the book. I look up every time a new train comes down the tracks. Leah and I look for the J or M sign, counting how many of each there are in an hour. We hear them coming when they stop five blocks away at Hewes Street; their screeching brakes sound distant, but the tracks outside our windows rumble. We can see into the cars. There are people going places in the middle of the night, mostly men. In my book, escaped American and British prisoners steal the German train and try to take it through Germany, across the border into Switzerland. They crawl onto the roof of the moving train and kill all the German soldiers guarding the cars. I ride on the roof of the J train in my dream.

Father and David come home from early-morning prayers at the synagogue with a dozen fresh hard rolls, cream cheese, butter, and milk, and Ma laughs at how fast we eat the rolls. They're so soft inside, it's like eating air.

Father says, "It feels good walking in the fresh morning air, not driving. The air feels pure this morning, maybe in honor of the New Year. You can feel the holy rebbe's presence in the air."

Ma wants to get an early start. She says, "Later in the day, there will be crowds everywhere. Rachel, you can come with me in the morning, and Leah will come with me in the afternoon."

I want our first stop to be Fixler's Dresses, but Ma says it won't be open this early. Not until ten. We walk down Lee to the fruit and vegetable store, and Ma buys ripe cactus fruit, kiwi, fresh purple figs, pomegranate, papaya, and mango. The cactus fruit, Ma says, are never the way they are in Israel, blood-red sabras dripping juice. Even though these fruits are very expensive, women crowd around the baskets, sniffing, pinching, and picking. Everyone wants to say the blessing for new fruit on the New Year.

Our next stop is the bookstore, where Ma buys new yarmulkes and fringes for Father and the boys. At Wiesner's Dry Goods, I pick out lacy white tights for Esther and, for Leah, Sarah, and me, tights with a new diamond pattern. Everyone will be wearing them tonight and tomorrow. Williamsburg girls always wear the latest styles. For herself, Ma buys two pairs of black stockings with seams and a new white apron and kerchief. Then we walk to Fixler's Dresses. I am so excited I feel like skipping.

Mrs. Fixler shows us a high-waisted navy pleated dress with white cuffs, a round collar, and a thin red ribbon bow. "This is a very fine dress," she says. "From England."

Ma says, "You have anything with a regular waist? She has a nice figure. Why hide it?"

Mrs. Fixler says, "I don't have any holiday dresses with a lower waist. This is what young girls are wearing these days. I do have it in another color."

With a metal hook, she reaches up to a rack and brings out the same dress in beautiful pale gray, and right away I love it. I don't have any gray. All my clothes are navy or plaid. This is different, soft.

Mrs. Fixler says, "Let her try it on. It suits girls well."

Ma nods and sends me to the back with Mrs. Fixler, who doesn't hand me the dress to put on by myself. She comes with me as if I can't dress myself, and I'm glad I thought to wear a slip so she doesn't see me in my underwear. Her dry fingers on my skin are like rough grass, and preparing for the next touch, trying to figure out where it will be, is like following a moving itch. She zips me up and walks out with me to show Ma.

"Very elegant," Ma says. "Father will certainly like it. Turn around, let me see you."

"Is there a mirror anywhere?" I ask Mrs. Fixler.

She points to the back of a door, but the store is dark and so full of dresses that it's hard to see. I wish I could buy seven new dresses at once, one for every day of the week. I could be completely new each day. I walk back and forth in front of the mirror, watching the way the wide pleats flap and fall back in place. I want to hop up and down, see how it will look during jump rope or sticks, but I don't in front of Mrs. Fixler.

When Ma hears that the dress is forty dollars, her lips get tight and thin, a line. She can't afford it.

The phone rings, and while Mrs. Fixler talks, I walk over to Ma and quietly say I have enough saved up for this dress. She smiles and puts her hand on my hair to move the bangs off my forehead. I take all the bills out of my purse and give them to her. She counts them quickly, gives me back two fives, slips the rest into her pocket, and walks over to look at dresses in her size as if nothing happened. She doesn't want Mrs. Fixler to know I'm paying.

Mrs. Fixler finishes on the phone and asks, "Is there anything else I can show you today, Mrs. Benjamin?"

Ma smiles. "Unfortunately I don't fit into dresses as nicely as my daughter does. I have a younger daughter, who will want a new dress too. I'll bring her in before Yom Kippur."

Ma unzips the dress for me, and the sound of the zipper and the cool air rushing in on my shoulders and back make shivers go up and down my spine. I'm sorry the zipper is so short, a girl's-size zipper. I want Ma to keep going up and down, up and down, to make it last longer, her soft fingers on my back.

Now that I am buying the dress, Mrs. Fixler lets me take it off by myself.

I come out wearing my blouse and skirt and walk up to the counter where Ma is standing. Mrs. Fixler folds the dress and wraps it in white tissue paper, and I walk out, swinging the crinkling bag.

Ma stops in front of Zelda's Buttons and says, "Let's go in here for a minute. I haven't been here in a long time."

She talks to Mrs. Zelda like they're old friends. Mrs. Zelda waves her hand over all the ribbon, and Ma sorts through rolls and finally asks for three yard-long pieces of black velvet, the one-inch width. She puts one around my head and turns me toward the mirror to see how I look with my hair pulled back in a ribbon. In old photographs, Leah and I have big white bows in our hair.

"It will go with your new dress," Ma says.

I agree, but it makes my shag look little-girlish, not like a shag is supposed to look. But for the holiday, black velvet ribbon seems right. The girls in Williamsburg have their hair in pageboys and China dolls, no shags. The beauty salons here don't even show pictures of shags in the windows.

For every day, Ma buys a yard of navy with white polka dots and red with white polka dots. Mrs. Zelda folds all the ribbon and puts it in a small brown bag. Ma pats the bag smooth and places it in a compartment in her black pocketbook. She snaps her pocketbook closed and smiles. I think she wanted to buy something with her own money, something to add to my dress.

On Lee, Ma keeps meeting women she knows. They stop to talk and wish each other a good and blessed year. Even busy days are fun in a city. Here, women aren't stuck in the house, cleaning and cooking all day. Ma talks about the people she meets, where they're from, whom they married, and how many children they have.

Here in Williamsburg she's different, and I wish we could live here. Here she wouldn't be so alone, without friends. Here she'd be happy.

In the afternoon, Ma's too tired to walk down the stairs again. "I'm not used to the city pace anymore. I used to keep going all day."

Leah and I go to Flaum's Herring to buy sweet roasted peppers and matjas herring. After Flaum's, we stop at Green's candy store and buy ten Paskez bubble gums, wrapped like coins. They're ten cents each. We each put five in our pocketbooks. I feel rich today.

"Your teeth will rot and fall out, chewing so much sugar," Leah says, imitating Ma.

"But I'm sure to have a sweet year," I say.

"A sweet year without teeth," Leah says and laughs.

We all dip a piece of apple in the honey dish and say the prayer for a sweet year. Father holds his apple up, and the honey drips down the sides, over his fingers. His eyes are shut tight; he's concentrating, praying.

Ma whispers, "Amen."

They're both hoping and wishing for the best year. Watching them, I can almost believe that we will have a sweet new year. That there will be no fighting over the new synagogue, over money, over Father being away from home so much, away in his car. At home, Ma turns against everything. I wonder which one of them makes things go wrong. We could have a happy year, their prayers could be answered, if Father stopped wanting a synagogue, moved to Williamsburg, and got a real job teaching. If. Then Ma could pay the bills. She wouldn't sit at the kitchen table after dinner, adding numbers, seeing who has to be paid before she can place another order. She's always switching from Frank's to Stern's, depending on where she owes less that week. And when she owes too much everywhere, she calls and says the check is ready and she'll send it with the delivery boy.

After eating, Ma says, "For a change, the women will go for a walk and the men will stay home and baby-sit."

Both sides of Lee Avenue are crowded with Chassidic people. Everyone's out walking. The streets are all dark satin and white silk. And baby carriages, so many carriages and strollers we have to keep making room for them. Some women recognize Ma, and they wish her a good signed and sealed year. Their husbands nod their heads in greeting.

Ma says, "They're visiting parents and grandparents, to wish them a happy New Year. That's what we used to do in Jerusalem after the meal. We walked all the way into the old city, where our grandfather still lived. My father and brothers would sing zemiros all the way there and back. There were always other families walking and singing."

We talk about what it would be like to have grandparents, aunts, and uncles here in Williamsburg, and I look at Ma to see how much she misses her parents, sisters, and brothers. When a streetlight shines in her eye, I think it's a tear. She's wearing her new white apron and kerchief out in the street. That's what all the married women here wear on Friday and holiday nights. It's what their mothers and grandmothers wore in Eastern Europe. Williamsburg is like a European shtetl, and it's where we belong. It's the largest Chassidic community in the world. Here people are like us, we're like them. I don't understand why Father doesn't want to live here. He can't have his own synagogue here, but he could be like everyone else, a Chassid who lives near his rebbe, who prays with his rebbe every day. But Father doesn't want to be just a Chassid. He wants to be the rebbe.

By the time I am in bed, I'm so tired that I don't read a single page of *Von Ryan's Express*. If I lived here, I'd read less, be what Ma wants me to be. There is so much to do in a city. I watch the lights crisscross on the ceiling. They come and go with the trains and the traffic, and I fall asleep liking the noise.

In the morning, the tires sound different, swishing, and when I open my eyes I see that it's drizzling. It's gray outside. Soft gray like my dress. Should I wear my new dress in this rain?

Ma comes in, and I don't have to hide anything, I don't have to push a book under my pillow. I look into her yellow-green eyes without shame, with nothing to hide. She's already dressed for synagogue.

She whispers, "It's nine-thirty. I'm going now. Aaron and Esther already ate breakfast. Dress them, and if it stops raining, bring them to the synagogue."

I nod and sit up, watching her. She looks good in her wool jersey dress. She dieted all summer to fit into it.

"Come lock the door behind me," she says. "Don't open up for anyone unless you know their voice. This is a city. You have to be careful."

I get up and follow her through the rooms. At the door, Ma buttons her raincoat. She's carrying her new brown leather prayer book, a holiday gift from Father. She opens the leather flap and checks to see if her thin white perfumed handkerchief is still there.

I say, "You'll look good in the synagogue today, as good as any Williamsburg woman."

"You think so?" She smiles. "Remember, lock the door with the chain."

I don't feel like reading. If we lived here, I'd be doing things, not reading about other people doing things. I want to go out, even though it's raining. I put on my everyday clothes and tell Leah I'm going out to explore.

In the street, it's quiet. A few cars stop and start at the lights, but it's as if everyone knows it's a holiday, even non-Jews. The trains overhead are the only things that keep going, riding, riding, to the end. But where is the end? And do they turn around and start again when they've reached it? I make sure Leah's not at the window and run up the black metal stairs. There's a turnstile at the top of the stairs, and I need money to get in, but it's Rosh Hashanah and I didn't bring my pocketbook. Thinking about getting on a train but not wanting to touch money, as if one sin is worse than the other, is ridiculous. I watch some kids go through the gate without paying and decide to try it too. No one stops me. I follow them to the platform and wait for a train. I want to see how it comes and what it looks like up close. Von Ryan's Express stops only once in every town, and I wonder how far this train goes before stopping.

The kids are giggling, and I think they're laughing at me. I turn my back and watch a train arrive, screeching so high my ears hurt. My hands go to cover them, but I hold them down at my sides. There are no Jews here: everyone's in the synagogue;

there's no one to see me. And if there were a Jew, he'd also be a sinner not wanting to be seen. Two sinners, meeting; would we become friends?

The doors open, and I step in to look. I hold on to a pole. Just when I get scared and change my mind about staying, the doors close and the train starts moving. I have to hold tight to keep from falling.

The train moves slowly, then faster, then it stops. The conductor says, "Hewes Street," and when the doors open I run, afraid they will close on me. My heart is beating fast, faster than I can run. I race down the metal steps, into the street, and look around to make sure no one saw me. On Broadway, I walk the five blocks back to the apartment slowly, to slow my beating heart. I don't want Leah to see me scared.

Walking up the two flights, it seems like hours since I came down these stairs.

"Was it worth going out?" Leah asks.

I shake my head. "Just rain and cars outside."

"What did you expect on Broadway?" she says. "I'll go out in the afternoon, when everyone's out walking on Lee Avenue, dressed up."

When we're packing to leave, Ma says, "I met Yehudit Greenberg in the synagogue, and it was so nice to see each other again. To sit near each other. Maybe we should move back here to Williamsburg. I forgot how much I like it here."

We start talking about where to rent an apartment.

Ma says, "The best street to live on is Lee, where just looking out the window you see a whole world. Here on Broadway, it's dark and there's too much noise from the trains. With a window on Lee, you never get lonely. Just sitting there, looking out, is as good as being outside all day. In Ashley, I look out on white snow all winter, squirrels and lost dogs, only things on four legs. Not another human being all day long. A wasteland. An American Siberia."

"Why did you agree to move to Ashley in the first place?" Leah asks.

"Your father, he's too smart for me sometimes. We moved there in the summer, when the city was hot and empty. In the country, all the bungalows were full; Ashley was lively. But everyone else was just renting. They left, and we stayed."

In the car on the way home, Ma says, "I want to live either in Williamsburg or in Jerusalem."

Father doesn't answer, as if he's paying close attention to driving.

"You hear me?" Ma says. "I want to live around my own kind. I do not want to live where I'm always a stranger."

The tires keep turning, taking us back to Ashley.

"Listen to me. What else do you have two ears for?" Ma yells.

"You're not the stranger," Father says slowly. "The others are. They're the ones who are not living the right way."

He always twists conversations and doesn't get the point. What he says doesn't even make sense. If you're the only one who's different, you're the stranger.

Ma says, "Fine. Say it your way. I don't want to stay in forsaken Ashley. I'm warning you. Later you'll come begging. I will not stay and live there."

"Very soon Ashley will be all built up. We will have a nice big synagogue. And soon there will be neighbors. You will be their rebbetzin."

"Again he starts with his own shtick," Ma says, as if Father's not there to hear it, as if she's talking to herself or to us only. "I don't want to be a rebbetzin. You have rabbonis on your mind like a sickness. I am not staying in Ashley to wait until you have a big synagogue with no minyan. I will not be the joke in every mouth."

We all know to remain silent when Ma starts up like this, not to take sides. We know to wait until it's over. Father's silent too. I want us to move to Williamsburg, but without the fighting.

Ma screams, "Why do I have to be unhappy all my life, tell me? Why can't I have a little joy, like other mothers, like my mother? I don't deserve this. I work hard enough, raising seven children. Why do I have to live in hell, a burning hell? I should have burned our bungalow down along with the others that night. With my own hands, I should have lit my own home and watched it burn down to the ground. I could've said a flying spark started it. Then I could've taken the insurance money, packed myself and my children, and gotten on the first plane to Israel."

Father remains silent, and no one says anything the rest of the way home. The prayers for a sweet year don't mean anything in our family. Our year goes sour in less than an hour. A rhyme. I want to repeat it. Our year goes sour in less than an hour. It's true. It's our family anthem.

We unload the car slowly, not as happy as we were loading it.

Ma keeps talking, complaining. "Look at this. I can't live like this, in mud and the constant noise of tractors. In a yard heaped with junk."

Father's not answering; he's keeping his head down, trying to let her words pass. I wish he would do something. He could promise to do what she wants, move to the city, or he could tell her to shut up. Anything is better than just listening.

"Look at him," Ma says. "He doesn't hear a thing. In one ear and out the other. Like a piece of wood, a wall. I can keep talking till my voice gives out. He won't change."

I look at Father. He does look like a piece of wood, not listening, carrying bags in. I follow him with a box in my arms. Ma's voice gets higher and higher, and when I come into the kitchen, she's holding a big meat knife in her hand.

"You see this?" she screams. "I will kill myself. I will take my own life. I will leave you with all the children on your hands."

We all stop and stare. Ma shrieks, "Just stand there and watch me. All of you. You can be my witnesses. Watch the blood come spurting out. I have to bleed to death before he will listen." She sticks the point of the knife into the soft, pale skin at her throat.

Sarah grabs my skirt and starts crying. Aaron hides behind Leah.

David says, "Stop her, Father." His voice cracks.

Levi cries, "No, Mama, no."

Father holds his hands down at his sides as if they can't move. He doesn't step closer to Ma, afraid she will knife him. He says, "Put the knife down, Tovele. I'll do whatever you want. Just put the knife down."

"Don't give me Tovele. Swear you'll go and buy airplane tickets to Israel. Swear you will come and live in Israel. I want to live with my old mother."

"I can't swear. I give you my word. I will buy tickets. Put down the knife. I'll send you to Israel for a visit. You need the rest."

Ma holds the blade edge against her skin. "Promise. Promise me you will go tomorrow and buy tickets."

"My word is a promise. You have my word."

Ma lets her hand fall limp, and the knife hangs against her dress, pointing. I am afraid she'll cut her leg.

"Put the knife back in the drawer. You're scaring the children," Father says.

"If you don't bring the tickets tomorrow, I'll hang myself. I'll hang myself on the step from the hall to the new room. Your children will come home from school and find their mother hanging there, my eyes and mouth open, rolled back, like this."

Ma throws her head back and rolls her eyes, and only the whites show. Levi and Sarah cry.

"Put the knife down and I promise I'll bring the tickets," Father says. "Enough is enough."

Ma puts the knife on the counter, and Father reaches for it and puts it away where it belongs, in the meat drawer.

"Who do you want to live with?" Ma asks, looking at us.

"Don't bring the children into this," Father says. "Leave them alone."

Ma continues, "Esther and Aaron will come with me. They're my babies. David can stay in yeshiva. Sarah, who do you want to live with, Mama or Father?"

Sarah looks at Father, feeling bad for him, and chooses Ma. We all look at Father sitting there, his hand over his eyes, the creases on his forehead deep and touching.

Levi and Leah choose Ma. Everyone looks at me for an answer. I'm angry. I am angry at Ma for asking, for making us choose just to hurt Father. All for nothing. As if things will ever change.

"Neither," I say. "Both or neither."

"Then stay with your father. You were always your father's daughter anyway."

She gets rid of me with these words. I'm not hers and never was. I look like Father's side of the family, I am like Father. She's insulted that I didn't choose her, even though I'm the only one, the one small gap in her triumph over him.

She says, "Look, you only have one child on your side. Your oldest daughter. She will take care of you. And you," she says, turning to me. "You'll be sorry. You will sleep here all alone, wondering where he is, whether he is still alive. He will forget to call you. He will forget to leave you money. You won't have food or clothes. That's what it's like, living with your father."

"I have my own money," I say, looking at her. "I'll buy clothes and food with my own money."

Ma looks at me. "You're a little stinker to be talking about your own money. My mother would have taken my money from me as soon as I earned it. I wouldn't have had the nerve to call it my own money. I would have come home from work and given it to her, and I would've done it gladly, with a smile."

Father shakes his head. "Leave her alone. What do you want from her? Go to Israel for a few weeks. After the holidays, take a vacation."

Ma goes to her room and the house becomes quiet, so quiet I hear her screams over and over in my head. Everyone walks around on tiptoe, whispering, as if to make up for the screaming. I help Sarah lay out her clothes for school tomorrow, listen to her read a page in her reader; I initial the page, using Ma's signature. No one says anything, but we're all thinking what if Father doesn't keep his promise. We've heard this before, Ma threatening to leave, to take only the baby and go live in Israel. But what if this time it's for real, if this time she means it and Father doesn't know, if this time we'll come home and find her swinging, her mouth open and her tongue hanging out.

CHAPTER TEN

WE ALL STAND waving, watching Ma push the stroller with Esther in it up the ramp to El Al's 747. There's a stewardess at her side, hurrying her, helping with the carry-on bag. Before turning the corner, Ma stops and blows kisses the way old Hungarian ladies do, and already she's someone I don't know, a stranger getting on an airplane. Father sways, his eyes closed, whispering a prayer.

"Dov Ber," Ma calls, and when he looks up, she throws a last kiss to him.

They didn't kiss when they were close up. Going around, kissing each one of us on the forehead, saying be good, Ma left Father out, and I wondered, Did they kiss in their bedroom in privacy, before leaving home?

Ma kissed me and said, "I leave everything in your hands. Take good care of your father. See that he eats hot meals. Don't let him travel too much. Insist that he comes home for Shabbat."

While Ma's away, Father will fly to Brazil to sell books. Still I feel bad for him. I expect them to change their minds at the last minute. Ma could say, I'm not going, or Father could say, I'm coming with you. But they don't. Everything goes exactly as planned, and after standing there, held back by the El Al guard and a thick velvet rope, looking at the top of the ramp where Ma was last seen, Leah remembers that we can watch the plane take off from the windows.

We run.

I lift Aaron up in my arms so he can see the jets backing away from the terminal, and we wave and wave and wave even though we don't know for sure which plane Ma's in. There could be a hijacker in any one of the planes, or a PLO agent with a bomb in his suitcase, prepared to die for his cause. A kamikaze.

"El Al," Father says, "is the safest airline. They're the only ones who haven't been hijacked, because they're careful and because they fly nonstop."

Several planes take off, and we give each one a family good-bye and prayers for a safe trip. On the way home, Aaron and Sarah fall asleep. Levi sits in the front seat with Father, in Ma's place, and recites passages of mishnayos in the same chant David used. Father questions Levi about the exact words of a passage, and I listen to them debate, knowing that Levi is always right; his memory is photographic, everyone says. Leah and I sit at the doors and look out. I watch the road and the passing houses. At night, in the dark, things look different. At night you see deep, all the way into the yellow-lit homes, into the rooms where people sit, eat, move around. For once, I wouldn't mind being stopped in traffic so I can watch for more than a second. But we pass house after house, too quickly, and the people and their rooms are gone before I can get to know them even a little, before I can figure out their stories. Seeing so much so quickly makes me dizzy, and I put my head back and close my eyes.

———

There are streetlights now in Ashley, but the bungalow is dark and quiet, and inside, it seems empty without Ma, as if she alone fills the rooms. Aaron and Sarah go straight to bed. Father and Levi go to the synagogue to look up the passage they're discussing, and Leah and I sit at the kitchen table.

"It's her voice that's missing," I say. "It's too quiet here without her constant warning voice, telling Sarah, Levi, and Aaron to sleep already, tomorrow's another day. You think she'll come back?"

"Ma?" Leah says, as if there's anyone else we could be talking about. "She can't stay away from Father."

"He's leaving the day after tomorrow."

"That soon? Good. We'll have some peace. And it will be fun keeping house."

"Easy for you to say. You don't have to wake up in the morning and get everyone off to school. You lie there sleeping like the dead until the last minute."

"I'm a night person. I can't help it. I can prepare everyone's lunch at night." She jumps up and takes the bread out of the freezer. I sit there watching her. As soon as Father's gone, I'll go to the library.

I say, "Ma gave me spending money, she said for emergencies and for fun. Two hundred and fifty dollars. She said groceries can go on the bill. On our way home from school tomorrow, we'll stop at Waldbaum's. I'll buy eight pairs of sheer panty hose, four for you and four for me. We'll look good while Ma's away."

"What colors?" Leah asks.

"Navy, black, and one beige. Gella Jacobs wore beige one day, and she looked so grown up."

"If Ma finds out, she'll kill us."

"She won't find out. Beige will look good with my new gray dress, and I'm going to wear that dress to school. What is there to save it for? So I outgrow it, so you and Sarah get to wear it?"

Leah shakes her head. "What about the kids? Sarah will tell."

"We'll buy her a pair too. She'll like that, big-girl stockings."

The phone rings before the alarm clock in the morning, and I run into the kitchen to answer it. Father picks up in his bedroom, and we both listen to a woman's voice, the operator, reading a telegram from Ma.

Everyone's gathered around me in the kitchen, waiting. I hang up and repeat the message. Father comes into the kitchen in his long white underwear and says, "Mama and Esther are safe in Jerusalem." He rubs his hand over his face, starting with his brows, and brings it all the way down to the point of his beard.

Aaron asks, "When is Mama coming home?"

Father smiles. "In a few weeks."

I look at him. Is he worried about Ma not coming back? She might send a letter saying she's staying, that if he wants his children to have a mother, he should pack everything and move there. That's what I would do in Ma's place. I'd stay until Father gives in.

"How many days are in a few weeks?" Aaron asks. Father puts his hand on Aaron's head and doesn't answer.

"A few weeks is not a couple, so it's at least three," Levi says. He adds seven plus seven plus seven, using his fingers, and says, "At least twenty-one days."

Aaron puts his fingers out for Levi to show him how many.

PART

TWO

CHAPTER ELEVEN

WITH MA AND Father both away, Leah and I sign up for a lifeguarding course. Last year when it was offered, we were afraid to ask. We're using a hundred dollars of Ma's money to pay for equipment and classes. With licenses, we can get jobs as lifeguards this summer and pay Ma back. We'll swim and sit in the sun instead of baby-sitting.

Classes are on Sunday nights at Bader's Hotel. We promise Sarah and Levi a trip to Toys "R" Us if they take good care of Aaron. It's two and a half hours every Sunday, not such a long time, still I worry. Ma wouldn't leave them alone. Before we go, I serve dinner and get them into pajamas. At seven o'clock our ride picks us up.

There are nine of us, plus our teacher, Ricki. Seven are from our school, and two are Beth Yaakov girls. I wish I were a Beth Yaakov girl. At seventeen, only two years older than me, Ricki has an instructor's license and drives her mother's car; next year, she's going away to Hebrew seminary in Israel. Away in seminary, I could be anyone, do anything.

As soon as the elevator door opens, I can smell the pool, a heavy, warm cloud of chlorine. Leah has on the old blue bathing suit I used to wear with a jumper over it, and I have a new red one from Avon. The only way to get in is to jump, and we do it, shivering. Once inside, the water feels warm, like a bath. It's heated.

Ricki explains that warm water is heavier and harder to swim in than cold. The first thing she teaches is the quick return, a basic technique to keep the lifeguard safe, she says. You swim up to the victim from behind whenever possible, and when at arm's distance away, you stop yourself so the victim can't grab you. You push hard against the water, and for a second your body is completely upright, you are standing in water. Then you're ready to continue.

Ricki says, "If you forget to do this before you begin a rescue, you automatically fail."

She wants to see us swim laps. We line up at one end of the pool, and she says to swim back and forth five times. "This is not a race," she says, "so stagger yourselves."

I'm happy not to be racing, because even though I'm older, Leah is a faster swimmer than I am. Her arms and legs are stronger.

Ricki tells us, "You're both good swimmers. You can hold your breath a long time, which is good for a lifeguard."

I am surprised to hear her say this and look to see if she doesn't mean it more about Leah. She has us tread water for ten minutes straight. That's easy. While we're treading, Ricki teaches us the jellyfish.

"Knowing this technique," she says, "can determine whether you become a survivor or a victim. People have survived hours in the ocean, staying relaxed, doing the jellyfish."

We hang our heads and arms and legs and float. The water sways, and my body moves with it. This is the way to live, I think. Like a jellyfish. Not fighting, just floating, letting your body turn and twist.

We learn how to jump into deep water without submerging, so our eyes remain on our victims. The surface jump. We all do it twice, smack down on the water with our open palms, splashing.

"Now you're ready for the first save," Ricki says. "This is the easiest one, the chin pull."

We split up into victims and saviors. I am the savior, and Leah is my victim. I do a surface jump, swim the American crawl, do a quick return a foot away from Leah, who has her back to me, then the hard part. I wrap one arm around her chest and use the other to get her into a floating position. Then, still holding her—Ricki says never to let go of the victim's body—I cup her chin with my other hand. I start scissor-kicking, and Leah floats along with me, and now that I have her cupped and floating, I release the other arm and use it to sidestroke to safety. It's slippery, holding a person's wet, slimy chin in the water.

When I get near the edge I let go, and Leah floats away.

Ricki says, "No, no, no. Never let go of your victim until you have her out of the water. Think about it. You could end up having to perform the rescue all over again."

She shows me how to put Leah's hands up on the edge of the pool, one on top of the other, and with one of my hands over both of hers, I lift myself out of the water in one heave. Then I have to lift the victim out up to her waist. I am tired and out of breath by the time I finish, and then it's my turn to be a victim.

Leah goes through the same steps, bringing me all the way to safety, and her hold on me feels strong and sure. When I tell her, she says, "Yours felt strong too."

Ricki says, "Continue practicing on each other. And when you're done, start swimming laps, using your sidestroke. That's one stroke that must be strong. You need it for all the carries."

We take turns on each other, then switch partners, so we don't get used to just one size. Ricki says there are always adjustments for size, yours and your victim's. If your victim is a lot larger than you are, you have to be extra careful. A panicked victim will try to climb on top of you.

Once class is over, I'm in a hurry to get home. Ma would never leave Levi or Sarah in charge. I worry that the bungalow is on fire, or that Aaron fell and broke a leg. Ricki asks where we want to get off, and I say Suzanne and Maple. Leah says 306 and Ashley. Ricki laughs. "Which one will it be?"

"Suzanne," I say. "We'll be home sooner."

When we get out, Leah says, "If we stayed in the car longer, we wouldn't miss what she's telling the others." She's not worried about the kids home alone. She's not the oldest.

We go through the moves a hundred times that night, walking instead of swimming across our room, practicing the order, remembering to do the quick return. Ricki said Leah and I could share the book and equipment. She said to go to the Red Cross chapter on 9W for everything.

At the end, there'll be a written test based on the book and a practical test in the water. We have to study for the written test on our own time. I'm not worried about the written part. It's the practical part that will be hard. I've never studied anything like this, anything I have to do with my whole body.

Leah doesn't stop talking. She keeps saying, "I can't wait for next week." She worries. "What if Ma comes home? What are we going to tell her?"

I look at her. This is the first time I can remember her trying to think of ways to get around Ma. Usually it's me thinking, planning.

"We have three weeks to worry about that," I say.

She says, "We can tell her it's required. That it's part of Science. That everyone in our school has to learn it."

I laugh. She's coming up with the worst ideas. "It shows you don't have practice. How long do you think Ma will believe that? She just has to ask Mrs. Sklar to find out it's a lie."

But this time Leah's willing to try anything. She says, "By the time she talks to Mrs. Sklar it will be too late to stop us. We'll be halfway through."

She says, "Marla Rappaport says you can get ten dollars an hour for lifeguarding in the summer. At Gartner's Inn off Old Nyack Turnpike. She's going to camp, so she's not applying. But we can. Ten dollars an hour. We can tell Ma that. She won't be able to complain too much about that."

I agree. Money talks.

CHAPTER TWELVE

WE TAKE SARAH, Levi, and Aaron with us to Nyack on Friday. They talk about what they want from Toys "R" Us all the way there.

At the Red Cross, Leah adds to our purchases two black lifeguard whistles for the summer, when we're both lifeguards. Even though the books are four dollars each, we buy two so we can study at the same time. We have the whole weekend to read, and no one to stop us. I add a thin book titled *Teaching Johnny to Swim*, and the bill comes to forty-nine dollars instead of thirty-five. The mask, fins, and snorkel are expensive.

We get on the bus back to the mall carrying our bag of equipment and the books. I look at pictures of jellyfish and stingrays and horseshoe crabs, animals I've never seen before. I read about whirlpools and currents and how to swim not against but with them. Not fighting. I imagine Ma a victim, how she'd fight, paddle, and kick, and how she'd drown in panic. She doesn't even know how to swim.

At Toys "R" Us, Sarah chooses a spirograph, and Aaron a long fire engine with ladders that unfold and firemen that snap off.

Levi wants a calligraphy set from the art supply store. He wants to be a scribe when he grows up. He's been practicing writing fancy aleph beth with an old turkey quill Father gave him.

Leah and I buy two heavy zip-up sweatshirts with hoods. That's what Ricki wears walking around the pool, giving directions. Ma would say who ever heard of Chassidishe girls wearing sweatshirts, but she is far, far away.

We're excited to get home, to try our new things before Shabbat. Leah and I want to put on our new sweatshirts, with our bathing suits underneath, and see ourselves as lifeguards with whistles on long strings hanging around our necks, looking official. Leah tries on the mask and snorkel right there on the bus, and people turn to look at us.

"Let them," she says. She's never embarrassed by people.

Walking home from the bus stop, not worrying about hiding anything or coming up with what to say, makes me want to skip and run. I add all the numbers in my head and figure out that after paying for classes, we'll still have fifty dollars for other things. Sarah runs ahead, and when we get there, David is standing at the door beside her.

"What are you doing here?" I ask. "Who gave you permission to leave yeshiva?"

"Father called Reb Blau. He wanted someone home to make kiddish and lead at the Shabbat table. And to gather minyan."

Leah and I look at each other. Who needs David to lead us? To see everything we do all day. I don't care about kiddish; I wouldn't have minded reciting it as the oldest in the family. Even if I am a girl. Or Levi could have said it, even though he's not bar mitzvah yet. I want to say, Get in a taxi and go back to your yeshiva. We don't need you. This is our own Shabbat.

"Where were you?" David asks. "I've been here an hour. I was starting to think you went away for Shabbat."

"Shopping," I answer, without saying where or for what.

Levi shows David his new calligraphy set, and they go into the boys' room to try it. Sarah sits at the kitchen table and unwraps her spirograph. Aaron sits on the floor in the hallway with his jacket still on, unfolding and folding the ladders on his fire engine. I close the door to our room and lean against it. Leah and I look at each other.

"At least he leaves early Sunday morning, before swimming," Leah says.

"That's all you worry about. Swimming. I hate Father for calling him to lead us. I can make kiddish as well as David."

"It's not that bad. Maybe he's happy to be home without Ma and Father too. He can be free. We can have fun."

"What about bowling? We were planning to go bowling on Saturday night."

"We'll go another time," Leah says.

I go into the boys' room. "You hungry?" I ask David.

He nods. "Is there any cake?"

He follows me into the kitchen. With Ma not home, it's like I am in her place. I am expected to be like Ma, offer food, make sure everyone eats. And I do. I take Ma's marble cake out of the freezer, unwrap it, and cut two slices. David stands behind me.

"Do you still eat trafe?" he asks.

"No," I lie. He's become so good I don't trust him.

"Then it worked. The dybbuk didn't come back." We laugh.

"I read somewhere that eating trafe changes you inside," he says. "You become less Jewish. Also reading goyishe books."

It's strange hearing him talk like this, and I laugh again. He looks at me to see whether I'm lying.

"I'm serious," he says. He takes a bite of cake, chews. Leah comes in. "You must be having fun by yourselves," he says. "You can eat whatever you want and go to sleep whenever you want."

"Yes, but it's work too. I have to come home right after school, because Aaron and Sarah are home alone."

Leah says, "She has to wake up at six o'clock to get everyone ready. I prepare lunches at night."

David nods and bends over his plate to catch the crumbs. His new mustache is white with milk. Leah and I look at each other and smile. We both know we're enjoying every minute of our three weeks. The hard part is knowing it will be over, knowing Father will be home. We're not sure about Ma. With Father home, seeing things, and Ma away, we'll have to continue doing all the work, without the fun. It will be like being Ma, staying home all the time, washing laundry, cooking.

"Were you happy to come home?" I ask.

He nods. "Sometimes I feel if I don't leave right that minute, I will go crazy. Like I am in jail."

I pull out a chair and sit across from him. "What do you do then?"

"I walk in the woods."

"Alone?"

He nods. "I talk to the trees. I talk to them as if they were people. One tree is you and the other Leah."

"Like the Baal Shem Tov," I say, "praying and singing in the woods."

He laughs. Leah and I look at him.

"Would you rather stay home?" Leah asks.

"No. I like it there. But sometimes, some days, I need something different. Like coming home today."

Together David and Levi manage a minyan, and I watch David walk over to Mr. Dorf and ask him to lead the prayers. It's always Father's voice we hear Friday nights, Father's voice welcoming the holy Shabbat, calling it a woman. Today Mr. Dorf's Litvak tunes make me want to correct him, to shout and drown out his voice.

At the table, David tells stories about yeshiva, and Levi asks questions. He can't wait to go. Having an older brother will make yeshiva easier for Levi. They talk about sharing a room in the dormitory.

We stay up late, playing chess and talking. After Sarah and Aaron fall asleep, we talk about Ma and how she went crazy with the knife. We debate who's right in the argument between Ma and Father and don't come to any conclusions. David takes Father's side, saying, "There isn't anything she lets him do without a fight. If he listened to her, he wouldn't get anything done."

I agree that Ma stands in the way of things, but Father makes things worse, I say, leaving her alone all week after moving her to forsaken Ashley, away from family and friends, away from everything she knows. "Look at you: you don't like being alone in yeshiva. Put yourself in Ma's shoes, living here without anyone."

David shakes his head. "It's different. She has us, and Father comes home for Shabbat. You should see how my rebbe's wife respects her husband. She knows he's the man in the house. He doesn't always go home during the week either. She never raises her voice. She's a true aishes chayil."

Leah and I laugh at him, talking about the man in the house and quoting the song. Anything like that coming from David is funny. He never sounds like a scholar or a great man. He's just David.

He doesn't stop. "Ma needs a lesson. If she respected Father more, then maybe things would be better. A good wife and mother doesn't threaten to leave her husband and children."

"If I were Ma, I wouldn't just threaten," Leah says. "I'd stay away until Father learns his lesson."

"You both learned this from Ma. You're as bad as her already."

"And you," I say, "you're like Father. You do everything he does. It's like you don't have a mind of your own anymore."

"That's what a good son does. He does what his father does. You're doubly bad. You only learn the bad things from Ma. You don't listen to her tell you not to read. You think I don't know you and Leah read goyishe books all Shabbat? And you're always speaking English so Ma doesn't understand. Father told you a thousand times not to bring a goyishe language into our house."

Leah and I look at each other. It's a good thing we didn't tell him about swimming. The less he knows, the better. He sees us looking at each other, hating him, and he says, "Don't worry, I won't tell. I'm not a tattletale. But I'm your brother, and I know what's right and wrong."

Saturday night, we order a whole pizza from Heshy's. We take out Ma's old record player and play all her albums. We sing along with the old Viznitzer Kol Nidre and Yom Tom Ehrlich's Yiddish songs. David bites into his slice and, with his mouth full, asks, "Does anyone miss Ma right now?"

No one answers, and we look at each other around the kitchen table. I look at Sarah's face, then Aaron's. I think they miss Ma. Every night, when I kiss Aaron good night, he asks, When is Mama coming home? Sarah doesn't ask; she listens. She stops what she's doing and waits for my answer. I miss Ma for them. I miss Ma taking care of things, worrying. I miss Ma's voice waking me every morning. I miss her sunny-side-ups, shiny and unbroken. I don't miss her hot milk with skin formed on the surface.

I wrap seven thick slices of cake, one for every day of the week, and David packs it. I'm glad and not glad he's leaving. With him home, I'm not the only one responsible; with him home

Sunday night, the kids wouldn't be alone. But then he'd know about swimming. I give him the leftover pizza too. He says, "In yeshiva, even cold pizza will be good."

Sunday night, Leah and I learn how to use the snorkel and mask. It's not easy, breathing like a whale. We spend half the class swimming laps, learning to breathe through a snorkel, inhaling air and spewing water. Ricki lets me use her snorkel and mask so we can all practice at the same time. Then she teaches us the chest carry. She says if you can do this one, the others are easy. This time, the victim faces us, and we have to surface dive and come up from behind, slide our hands up the victim's sides while still underwater, then surface, cross one arm over the victim's chest, and sidestroke to safety. If we forget the quick return, she makes us start all over. We also learn the hair carry, which is fun if you're not the victim.

At the end of the two and a half hours, everyone's eyes are red from chlorine. My lungs feel raspy, like I've been running in the cold. Leah says hers feel that way too.

Ricki says, "It's the chlorine. It burns. But it doesn't hurt you. Put moisturizer on your skin and conditioner in your hair after swimming."

The sweatshirt feels soft and warm when I come out of the water. When all of us are showered and dressed, Ricki reviews everything we've learned so far. She asks about the reading, and it turns out Leah and I are farthest along in the book.

"You two will have no problem passing," Ricki says in the car on our way home. She's taking us all the way tonight, because it's cold out. I sit in the front and watch how she presses for gas with her toe, moves the wheel quickly and lightly, and pulls up in front of our bungalow.

She says, "I didn't know anyone lived here during the winter."

"We used to be the only ones," Leah says. "Now there are four other families."

Inside, Sarah says, "Father called."

Leah and I look at each other. We never thought of this possibility. We could have left the phone off the hook.

"What did you tell him?" I ask.

"That you're doing something for school and you would be home in an hour. He said he'll call again later."

Leah and I grab Sarah and kiss her, and she looks at us, happy to get so much attention. She shows us ten sheets of paper, each with a different spirograph pattern, made with different-color pens.

"It's beautiful," I tell her. "What else did you talk about?"

"I told him about my new spirograph and about Levi's calligraphy. Levi was in the bathroom, so he couldn't come to the telephone. Aaron held the phone and nodded, but he wouldn't say anything."

"At least it was Father, not Ma. She'd raise a mountain about us leaving the kids alone," I tell Leah.

"Yeah," she says. "Father won't think much of it."

At ten-thirty, the phone rings, and it's Father. "Was it so important, you both had to be out at the same time?" he asks.

"It was only for a little more than an hour, and we called to check several times."

He asks how things are going, if everyone's healthy, and how Shabbat went with David. Was there minyan? he wants to know. My answers satisfy him, and I ask how he's doing in Brazil. He explains that an old friend he hoped to meet is away on vacation and he wants to wait for him, so he won't be home for Shabbat. The extra time will be profitable, he says. He asks if we've heard from Ma about when she's arriving and says he'll call again at the end of the week, to see if there's news. Listening to him say this, I think he's not so sure she's coming home, and for a minute I'm afraid. I'm afraid that with Father home, I'll have to be even more of Ma, Ma's replacement, a wife to Father.

I hang up and tell Leah we have only one more week on our own. I don't know what I want, Ma home or not. I rinse our bathing suits in the bathroom sink and hang them up to dry in the laundry room. If Ma comes home, Leah and I have figured, we can rinse them at Bader's and hang them on a nail outside our bedroom window to dry. Ma will never think to look there in the middle of the night. In the morning, first thing, we'll bring them in and hide them.

Ma's Pond's moisturizer goes on smooth and cold on my face, arms, and legs. It feels good smoothing it over my whole body, being nice to my body, and I sit naked, stroking the lotion into my skin, letting it dry before putting on my nightgown. There are things women do for their bodies that I never thought to do before. Moisturizing. Shaving. Mrs. Glickman shaves her arms and legs, and when the hair grows back, it looks like a beard. I saw this bottle at Pathmark, Nair for "no hair." I want to get rid of the hair under my arms before next Sunday. No one wants to touch hair when we do the armpit carry. I don't even want to touch my own. Ricki doesn't have hair. I knew about hairless armpits and how I liked them that way, smooth and hairless, but I didn't think to do it. It's strange how you know something but you don't know it for sure until a certain moment. Then suddenly you're in a hurry.

CHAPTER THIRTEEN

THE INSTRUCTIONS ON the bottle of lemon-scented Nair say to leave it on for twenty minutes. I have to sit in the bathroom naked for twenty minutes.

"Bring me the book," I tell Leah. "I'll read."

It smells so bad I have to hold my breath until I can't and stick my head out the window for fresh air. It's worse than chlorine. I try reading, but it's hard to concentrate with the fumes.

Leah knocks on the door. "Twenty minutes now."

I wet a washcloth and wipe off the Nair and rinse with warm water. I raise my arms up to the mirror above the sink, and my skin is hairless and smooth and red. I powder it with Shower to Shower and wash the sink and counter.

Leah's waiting right outside the door.

"It stinks and it's messy, but it works."

"Let me see," she says and follows me into our room.

I take one arm out of the sleeve of my bathrobe and show her. "It's my turn," she says, and I time her.

———

Levi and Aaron skip school again on Friday, and we go bowling. We have to walk there and back, because taking a taxi would leave us without enough money to play. The man gives us our own lane, and we give him our shoes and tell him what size. We look at each other, all of us in the same red-and-blue shoes with numbers on the back, and laugh. They feel like flat tires. The man has even found a pair for Aaron, whose feet are still small. I read the rules of the game and explain it to the others. We find the smallest balls for Levi, Sarah, and Aaron, with holes the size of their fingers.

All our first balls fall into the gutter, and we stop to watch how others do it. I think maybe bowling was a mistake; it's too hard. We should've gone skating instead. I try again.

I hold the ball up, centering it, take my steps carefully, one, two, and, on the third, swing forward and let go. The ball rolls straight, but slow, and then stops. I try again, this time swinging hard and fast, and four pins go down. Levi screams and Aaron jumps up and down. Now everyone wants to try again.

This time Leah knocks down seven pins. She takes her steps smoothly and swings. The ball rolls straight and fast, as if in the air. Now she's the expert, we listen to her, let her center us and show how to hold the ball. She looks at the man in the lane near us and does what he does, bending one knee low as she lets go of the ball. Levi gets two pins down. Instead of walking and swinging the ball, Aaron sits down in front of the lane and just rolls it out between his legs. The ball rolls slowly but straight down the side and knocks down two pins. Sarah's ball rolls into the gutter, and we let her have another turn, and another. She finally does it Aaron's way and hits three pins.

The man we're watching comes over and shows me how to keep score, how each turn consists of two throws and if a player gets all ten pins down, it's called a strike and the player gets another turn. He bends over our table to show me how to fill in the boxes, and his smell is all over me. I look at the big gold ring and the short black hair on his fingers. On a man's skin, hair looks good.

On our way home, we walk past the Pals' house, and I suddenly want to see Gita, to hear her talk, hear her sound like Ma but different, happy. As soon as we turn into their steep driveway, Aaron lets go of my hand and falls behind. Gita opens the door, smiling and happy to see us, even though it's Friday afternoon and there's always too much to do before Shabbat.

"Rachele, Leahle. Come in. Don't stand at the door like strangers."

She sees Aaron hiding behind Levi and scoops him up for a hug. Aaron makes himself heavy and slides right out of Gita's arms. "Look at you. You've grown so much I can't hold you anymore," she says.

"Come in," she says again, opening the door wider, and I step inside. Leah, Sarah, and Levi follow; Aaron won't. Gita stands at the door and looks at him. "He's afraid you'll leave him here," she says softly in Hebrew. "He's afraid of being left again, poor child."

She walks over to the stairs to the second floor and calls, "Itzi, come see who's here. Bring your jacket."

"We're just here for two minutes," I say. "He can wait outside."

"So how are you two managing everything and going to school?" she asks, smiling, looking from me to Leah. "Especially now that you're in high school. It's not so easy when you're in tenth grade."

She's always cheerful. I want to hug her.

"I prepare lunches at night, and Rachel makes breakfast in the morning," Leah says. "Because I like to sleep late in the morning."

Gita smiles. "It's nice you two get along so well. I just remembered: I baked fresh rugelach yesterday. Let me give you a bag for Shabbat." She walks into the kitchen and I follow her, with my coat still on. I wonder what she'd say if I told her about lifeguarding classes and about the sheer stockings under my boots. Gita wears thick black stockings with seams like Ma. I want to tell her. I always want to tell Gita everything, but I don't.

When I'm about to light candles for Shabbat, the phone rings, and I think it's Father calling or Ma sending a telegram. I put the match down and run to answer. It's Rabbi Beyer, asking why Levi and Aaron haven't been coming to school on Fridays. He says he's concerned because they've never missed classes for anything other than sickness, and knowing our parents aren't home, he worried.

I explain that we had to be somewhere important and didn't want them to come home to an empty house. He asks when we're expecting our parents back and I say next week sometime and he wishes us a Good Shabbat. Just before I hang up, he asks whether we want to come and eat one meal at his house, with his family. He says he knows his wife would love to have us to lunch tomorrow.

I think quickly: what would Ma say? "Thank you," I say, "but we already cooked everything. Maybe another time."

Levi worries that now he's in trouble. I worry about Rabbi Beyer telling Ma. I say, "I'll write you a note for your English teacher. And if Rabbi Beyer asks where you went that was so important, say to a big doctor, a specialist."

I dive into the water and swim along the bottom, my underarms bare and smooth. Leah follows, and we watch each other underwater, our eyes watery, our hair like seaweed. Leah looks like a surfacing seal, her black hair shiny wet and sleek. We come up for air, turn, and go down again, sharply, headfirst. Leah puts her hand out, and I take it. We breaststroke together, one-handed, staying along the white line at the bottom, living on one breath of air all the way to the end. We come up tired, laughing and gulping, and lie faceup in the water to rest. If we were fish, we could stay in the water forever.

When we get home, Aaron is awake and crying. I pick him up, and he asks, "Is Mama coming home?"

He's asking not when but whether. I don't know what to say. Even Father's not sure Ma's coming back.

Sarah says he woke up just like that; she swears she wasn't doing anything.

"You weren't making noise?"

"Maybe a little, because Levi said calligraphy is more important than a spirograph because he can write Torah."

Aaron falls asleep in my bed, his thin blue lids closed over his green eyes like Ma's.

In the morning, we get a telegram. ARRIVING TUESDAY 8 P.M. STOP A VIDER ZEN STOP KISSES MAMA STOP.

I repeat the telegram, and suddenly, knowing for sure Ma's coming home makes me nervous. Now that I'm used to keeping house, being in charge, I want her to stay longer. I don't want her home. I don't want Rabbi Beyer telling her the boys missed school. I don't want to stop swimming. I want her to stay away, or die.

Leah says, "I told you she'd come running. She can't live without Father."

How easy it is getting used to doing things without asking. Going back is hard. Going from skin-color legs, as if bare, to opaque blue tights is impossible. When Ma's home, I'll have to wear tights over my sheer in the morning and take them off on my way to school.

"You're crazy," Leah says. "It's not worth the trouble, not for every day. Swimming will be enough of a fight."

"You haven't worn them as much as I have. I have to continue. If I stop now, the girls in my class will know it's because Ma's home. They're wondering enough already. They're wondering how, with a rabbi for a father, I can get away with swimming and with wearing sheer beige every day."

"I told you beige was too much in the first place," Leah says. "You always go too far. But what will we say about swimming? I definitely will not stop swimming."

We look at each other, afraid. "If only she were dead," Leah says. "If only we were orphans."

We wash, dry, and pack away everything that night. I close the door to our room and pull out our big textbooks and spirals. Our shelves are packed so full, Ma will never think to look back here. I roll up all the panty hose and the bathing suits and organize it so that there's enough room and so I can reach in and get what I need quickly. The Nair goes in first; we won't need that for another month.

I bring two psalm books into our room, and we sit on our beds facing each other, reading psalms, hoping and praying that a war starts in Israel and Ma can't come home. Or that her plane crashes.

"What about Father's plane?" Leah says, and we laugh nervously. Father's arriving two hours before Ma so he can meet her at the airport.

"Pray for one thing at a time. Father we can deal with." We whisper the prayer to the end.

But I don't want Esther to die, and she will be on the plane with Ma. I read about a boy whose parents died in a plane crash when he was a baby. They all jumped out of the plane together, but the boy landed in a tree and survived. I pray Esther gets caught in a tree.

CHAPTER FOURTEEN

———————

THEY ARRIVE HOME tired. Father gives each of us a hot, humid kiss that tickles, and we kiss his hand. Ma hugs and kisses Aaron, puts her hand on Sarah's head, and watching them so happy to have her back frightens me. I am afraid of the possibility of her death, of my prayers for her death.

She asks about everyone's health and whether we were able to go to school every day. I look at Levi to make sure he doesn't say anything about Fridays. Talking about the three weeks makes them seem like a long time.

"Did you miss me?" Ma asks. "It sounds like you didn't even miss me."

Leah and I look at each other quickly, and Ma sees us. Her eyes narrow. "You hear that, Dov Ber? Your children enjoyed not having a mother and father, didn't you?"

I shake my head, not knowing what to say, feeling angry and guilty.

"It was a lot of work," Leah says. "Making lunches at night, breakfasts in the morning."

"We ate burned chicken almost every night," Sarah complains, for once saying the right thing at the right time.

Ma looks at me questioningly.

"We overbroiled the chicken some nights because we wanted it to be brown," I explain. "We wanted it crispy."

"For the younger ones, I take the pieces out earlier, before the meat becomes tough," Ma explains.

There are gifts for everyone. Silver rings for Leah and me, a small red leather briefcase with shoulder straps for Sarah. Levi and Aaron get small Torah scrolls wrapped in embroidered velvet like the real thing; also for the boys, there are prayer books with silver covers and turquoise stones inset.

"And from Baba," Ma says, "I have a surprise for the girls. Look at Esther. Did you notice something different about her?"

We look at Esther. "Earrings," Leah says. In Esther's smooth brown earlobes are tiny red earrings.

Ma smiles. "Baba wouldn't let me take her out without something red to keep off the evil eye. She tied a red string around her wrist, but Esther chewed on it. So she bought red earrings. I have a pair for each one of you. We'll go have your ears pierced."

I touch my earlobe. It's fleshy like Ma's. The boys in our family have thin lobes, and the girls have thick ones. It should have been the other way around. It would be less painful, I think, if my earlobes were thin.

Father says, "Why do you want to deform your children's bodies, put holes in their bodies? Gypsies wear rings in their ears and noses."

Ma laughs and waves her hand, indicating what do men know? "We'll go to the mall. They do it for five dollars there."

"It will hurt," Levi says.

"The younger you are, the less it hurts," Ma says. "Esther

hardly felt it. She didn't even cry on the first ear. She just looked surprised."

"I don't want a hole in my ear," Sarah says. "Not if it hurts."

"Don't listen to him or your father. They're men," Ma says. She shows us the earrings. Tiny white pearls with gold trim for Sarah and Leah. Because I'm older, mine have a gold wire that hangs off the earlobe.

Ma says, "You can't wear this kind right away. You'll have to wear gold studs first."

In the morning, I wear a pair of sheer panty hose under my tights and feel Ma's prying eyes all over me, looking, searching for what's different, burning through to my skin. I hurry Leah out of the house early, and we take a back way to school, cutting through backyards, jumping over the brook. Leah stands in front of me to block me from view, and I lean against a tree, pull my tights off quickly, and bunch them up in my schoolbag. Getting them back on after school will be harder. I'll need more time; I'll need a place to sit. We'll have to walk farther out of our way. With families now living on the hill, we must be careful.

"We'll have to tell her about swimming pretty soon," Leah says while I'm changing. "Before Sunday comes. I don't want to miss class."

As soon as we walk into the house after school, I know something's wrong. It's too quiet, and Ma's in her room, resting. I rush into the bathroom and lock the door. I pull off my tights, then my panty hose, which I hide in the cabinet under the sink, then I put my tights back on. My arms and legs are weak.

Leah meets me at the door to our room. She doesn't say anything, just points to her bed, to a pile of panty hose in bits and pieces, blue, black, and beige, all cut up. Beside it is the snorkel, mask, and fins.

I walk over to our shelf. It's a mess. My hand trembles, reaching behind the books to the bottom corner. The bottle of Nair is still there. I take it out, climb up on a chair, and hide it higher up, on the top shelf in our closet, behind piles of old sheets and blankets.

"What about our bathing suits?"

"I checked," Leah whispers. "They're still under the mattress. She didn't find them."

We hear the springs of Ma's bed and wait for her to come in. Standing in the doorway to our room, in her flowered robe, she looks pale and tired. But her eyes are angry green.

"What did you think? A mother wouldn't know? I knew last night. A mother feels. Stockings so see-through you may as well not wear any. What do you want to be, two shiksas? Outcasts? Your father's calling your principal and all your teachers. You will not grow up in this home wearing such stockings." She stops for breath.

"Everyone in our school wears them." My voice comes out thin and scared. "They're not different from what our teachers wear. They won't understand what he's talking about."

"They won't understand? We'll see about that. Father always said your school is too modern. And now we see the results. I send you to school and do everything myself because I want you to have more than I had, I don't want you to feel less than anyone, and this is my reward. Daughters who are shiksas. Just wait until Father comes home."

She points to the mask. "And what's all this? What's that

black mask for? Is that what you spent my money on? Masks and see-through stockings. I should've known better. I should've left you without a penny."

"They're for swimming," Leah explains. "So you can see underwater."

"And all the books in your closet? Father threatened to remove you from school because of those books. He says he warned you last time. I said no. I don't want my daughters sitting home. I want you to finish school. You're lucky to have me as a mother. You should get down on your knees to thank me."

"They're schoolbooks," I say. "History, literature, science."

Ma looks at me, not believing. "Schoolbooks. You think your mother's a fool? And another thing. Rabbi Beyer called. He says Levi and Aaron weren't in school Fridays. What did you do, take them to the mall? Who gave you permission to take them out of cheder? You think when your mother's away it's a free-for-all?"

She walks out and slams the door hard behind her, not waiting for answers. Leah and I sit on our beds, across from each other, the bits and pieces of nylon in a pile beside her. I'm trembling I'm so angry. I'm angry at having to feel grateful. They have no right to stop me from going to school.

"She should've died," I say, not sure I mean it. "The nerve. Cutting everything up." Leah looks at me, saying nothing.

"I should go to her dresser and tear every one of her stockings, her thick black seamed stockings like sacks. I want to split them right down the seams. Then she'll have to go spend money buying new pairs. The way I will."

"We'll have to tell Father about lifeguarding," Leah says. "If we get him on our side, talk about the importance of saving people, he'll help us with Ma. He'll understand."

"It's always like this. When Ma's not fighting with Father,

she's fighting with us. She has to yell at someone. You'd think she'd be more grateful. We took care of everything while she was on vacation. So what if the boys have a day off." I stop and take a deep breath. "Now she's home, she has to show who's boss."

"I don't care about the stockings," Leah says. "I just want to continue swimming."

I take my new ring off. I want to throw it at the door, follow Ma and throw it at her. But it's a gift from her, it's silver, and it's my first ring. I leave it on top of the dresser as if I don't care what happens to it. I don't want Ma's gifts, not now.

Father comes into our room later that night and closes the door. In his hand is a brown paper bag, and I wonder what's in it. He sits on Leah's bed and lectures us on the importance of a woman's modesty. "The Jews escaped slavery in Egypt because of three things," he says, quoting from the Chumash, swaying as if he's studying. "Name, dress, and language. You two call each other by your goyishe names, Rachel instead of Ruchel; you speak a goyishe language; and now you're changing the way you dress. I will not have any of that in this house. This is a Chassidishe home."

He opens the bag slowly and pulls out six new pairs of thick beige stockings with seams. "I went all the way to Williamsburg to buy these," he says. "If you're old enough to wear beige, you'll wear beige with seams. So everyone knows your legs are covered. So there's no question about it, no talk."

Leah and I look at each other.

"I will never wear stockings with seams," I say. "No one in our school wears seams."

"In Williamsburg, all the Satmar girls wear seams. I visited

Reb Berkovitz, the principal of the girls' school, and asked him. He told me where to buy them. You and Leah will look like fine Satmar girls."

He went to Williamsburg to talk to a man about girls' stockings. Two men talking about what I should put on my legs. What do they know about girls' legs, about what's comfortable, what looks good?

"We don't live in Williamsburg. If you wanted us to look like Williamsburg girls, you shouldn't have moved away from Williamsburg." I sound like Ma. But it's true. We wouldn't have had so many problems if we'd lived in Williamsburg. Ma would've liked it better. We all would've liked it better.

"What do you mean, you don't live in Williamsburg? God is everywhere," Father says. "The same God is here and in Williamsburg. You will behave the same way in whatever country or city you're in."

I don't answer.

"And this," Father says, lifting the mask. "What new thing is this?"

Leah explains about lifeguarding. About learning to save people who are drowning.

Father nods. "A very good thing to know. Who's teaching it?"

"The Nussbaum girl."

"And there are only women in the swimming pool?" Father asks.

Leah and I nod. "It's once a week, on Sunday night. We have the whole swimming pool to ourselves for two and a half hours. And we practice."

"That's good. But no more of these see-through stockings, you hear?"

Leah nods, and Father gets up and walks out, leaving the six pairs of thick seamed stockings on the bed.

"He didn't say a word about the books," I say. "He was so busy driving to Williamsburg for those stockings, he forgot about everything else."

"I don't want him to call our teachers in school," Leah says. "It's embarrassing."

"I am never wearing those seams," I tell Leah. "Never."

"Then don't wear beige," she says. "Why'd you have to start wearing beige?"

At dinner, I don't talk to Ma. I hate her. Father fills the silence, explaining that Union National Bank is giving him money to build the synagogue, and when it's finished, he will pay a certain amount a month, plus interest.

"We'll be in debt all our lives paying interest," Ma says.

"It's called a mortgage," Father says. "We'll move into a big new apartment above the synagogue, and I'll rent this bungalow out. The money will help with monthly payments. That's how things are done in business."

"Why not borrow from a Jewish bank or fund, so there's no interest?" Ma says.

Father answers, smiling at what women don't know. "All banks charge interest. That's how they stay in business. And Jewish funds don't have enough money. I already owe the fund several thousand dollars for your trip."

"You're smiling as if I'm too stupid to understand," Ma says. "But just wait until the day they come and put you in chains because you can't pay your bills. Then who's going to laugh? I'll sit here laughing and crying at once."

Father shakes his head. "Not everything will come from the bank. There are people in Brazil and Montreal who have promised great sums. Berl Reichman is sending a truckload of tiles for the

showers and mikvah. All the way from Canada. How do you think
he made his money? He went into debt. To earn money you have
to spend money."

Father talks like a man who knows money, like someone
who's lived with money all his life. I watch Ma's face closing,
holding back. She can't threaten to leave again after coming home,
and suddenly I know why she's back. I know her mother said to go
home, to go back to her husband and children, because that's
where a wife and a mother of seven children belongs.

The next day, I wear my leather boots to school so the girls in my
class can't see my stockings. Which gives me an idea. I can wear
sheer panty hose under my boots, and Ma won't know. I could
take my shoes with me and change in school. It will seem normal
to everyone as long as it's cold out.

Ma complains that Sunday is the worst day for both Leah and
me to be out. It's after Shabbat and it's laundry day.

"So change the day for laundry," I tell her.

"If I don't do the laundry Sunday, right after Shabbat, the
children will have nothing to wear come Monday," she says.

Leah and I hurry home from school and do everything in two
hours. I run through the house with piles of folded underwear,
socks, and shirts, separating them and putting them into the right
drawers. Leah washes all the dishes, cleans the stove, and sweeps
the kitchen floor. By the time it's seven, the house is spotless and
we're ready to go. Ma can't say anything, but still she's not satisfied.

"What do the girls wear in the water? More important, what
do you wear?" she asks.

"Bathing suits," Leah answers, and I look at her, surprised to
hear her tell Ma the truth.

"Big girls walking around naked. Wait till I tell Father. He won't think it's so good then."

Ricki beeps, and we leave without answering.

When we get home, Father's sitting at the kitchen table. He looks up when we come in. "So what did you learn today?" he asks.

Leah and I describe all the saves and carries. We demonstrate on each other, walking back and forth across the kitchen, stumbling over each other, trying to be the one to do the talking and performing.

He smiles. "Maybe you could take turns. One of you could go one week and the other the next. You could teach each other what the other has missed. That way Mama won't be here alone with all the children. She needs your help. She doesn't like both of you leaving her."

I pull out a chair and sit down at the table. "It's only for ten weeks, and four are already gone. And we already paid for it. After ten weeks, we will be tested and then licensed. She can hold out for six more Sundays."

Father nods. "Is it modest? Are the girls in your class modest?"

"When we're not in the water, we're covered," I explain. "It's cold."

"What about in the water?" Father asks.

"What difference does it make what we wear in the water?" I say. "Men go to the mikvah completely naked. We're at least covered. It's impossible to swim quickly in a dress. The person will drown by the time you get there."

Father says, "As long as there are only women, it doesn't truly matter. You can wear what you like."

Leah and I look at each other. We can wear what we like. Father just pronounced it. I want to make him repeat it. Get Ma in here and make Father repeat it in front of her. We can wear what we like. Bathing suits for swimming. Like normal people.

"Tell Ma," Leah says. "Tell her we can wear whatever we like for swimming, even bathing suits. Tell her it's only for ten weeks. That we'll earn money after. That it's worth it."

"I'll tell her," Father says. "But let me tell you another thing. Mama says you called her an Indian. That she heard you saying, in English, 'She's such an Indian.' What does this mean? What kind of behavior is that, calling a mother names, an Indian?"

Leah and I try hard not to laugh. She must've heard the word "idiot." Aloud I say, "She must not have understood. Why would we call her an Indian? She can't be an Indian; she wasn't born one."

"Then speak Yiddish so she understands her own children in her own house. So she doesn't think you're talking about her."

We want to skip and leap we're so happy. But not in front of Father. We wait until we're in our room, sitting on our beds facing each other, looking into each other's chlorine-red eyes. Leah's are shiny, and I can see myself in her pupils. I unzip my bag, take out my wet bathing suit and towel, and drop them on the floor in a pile. Out in the open. No hiding. Leah follows.

"Let's put everything in the washing machine," I say. "They need to be washed and dried properly. With soap. They stink."

Ma lifts the blue bathing suit and then the red one with the tips of her fingers. "You're not embarrassed to wear these?" she asks. "If my mother saw me wearing a little nothing like this, she'd have pulled my hair out. She wouldn't have let me live. I wouldn't have dared. We went to the ocean wearing dresses. I thought a sleeveless jumper was bad enough. In America, things are modern. My mother always said every Jew in America has a little pig in his stomach."

She looks at me. I don't say anything. When things are going your way, there's nothing to say. I think I can even forgive her for the stockings. Ma knowing about our bathing suits will make this summer easy. We won't have to worry about someone calling her. We'll go to work wearing our bathing suits underneath our robes, earn ten dollars an hour, and come home to change.

I call Avon and they send me a new catalog. We'll need new bathing suits for the summer. I select a blue-and-white gingham for Sarah. With sisters as lifeguards, Sarah and Esther will swim free every day this summer. I want the bright-yellow sunflower suit. Leah picks a white one. Pure white. She says, "White will look great against a good tan. Lifeguards get really tanned."

I see Ma looking through the catalog, shaking her head. She doesn't like touching our bathing suits, but she's curious. She asks questions about lifeguarding. I tell her that it's important not to panic. She says, "Maybe I can come and watch sometime. Maybe Father can drive me to Bader's and wait in the car."

I don't say anything. I don't want her coming to see us. I don't want her to see me, to see my naked arms and thighs.

She asks what the girls do when it's their time of the month. I tell her they don't go into the water; they just watch.

"Has that happened to you?" she asks.

"Luckily, no." I don't tell her about tampons.

"Wouldn't you be embarrassed for everyone to know?" she asks.

Father comes home from Canada with two divers' watches, big, heavy black-and-chrome watches with wide black rubber bands and letters that glow in the dark. We can take these watches two hundred feet underwater. Ma says they're mannish, but Leah and I love them. They have manual timers, and we clock ourselves swimming laps, treading water, washing dishes, walking to school.

It takes me exactly one and a half minutes to slip my tights off on the way to school in the morning. It takes four minutes to put them back on.

This is the best gift we've ever gotten. Beautiful black divers' watches.

CHAPTER FIFTEEN

FATHER HIRES A Jewish architect to do blueprints for the synagogue, and they have long meetings in the dining room, with the door closed. The drawings are spread out on the table, and when the meeting is over, Leah and I bend over them. We're mostly interested in the third elevation, with plans for a large four-bedroom apartment. Every bedroom has a walk-in closet, and the master bedroom has its own full bath. The kitchen is large, with counters on all sides. There's also a dinette, a dining room, a long living room, a playroom, and an open front porch.

Ma's not interested. "I don't want anything to do with plans for a building I don't want in the first place," she says. "Your father doesn't listen to me; why should I listen to him?"

"Because if you don't look at them now," I tell her, "you'll be complaining later, about why the kitchen is here and the bathroom there."

"Say what you will, I'm not moving in there. I will not live above a synagogue like a rebbetzin. Let your father be a rabbi, I will not be a rebbetzin. I'm proud to be what my father is, simple and hardworking. I don't need honors. But why are we talking about it? You're getting excited over a piece of paper. As if the building's already built. It hasn't even been started. God knows it never will be."

Father asks what should be larger, the kitchen or the dinette. Ma won't say. I say what I think she would say: "A kitchen can never be large enough."

In the basement, Father's planning to build a matzo oven for Passover and a mikvah fed by water from the well. He had a dream about water running underground, and when he dug the earth with a shovel, he heard gurgling. He's putting everything into this building, everything a Chassidic community needs in one building.

The synagogue will be above the basement, with a separate entrance on the side for women. Leah says we can build a swimming pool on the roof because it's flat, a pool the whole length of the building.

Father smiles and nods. "With water from our own well," he says, "a swimming pool is possible."

Ma says, "You're all just like your father, crazy dreamers. You know how heavy water is?"

Father says, "I'll talk to the engineer. He can do the calculations."

"We can charge people," I say. "To help pay expenses."

"We can have double shifts: girls in the morning, boys in the afternoon," Leah says. "And family can swim any other time we feel like. We could even swim at night, in the dark."

"And break your neck falling over the side of the building," Ma says.

"The walls would have to be high, very high," Father says. "We'll see what the engineer says. Right now I'm waiting for the building department to straighten out the title. I can't get started until they grant me a permit."

The bungalow next door is almost taken apart. All the wood, doors, and windows are stacked in piles; everything's saved. The bathtub, toilet, and sink are sitting on our front lawn, an unusable bathroom. It's slow work, and I can understand why Kleinman used fire. Father won't hear of it. "Fire is wasteful, fire destroys," he says.

When he's not traveling, selling his book and collecting funds for the new synagogue, he's outside pulling nails, removing windows and doors. His arms are turning brown and strong, like a construction worker's. But suddenly there's a lien on the property, and work can't go on. Someone named Adler is claiming that he owns the title. Father has a signed bill of sale to prove we own the lot, but Mr. Adler's papers also have the right signatures, and Yosel Kleinman isn't returning phone calls.

Ma says, "I knew there'd be trouble. Call the Viznitzer Rebbe. That ganef won't ignore his own rebbe's phone calls."

Father says, "I don't want to involve the Viznitz community. I'll take Kleinman to Din Torah. I'll go to Williamsburg and talk to the rabbis who sit on the Beth Din."

"Why not court?" I say. "That's what they suggested at the Building Department. Take Kleinman to court. He's a thief."

"A Yid doesn't take another Yid to court. It would be a chillul hashem. That's why we have our own court."

"Beth Din," Ma says. "They never make a real decision. It's always a compromise. And Yosel Kleinman's money will impress the judges. Just wait and see. You'll lose everything. If Viznitz finds out you're planning to build a synagogue, they'll work twice as hard against you."

Father says, "We're Yidden. We have to trust one another."

Our lifeguard test is scheduled in two weeks, and Leah and I are nervous. Swimming classes were over a month ago, and we haven't been practicing. It's May, and indoor pools are already closed for the season, but outdoor pools haven't opened yet. It's still too cold to swim outside, but Ricki convinced her parents to fill their pool early so we can take the test. She says not to expect anything less than freezing water.

Leah and I spend every night reviewing, talking through the maneuvers, going through the motions, practicing them walking instead of swimming. After the practical exam, we'll take the written. Ricki will send in the scores to the Red Cross, and they'll send us our licenses. Then we can apply for summer jobs. Leah and I take turns testing each other.

Father spends hours writing notes for the Din Torah, arguments to convince the judges he's right. Some nights he reads them aloud.

"I can't understand what there is to argue," I tell him. "You bought the place in 1967, so it was no longer Kleinman's to sell."

Father smiles and says, "I wish it were that simple and without complications. The problem is I bought both bungalows for the cost of one and a half. It was an agreement we came to." He stops and thinks about this, remembering. His stories always take three times longer than they should. Whatever he says, he makes it sound as if he's solving a puzzle or figuring out a passage of the Talmud. "But Yosel Kleinman only gave me the title to number nineteen, and promised the other at a later date. He never signed over the title."

"Why didn't you ask for the title right away?"

"I did, and he said then that he didn't have it with him. Now I know why."

"What happens if he wins?"

"I don't know what happens." Father sways and pulls his beard. "I already spent money taking the bungalow apart, drawing up plans. God knows what happens. With his help, the right thing will happen."

It's sunny and cold the afternoon we take the test, and we all stand at the edge, shivering. I dip my toes in, and the water is clear and cruel. Ricki says, "I won't make you tread or swim laps. I've seen you do it enough."

We stand there listening to her and hugging ourselves. It's indecent being out in a bathing suit in this weather.

"I want each of you to do a shallow dive, swim halfway across, and do a quick return. You can line up and do it one after the other."

Everyone passes this one.

"Now team up," Ricki says. "The victim won't be facing you, so you can't tell whether she's panicked. Victims, don't be afraid to struggle. Lifeguards, decide on your strategy and proceed. One team at a time."

I do a surface jump to keep my eyes on the victim, swim up behind her, remember my quick return, and do a chest carry so she can't get away from me if she panics. She kicks her legs and waves her arms a bit, then stops, as if trusting that I am in control. If your touch is strong and sure, the book says, the victim often calms down. The water is cold; I have to keep moving. I side-stroke to safety and remember not to let go of my victim until I have her hands over the edge of the pool, my hands over hers.

Ricki says, "Good. That's enough. Stay in and switch: you're the victim now."

I swim out to the middle of the pool and tread water, trying to decide how much to struggle. Leah and I aren't working together today; Ricki doesn't want us making it easy for each other.

I flail about until I feel strong, sure arms holding me, as if I'm a real victim.

We do more carries, then we dive with our masks and snorkels, find coins Ricki throws in, surface, spouting water through the snorkel, breathing without bringing our heads out of the water, then go down again, diving and surfacing, up and down, across the length of the pool and back. I'm warming up.

We each have to show that we know how to throw the Styrofoam ring to the victim, then draw in the rope hand over hand, like a lasso. Then the long aluminum body hook. These are the first tools to consider in every emergency. A lifeguard should enter the water only when there's no other choice.

"You're done and I'm proud of all of you," Ricki says. "You did well. The written exam is on Thursday night, here at my house. Then I'll send the scores in, and the results should be back in a week or so."

Leah and I walk home, talking about exactly what we did for each of the emergencies. It's cold, and even with our hoods up over our wet hair, our teeth are chattering.

"We're almost lifeguards," I say.

"Yes. We definitely passed," Leah says. "We did every single thing right."

"I'll have two cards in my wallet," I tell Leah. "A library card and a lifeguard's card. The next card I want is a driver's license. I'll be sixteen in September. Which is when I can get a junior permit, Ricki said. She never takes buses."

"You're crazy," Leah says. "Father will never let a woman drive. How are you going to keep that a secret?"

"If I drove, everyone would enjoy it. Ma would love it. I could take her to the mall and on family trips."

"You're dreaming. Where do you get these ideas?"

"We won't need rides everywhere. We won't have to depend on Father."

The trial at the Beth Din goes on and on. Mornings, Ma packs Father's lunch in his black leather briefcase, along with all the notes he wrote the night before. She worries about him. He's losing weight, and already he was too skinny. He's so worried about the Din Torah, about losing the bungalow, losing the possibility of a big synagogue, losing everything he's been hoping for, he doesn't sleep at night. Even though she never wanted the synagogue, Ma wishes him good luck on his way out.

On the last day of the trial, I stay home from school with Esther, so Ma can be with Father. Although there's no place for women in the courtroom, Ma wants to be waiting when he comes out. She says she'll run errands, visit an old friend, and then come back and wait in the car. Father says it's not necessary, that there won't be a final decision for a month or so, and when it does come it will be a compromise. He says not to expect a win. Still he's hoping.

Before they leave in the morning, Father says to me, "Pray that God puts the right words into my mouth today. God listens to the prayers of innocent children."

I start praying at eleven o'clock, when the trial's scheduled to begin, worrying that Father might be better off without my prayers. I am not an innocent child. I start at the back of the book, avoiding the psalms I've tried before, those that didn't work. Then I go back to my other book. With Ma and Father away, I can sit at the kitchen table and read.

Father comes home happy. "It'll be a good compromise," he says. "I'll have the synagogue." He explains that he agreed to give up certain rights to the lake in exchange for the title. Kleinman wants to fill in the lake and donate his share of the land to Viznitz for a new boys' yeshiva.

I don't think we should compromise, since we're right in the first place. Part of Ashley Lake is ours. It's been in back of our bungalows for years. Ashley was built around this lake which is fed by underground streams and runs into Francis Lake. All flowing water in Monhegan ends up in Francis Lake.

Father says, "We'll still own the part that's ours, but as land instead of water. I told the judges that the lake is fed by running water and the water will find another place to flow, the way water does. I showed them the engineer's statement about the damage it could cause, and Kleinman agreed to install special water pipes underground, the way they did on Hopal Lane. What more could I ask for?"

"I wouldn't have given up the lake," I tell Father.

"We're gaining land," he says. "Land is more valuable than water."

"Water looks better than land."

Ma says, "What you should worry about is the boundaries. Without water between us, you'll have Viznitz in your own back-yard. Right under your nose, a Viznitz yeshiva."

Father says, "That's true. I'll write to the judges about that. I'll ask for a high fence to separate us. I am in a good position to ask for things."

"Instead of a lake, we will be seeing an ugly fence from our bedroom window," I say. "The lake was something to look at. We caught a carp once, remember?"

"When the new building is finished, you'll have a view of all of Ashley from the third floor. You won't see the fence from up there. Thank God we got the main thing. The title."

"You brought all this trouble on yourself," Ma says. "I warned you not to start with that bungalow and a synagogue in the first place. All dreams and fantasies. You should listen to your wife more. I know what I'm saying. I'm always right."

"You were wrong about the book," I say. "It's selling. We get checks in the mail almost every day now."

"Bubkes," Ma says. "What do those checks pay for? Printing and mailing costs. We haven't broken even yet, and already your father's ordering another printing."

No one bothers to say that the second printing is cheaper, that the fact that there's going to be another printing is a good sign. Somehow Ma is always in a position to say, "I warned you."

CHAPTER SIXTEEN

OUR RED CROSS LICENSES arrive in the mail. We sign and laminate them and schedule an interview with Mr. Gartner.

On the phone, he says, "You two being sisters could work out very well. I always hire two lifeguards, so one can cover for the other. And you won't even have to make a phone call."

Leah and I figure that we can get a second lifeguard job at different hours. So we can both work every day and still cover for each other.

Thursday night, we tell Father we'll need a ride the next day. We warn him that we have to be there by eleven.

At ten-thirty, he's still not home.

Ma says, "Now you see what I suffer with that man. You can't rely on him for anything. Let this be a lesson to you. If you get this job, you'll have to find someone else to give you a ride every day."

"Let's call a cab," Leah says. "We can't just wait."

"Who knows how long the cab will take to get here."

"We have no choice," Leah says. "What do you want to do? Just stand and wait?"

I dial Pete's Taxi and give him our address. It will take at least ten minutes, the dispatcher says.

Seven minutes later, Ma announces that Father's here. I call to cancel the cab, and the man says, "Ma'am, next time don't call unless you're sure you need one."

Leah is already in the car. I get in and close the door.

Father says, "I was talking to Yidel Weiss about my book. He saw me in the bookstore and stopped to ask a few questions. He wants to know if I would teach a class on Cabala writings."

"Let's go," I say. "It's on Sleepy Hollow, you know, off the turnpike. You can talk while you drive. Quick."

Father starts out quickly and then slows down. We should have taken the taxi anyway. We would have gotten there a lot sooner.

"You have to drive faster," I tell him. "We're late. We're not going to get hired if we can't even be on time for our interview."

"Who is this man Mr. Gartner?" Father asks. "Is he even a Yid? Gartner."

"Who knows," I say. "The important thing is that we get there."

"It's important that he's a Yid," Father says slowly. "I don't want my daughters working for a goy."

I look at Leah. She's biting her nails to the white moons. I want to scream. I want to put my foot over Father's and stomp down hard, give the car gas. I want to drive to Gartner's and get this job.

On Maple, we're lucky and we get the light. We're lucky again on Route 59.

"See," Father says. "If you drive at the right pace, you make all the lights. There's no reason to rush. It won't help. It only causes accidents, God forbid."

I imagine calling Mr. Gartner from the hospital to say we can't be at the interview because we were in a car accident.

Father pulls into the circular gravel driveway and asks if he should wait for us.

"No," I say. I don't want him here, looking around, deciding whether this is a good enough place for us to work. And I don't want Mr. Gartner to see him and think that's what we're like. Father's not the kind of man you imagine moving quickly to save a life.

"We'll either walk or take a taxi or both. I don't know how long we'll be."

Leah and I go up the stone steps in front of the inn. I can hear Father's tires on the gravel, moving slowly. He's looking around. It's so shady here it's a forest. A magical forest. Underneath the green ivy, the inn is all stone.

Inside, the smell of wood. There's a fire burning in the big stone fireplace; everything here is dark wood and stone. We walk up to the reception desk, to a girl with long straight brown hair, parted in the middle.

"We're here to meet Mr. Gartner," I say. "My name is Rachel Benjamin, and this is my sister Leah."

"You must be the lifeguards," she says, looking at us over the high desk. The phone rings, and she answers softly, "Gartner's."

I turn away to look around, to not stare at her. I want to see her better. Her eyelashes are long, black, and curly at the corners. I want to see what she's wearing all the way down to her shoes, but she's behind the long wood desk. I turn back to look. She covers the mouthpiece and says, "Have a seat near the fire."

Leah and I walk over to the big stone fireplace, to the burgundy leather sofas and chairs. I sit on the long sofa near the fire. Leah sits across from me in a chair.

"This place is gorgeous," she says. "Imagine coming here every day in the summer. It'll be like living in a castle."

I nod and tell her to be quiet. She always gets talkative at the wrong times. I want us to seem older, like we're used to all this. But it's true I've never seen anything like this place. It looks so old. I look at the girl behind the desk. She's so lucky to be working here. I wonder if she lives here too.

A tall, thin man walks into the inn and up to the desk like he knows exactly where he's going. The girl motions toward us with her chin. The man turns and takes long steps across the room. He's wearing cowboy boots under his pants.

"Hello. I am Mr. Gartner. You must be the Benjamin sisters."

He puts his hand out for me to shake and says, "And you are?"

"Rachel," I say and stand up to put my hand in his large hand. We shake.

Ma would never shake a man's hand. She would apologize and explain that she's religious and can't. The way she does with doctors. Mr. Gartner puts his hand out to Leah. She remains seated but shakes his hand and says, "I'm Leah."

Mr. Gartner sits in the chair near her. "Rachel and Leah. Leah and Rachel. Very biblical."

"It is," Leah says. Mr. Gartner looks at her.

"I mean, they are from the Bible," she says. "The wives of Jacob." I look at her to make her stop talking.

He smiles and nods. "Are you two religious? Are you Orthodox?"

We nod, and for once Leah keeps her mouth shut.

"I've never had religious lifeguards," he says. "But since the people you'll guard are religious, I can't see why that shouldn't work. On Saturdays, my guests have the swimming pool to themselves all day."

Gartner. I think he could be Jewish. A non-religious Jew.

He leans back in his chair. "I'll start by telling you about this inn," he says. "It was built in 1859, and it's been in my family since the 1920s. I've been running the place for fifteen years or so, the last five with the help of my wife, Judy, whom you met at the desk."

I'm sorry he has a wife. I wish he didn't. I don't know why, but he doesn't look like a man with a wife.

"We have twelve rooms in this inn. It's not large, but that's how we like it. Intimate." He breathes.

"Breakfasts are served buffet style. Dinners are served in the dining room, through those doors. You won't have much contact with our guests. You may see them sunning on the deck in the back or strolling. Be courteous and brief. I don't want the swimming pool crowd wandering near the inn. I want them to go straight up to the pool and stay within that area."

He stops and looks at each of us, and it is as if I am at a desk in a classroom, not sitting in this castle on this leather sofa in front of this burning fire.

"Now. Tell me about yourselves," he says, folding one leg over the other and letting it swing. "How old are you?"

Leah and I both have our mouths half open, ready to talk, waiting to see who will talk first. We look at each other and laugh. He laughs with us.

"I'm almost sixteen and Leah's fourteen. She has a junior license."

He nods and looks at me, as if he's expecting me to continue. I start by telling him we grew up in Ashley and how, winters, the whole place is ours. Leah looks at me. She knows I'm making Ashley seem better than it is, and that it doesn't compare to this place.

Leah keeps wanting to talk, and finally I let her. She tells him what school we go to and how we trained as lifeguards at Bader's Hotel. He nods like he knows the place. Hotel people must know each other, I think.

"So you both passed the test the first time?" he asks.

"Yes," we say together.

He smiles and stands up, his body long and hard. "Let me show you where the swimming pool is. It's still covered up, of course, but you'll make out the size."

We follow him out the back doors, white French doors with glass panes. Everything in this inn is so perfect. He looks at our shoes.

"It's still wet out here. The ground is wet from all the rain."

"We're used to wet ground from Ashley," Leah says.

He takes out a large ring of keys and unlocks the gate to the pool. I can see he has the Styrofoam tube that every pool is required to have.

"Do you have a hook too?" I ask, to show we take our lifeguarding seriously, that we know what's important.

"Yes. And there's a first-aid kit we keep out here in the summer. It's in storage now."

Leah and I walk around the perimeter of the pool, trying to look serious. He waits for us at the gate and locks the door behind us.

"Well, you two are hired. I open the pool on June twenty-fifth and close it on Labor Day. I will need either of you Sundays through Fridays, eleven to two. Then there's a boys' shift. Know any Orthodox boys who are lifeguards?"

I shake my head. I can't imagine David or Levi a lifeguard. They can hardly swim. We walk around to the front of the inn and stop. He looks at his watch. "I am driving past Saddle River Road and Route 59. Can I give you a ride to that corner?"

"That would be perfect," I say. I want to stop at Waldbaum's for *Wuthering Heights.* Gartner's Inn looks like the picture on the cover, and having it, reading it, will get me through the next days and nights. I decide to buy the book instead of stealing it. We'll be earning good money soon.

"Wait here," he says. "I'll bring the car around."

I watch him walk away, toward the other side of the inn. Leah is looking into the trees. She turns a full circle with her arms out.

"This place is gorgeous," she says. "It's like a fairy tale, this inn. It looks like a castle, only small."

Mr. Gartner pulls up in a dark, shiny car. He leans over and opens the passenger door. "One of you sit in the front. The front seat in a Jaguar is more fun."

Leah opens the back door for herself, leaving me the front. Before I get in, Mr. Gartner picks up a magazine off the seat and throws it behind him. I sink into the seat. It's low and soft. Leather. I can smell Mr. Gartner from where I am, a fancy rough perfume smell. If someone in Monhegan sees me riding in front like this, near a man, Ma will hear about it. I turn around to Leah, but she's looking at the magazine. A car magazine. She's not watching me, sitting in the front seat of this Jaguar, near this man.

"I knew Mr. Ashley," Mr. Gartner says suddenly. "He was a friend of my father's."

I look at him to see if he isn't just kidding. "Really?"

He nods. "He came to visit. He and my father would sit in front of the fireplace, smoking."

He turns to me. "This was before you were born. I was a boy."

I can't imagine him younger, different from now.

"What was Ashley like then?" I ask. "It's changing now. They're building ugly houses."

"Yes, I heard." He takes a deep breath. "Ashley was a beautiful country club. My father would speak of the Black Kat Casino.

He and Mom would go Saturday nights. I went swimming there once."

Mr. Gartner and I in the same swimming pool, only at different times. He was there before Ashley was Jewish, before separate swimming. I can imagine Ashley looking beautiful, a little like Gartner's Inn. Before roads. Before Yosel Kleinman. Before us.

"They stopped using the pool years ago," Leah says. "It was already crumbling when we moved in. Then they stopped filling it. Now they're digging it up."

"They're getting rid of the lake too," I tell him. "My brother and I used to ice skate on the lake."

"How many children are in your family?" he asks. "I already know of three. Are there more?"

I nod.

"How many?"

"Seven altogether."

"Seven," he repeats. "It must be wonderful having six brothers and sisters. I wish I had brothers and sisters."

"You don't even have one?" Leah asks.

"I was an only child," he says.

"You're lucky," I say. "Only children have their own rooms."

"You two share a room?" He looks at me and I nod. "Is it that bad?" he asks.

I laugh, and he pulls over to the side of the road at the corner of Saddle River and Route 59, and I'm sorry we got here so quickly. "Here we are," he says. "It was nice meeting you. See you June twenty-fifth."

Leah and I watch him turn left toward Suffern. The car shines and flashes on the road. I imagine myself driving his car, him sitting in the passenger seat, letting me drive his Jaguar.

CHAPTER SEVENTEEN

MR. GARTNER CALLS and asks to see me; only me, not Leah. He says he'll pick me up in Ashley. He asks which bungalow. I tell him I'll wait on the corner, even though I know the corner is not the place to be picked up by a man. I wear my soft gray dress from Fixler's. He pulls up in his Jaguar and leans over to open the door for me. I slide into the seat and sink lower and lower, a sinking like a dream. The soft leather and the smell of Mr. Gartner surround me. Mr. Gartner leans over and kisses me, and for a moment I feel his shaved dry skin against my skin. I want to rub against it, rub my face and my whole naked body against it. He speaks, and I can hardly hear him; all I hear is my skin asking to rub against his.

I watch his hands move on the wheel as he drives. I stare at his brown strong hands, the short black hairs on the back. We're on Saddle River Road, and he's taking me to his inn.

"I hope you're hungry," he says. "We have roasted pheasant for dinner. But first I'll show you to your room to dress."

"Dress?" I look down at my pleats.

He turns his head to me and takes one of his large hands off the wheel and encloses my hand in it. "Wait and see."

His hand is doing something to my stomach. I close my eyes and feel his hand and the movement of the car turning into the circular gravel driveway of Gartner's Inn. This car feels like a cat; It glides so smoothly, so low to the ground, and stops in front of the big wooden double doors.

I watch him stride across the front of the car and open my door. He helps me out.

I am in a fairy tale. He's wearing a brown leather jacket and jeans and cowboy boots. I want a pair of cowboy boots to stride in.

He doesn't let go of my hands, and we walk up the stairs together, jump-skipping up, one-two-three. Inside, the smell of wood burning. Mr. Gartner leads me to the leather sofa, not the chair. I sit. He walks to the table and lifts a dark bottle, pulls the cork out, and pours into two short glasses.

He hands me one and says, "Sherry. Try it."

I sip and he sips, we watch each other sipping, he standing in front of me, the gold liquid hot and burning.

He puts our glasses on the table, and we walk up the curving stairs, I in front of him, going up to I don't know where. On the landing, he steps in front of me and turns right, and I follow him down a long hallway. At the end, he opens a door to a large room with dark wood furniture and white lace coverings. The bed is so high it has a stool to get up to it. Will I sleep in this bed tonight?

Mr. Gartner steps into the room and walks to the bed. "Everything you'll need is here, I believe."

He takes long cowboy steps out the door and smiles when he turns to close it behind him. I stand staring at the door and then the bed. A long, thin red gown is laid out across it, and on the floor are red velvet shoes to match. There's also a red lace bra and panties on the bed, and my face turns red thinking about Mr. Gartner buying me panties. The stockings are silky and black.

Before I figure out what to do first, there's a knock, and a woman in a white apron enters. She smiles and takes my hand and leads me to the long mirror on the wardrobe door. I see myself, my white round collar, and look at the red dress on the bed. I am not made for such a dress. I wear pleated skirts.

The woman starts to unzip me, and I let her. I step out of the dress when it lands on the floor and stand there in my plain white cotton slip. I don't want her to see me in my white underwear. I walk over to the bed and, without taking my slip off, change out of my white panties into the red lace ones. She's not watching; she's busy at the dresser. I quickly pull my slip over my head, take off my bra, and put on the new one. The woman steps up behind me and clasps the hook. I walk to the mirror. I've never seen myself in red. She wraps a large towel around my shoulders and pushes a bench up for me to sit. I watch her brush my hair. My head sways forward and back with the rhythm of her brushing.

She hands me the black stockings, and I put them on carefully. They're so soft and silky, so easy to tear. She brings the red dress, and I step into it with my silky black-stocking feet. She zips me up, and the higher the zipper goes, the more my body shows. It is as if I've painted my naked body red. There are no sleeves on this dress; it's a jumper, and I'm wearing it without a blouse underneath.

The woman steps away and looks and puts her fingers to her lips and kisses them loudly, smackingly. "Beautiful," she says slowly, with an accent, the first thing I've heard her say. She puts the red velvet shoes in front of me, and I step into them. They are like slippers, not shoes. I walk across the floor, feeling them. The bottoms are so soft they hardly make a sound. I lift my foot to see the sole. Pale soft leather. And in gold lettering, six and a half, my size. Everything fits perfectly.

The woman opens the door, steps away for a minute, and comes back to say he's waiting in front of the fire. She follows me to the steps and whispers, "Hold on to the banister and walk slowly."

I do as she says and feel like Cinderella entering the ballroom. There are several men with Mr. Gartner, and they turn and watch me walk down the stairs. When I get near the bottom, Mr. Gartner comes over and takes my hand. In his printed silk jacket and black velvet pants, he looks like Mr. Rochester. He's wearing black patent-leather shoes now, not cowboy boots, but still he takes long strides with his long legs.

He leans over and puts his lips on my hair.

The men stand up when we approach, and they each shake my hand and tell me their names. I don't hear them. Mr. Gartner and I lead the way into the dining room and to the long table set with heavy white plates and candles in a row all the way down to the end. He pulls out the first chair on the left side, and I sit, the only woman at this table. He sits at the head. Other guests of the inn are sitting in couples, each couple alone at a small round table. Someone's playing the piano in the corner, and when we're all seated, he gets up and comes to sit with us. He's also wearing a silk jacket and black pants, all the men are, only the colors of their jackets are different.

Mr. Gartner reaches for a fat bottle and takes a small silver knife from his pocket to open it. The men are laughing at someone's joke, and I turn to listen. Mr. Gartner stands up and pours wine into our glasses. We sip, and the men talk about the age of the wine. I've never had wine like this. Burning wine.

The waiter puts sparkling white bowls down in front of us and serves thick white soup.

"Chowder," someone says.

A large platter with the largest-looking chicken I have ever seen arrives on a cart, and Mr. Gartner stands up to cut it. So this is pheasant. He puts two slices on my plate, and the waiter comes around and fills my plate with tiny potatoes and leafy vegetables.

"That's a good bird you caught this time, Henry. One shot too," the man across from me says.

"It was a good day for it," Mr. Gartner says. "I shot a good few that day."

"You have a gun?" I ask, and everyone laughs.

"I have several shotguns. I'll show them to you, if you like."

Everyone laughs, drinks, and eats, and the man sitting near me explains that they're hunting buddies, and the one who shoots the most birds hosts the dinner. Before I've finished eating, the music begins again, and Mr. Gartner stands up and takes my hand. He puts his arm around me and holds me, and we're so close together.

We dance like that, so close it's like one person dancing. Somehow he gets my feet to move where he wants them to go. I have to think of nothing. He lifts me right off the floor every time we spin and then sets me back down and we continue. He's tall, and standing this close I have to tilt my head up to see him. He puts his hand on my hair and leans my head against his chest and we dance across the room. There are other couples dancing like we are. I want his arms never to leave me. I see the others only in flashes, green, red, white. I wonder what Leah would say if she could see me. What would Ma say, me in the arms of a strange man?

I look up into his eyes and he looks into mine, all the way inside me. He puts my hands around his neck and his around my waist. We are not as close together now, but we can see each other better, and he's looking up and down my red body. He smooths his hands up my sides almost at my breasts and then down over my hips. He owns me, he has me, all of me. And without warning he just lifts me up into his arms and carries me back to my chair at the table.

After dessert, we sit in the front room, near the fire. Mr. Gartner fills everyone's glass with sherry. It is warm beside the fire, beside Mr. Gartner, and, listening to the men, I think about how much I like the voices of men talking, the sound of their deep, rumbling voices, low enough to sleep to.

Mr. Gartner says, "I better take her up to bed."

He carries me all the way across the room to the steps and up the steps and down the hall to my room, where he lets me stand. He walks around me and unzips my zipper and asks, "Do you want help?"

I shake my head. "I've been dressing and undressing myself for a long time now."

He laughs and says. "There's a nightgown under the pillow. Sleep well."

I watch him walk out the door and close it behind him. Now that I'm alone, I'm wide awake, and I look in the mirror and zip myself back up to see how I looked. I get the nightgown out from under my pillow, and it isn't a nightgown at all. It's a long white silk slip. I take everything off and put on the cold slippery slip and climb up into bed and wish he were there beside me. Then it's the middle of the night, and I wake up and hear the door, and Mr. Gartner walks in and starts to undress right there in front of me. Is he coming into bed with me? I sit up, scared. I don't know how things go from here, what happens next. I'm in my own bed at home, in my old blue nightgown. It's early. I can hear Leah's breathing.

I close my eyes and try to bring Mr. Gartner back, but it doesn't work. Once my eyes are open, even if it's just for a second, I can't do it. I try to think of him with a beard and peyess, someone Father could accept as my husband, and laugh. He could never pass for a Chassid. Everyone could tell he's not by his smell, and his body, and the way he walks.

CHAPTER EIGHTEEN

THE TWENTY-FIFTH IS a sunny June day, not too hot. Leah is taking the first days at Gartner's because I am scheduled to teach my first swimming class at the Weiss pool. She and Sarah are already on their way; the boys are in cheder, and Esther's playing outside. The house is quiet. I go from room to room, making beds. This is our first real day of vacation. Ma's in the kitchen, cleaning up after breakfast. I can hear her humming. With Esther growing up and no new baby on the way, this will be a good summer for her too. The windows and doors are open, and a strong breeze skims through the house. I am still in my nightgown, and goose bumps rise on my neck, legs, and arms.

When I get dressed, it is a bathing suit I put on, and I think about all of us in bathing suits all day. Leah, Sarah, Esther, and I. We'll spend most of our day undressed, near our bodies. People who live by the ocean are always near their bodies; they must get so used to it they're unashamed. It could happen to us this summer.

I walk to the Weiss pool in my long tie-dyed robe with a hood, perfect for the pool. It's blue-green-red-yellow, every color of the rainbow. Leah has one too. They come all the way down to our ankles, so we don't have to wear tights on our way to the pool and back. Our bare legs are under our long robes; on our feet, we wear clogs.

Ma thinks we should wear something anyway, in case. She says, "Knot a pair of stockings at the knees. People will talk if they see your bare feet."

We decide on David's old socks. They come to the middle of our calves.

By the end of the first lesson at the Weiss pool, all five kids are floating facedown in the water and blowing bubbles. The Red Cross guide, *Teaching Johnny to Swim*, works. Next class, they'll learn to kick all the way across the pool, holding their breath as long as possible. Raisy Lender and one of the Weiss kids inhaled water and coughed and coughed. I thought they'd never learn.

Leah and Sarah come home from Gartner's, sunburned and happy. They look good. "Did you see Mr. Gartner?" I ask, careful not to sound too interested.

"No," Leah says. "Judy unlocked the gate and collected the money. There were twenty people today. She says to expect more tomorrow. You'll love it. It's great sitting there in the sun and getting paid for it."

Ma says, "Be careful you don't turn too brown. You'll start looking like an Arabke."

"I want to be brown," Leah says. "Tans look great."

"You're red, not brown," I tell her. "And you have freckles. Your face will turn into one big freckle."

Leah's skin is paler than mine, more like Ma's. In our room, she takes her robe off and shows me the lines where her bathing suit ends. She's proud of these lines that prove how tanned she is. I think she'd look better without lines, just a smooth brown body.

Gartner's gets more sun than the Weiss pool, and I can't wait to be there tomorrow. I want a brown body to walk around in.

"Judy said they'll pay us every Friday, at the end of the week," Leah says.

"If Mrs. Weiss asks, tell her also to pay on Fridays. That way we'll have it all at once."

"The teaching money is all yours. You're doing it."

I nod. I've already decided that. It will come to sixty dollars a week.

"Start saving for your wedding," Ma says. "Your father's certainly not worrying about it. Look at him. Instead of putting money away, knowing he has a sixteen-year-old daughter, and a son right after, he spends, spends, spends."

Father's spending everything on tractors and builders. A truckload of brown and white tiles arrived from Canada, and Father can't wait to build the mikvah. The water from the well is red with minerals and stinks of sulfur; still he plans to use it.

He says, "It's healthy, bathing in mineral waters. People used to travel all the way to Sharon Spring to bathe in such water."

There's the noise of tractors all day. They're digging the foundation, pouring cement, and our yard is a muddy mess. From the backyard, the sound of Yosel Kleinman's tractors installing water pipes and filling the lake. In front, the rumble of the cement truck.

"Look at him," Ma says. "Walks around with nothing but that cursed synagogue on his mind. I want to go in there, into his head, and tear the whole idea out by its roots."

"Don't worry about my wedding," I say.

"Just wait until next year," Ma says, "when the girls in your class start getting engaged one after the other. You'll find out what it feels like to want. You think we'll let all the best yeshiva boys go? You have to grab them while they're there. There are only so

many every year. You're not going to want someone older or
younger, the leftovers. Then there's David to think about. We
can't let you sit around, with David right behind you."

The next day, I get a ride to Gartner's with Mr. Lender. He tells
me Raisy enjoyed my lesson and talked of nothing else all evening. He says, "I've never seen her so excited. She practiced
blowing bubbles in the sink."

I laugh.

He says, "I'm very pleased she's learning how to swim. It's an
important skill, knowing how to swim."

He's an electrician, not a scholar, and I wonder if he knows
that Rashi says every father should teach his son how to swim,
how to survive.

"Swimming helped us escape the Nazis one night," Father
says. "We swam across the Timis River into the next town. Into
Lugoj."

When he was eleven, Father traveled with a group of boys his
age, sleeping in synagogues, basements, and fields. First they
were running from the Nazis, then from the Russians. Their instructions were to wait for their parents in Lugoj. Father waited a
month.

"An important thing to know," Father says, "is that water
always leads somewhere, to a village or city. If ever you're lost in
the woods, look and listen for water and follow the sounds. You'll
always come upon people. Since the beginning of time, mankind
has known to settle around a body of water. Water gives life."

Ma jokes about my teaching her to swim. She says, "I'll sink
like a sack of potatoes. Then what will you do?"

Leah and I laugh, talking about surface diving for her body,
pulling her up by her wrists, and getting her ready for the carry.

Her clothing would be heavy, dragging us down, because she wouldn't swim wearing anything less. We'd have to put her in a snug chest carry, because Ma would definitely panic.

There are thirty-four women at Gartner's. I sit in the sun, watching them, seeing every shape of woman, skinny and fat, their stomachs flat or round. My arms and legs and back are turning brown. I put lotion on my nose and lips to prevent their burning. My eyes are on the back door of the inn, and every time it opens there's a pounding in my chest and my ears, and I have to breathe and swallow to stop it.

By one-thirty, I realize there won't be a problem getting a ride home. From Gartners it's not far to the library, and I decide to go there on Wednesday or Friday after lifeguarding. I can choose my ride down Route 59, pick someone who doesn't know Ma or Father, someone who wouldn't think twice about my going to the library. And I can take the jitney bus home, the books in my swim bag along with my towel and wet things. Ma won't think to look in my swim bag. I can go and come quickly, to the library and then home in less than an hour.

When everyone's out of the water, I decide to walk into the inn. Judy smiles when she sees me and, without asking, points me toward the bathroom. I push the heavy, dark door open. It's beautiful in here. White marble counters and sinks. Big white tiles. The toilet seat is dark wood, like the door. I wash my hot face, careful to dry the sparkling white sink when I'm done. I don't see Mr. Gartner.

On Friday, I get a ride to the library with the Mullers. Inside, I hurry. There are so many people here it's dangerous. The way to avoid being noticed is to go straight to the stacks, not to wander around in open areas. In the D's, I find *Rebecca*. I loved *My Cousin Rachel*. In aisle H, I pick up a Victoria Holt novel. I'm lucky today: *Gone with the Wind* is on the shelf.

Before I walk up to the the librarian's desk, I make sure there's no line. She checks out the books, and I put them in my bag and leave quickly. I walk to the stop on Main Street so I'm not seen waiting in front of the library.

Ma's sitting under a tree in front of the Lenders' house, with the others. That's what the women here do summer afternoons, as if Ashley is still a summer place. They rotate every day, sitting in the shade of someone else's tree. Each woman brings her own canvas folding chair and some sewing or needlepoint.

I wave before I turn in at our walk. I want to put the books away before I join them. They like hearing how the day went at the pool. Leah and I are the oldest girls on the block, and everyone wants to know about our new lifeguarding jobs. Ma worries about all the talk. She says, "This isn't good, I tell you. Your names on every tongue."

I hide the books under Leah's mattress, put on my robe over my bathing suit, and brush my hair. Leah and I will do laps in the Weiss pool today. A lifeguard has to stay in shape.

I drink a glass of water and go out to Ma.

"You're turning brown like a Yemenite," she says.

Mrs. Lender picks up a little dress by the shoulders to show me the smocking.

"How did you do that?" I ask. "Do you have a special machine?"

She shakes her head. "It's easy. You use elasticized thread on the bobbin. When it goes on, you pull on the thread, stretching it to keep an even tension. The rest takes care of itself."

"Are you feeling tired," Ma asks, "sitting in the sun for so many hours?"

"No. Sitting isn't tiring. After swimming I'll be tired."

"Tell me," Mrs. Kahane says. "What do you wear when you swim? People are saying you swim in a bathing suit. I said I don't believe it. Not Rabbi Benjamin's daughters."

I look at Ma's red face. I wish she wouldn't shame so easily. I hate Mrs. Kahane. She's doing this on purpose, to embarrass Ma.

"It's none of your business," I say, "but I'll tell you anyway. We swim in bathing suits. My father says it's fine as long as there are only women."

"You can't be expected to save someone," Ma adds, "swimming in a long wet dress."

Mrs. Kahane's lips spread thin. "If your husband allows it. But I'm surprised. I wouldn't have expected it. Not with a mother who wears black stockings and a father in short pants. Never."

I say, "And what do you, Mrs. Holy of Holies, wear when you swim?" I don't know how Ma can stand this woman. I want to spit at her, I'm so angry.

"Listen to her," Mrs. Kahane says. "A little chutzpenyak. She's a lifeguard in a bathing suit, so now she can open her mouth and talk back. You should have respect for your elders."

I am about to tell her she has no respect for Ma, who's quite a few years older than she is, but I don't have to. Mrs. Lender says, "I'm surprised at you, Tili. How can you speak that way? Mrs. Benjamin is older than you. And she's a rebbetzin."

"My husband may be a rabbi," Ma says quickly, "but do me a favor, don't call me a rebbetzin. 'Mrs. Benjamin' is fine."

Mrs. Gantz leans forward. "Tell us, Tili, what *do* you wear when you swim? Do you wear a dress?"

"Me?" Mrs. Kahane says, gathering her things. She stands up, ready to leave the circle. "I always wore a bathing suit. That's what my mother wore. But I don't claim to be special. I'm not a rabbi's wife or daughter."

"Then you shouldn't talk," Mrs. Gantz says. "You should keep your mouth shut."

Mrs. Kahane folds her chair. She looks like she's about to cry. We watch her go inside and slam her door.

"She gives, but she can't take," Ma says.

"I'm the one who'll have to deal with this," Mrs. Lender says. "She's my tenant. But I think she was wrong, and I would say so again."

"I'm going," I tell Ma. I'm sorry I stopped by at all. I walk down the block in my clogs and robe. Now the women will gather up their chairs and bags and go home, each one to tell her husband what happened. Ma will tell Father.

At the pool, I tell Leah about it. She laughs. "Serves her right. She's such a kocher lefl. Her spoon in every pot."

We do laps, racing. First I'm ahead, then Leah is. I'm faster on the breaststroke, she's better at the crawl. We're even on the sidestroke. Swimming hard, inhaling and exhaling, using my arms and legs to move me through the water, feeling every inch of my body, the water knowing every inch of my body, I'm more alive than ever.

We finally turn on our backs and float, arms and legs limp, and water all around.

I speak with my head up, addressing the blue sky. "That Kahane has been this way since she moved in. What did we ever do to her?"

"It's her husband: he's a Viznitzer," Leah says. "They can't stand it that Father's building a big synagogue right in front of their noses."

"I got three fat books from the library today," I say. "That should be plenty for Shabbat."

Leah stands up right in the middle of the pool. "You went to the library? On a Friday? That's all we need."

"Don't worry. No one saw me."

"You're pure crazy. A hundred percent crazy. That's all we need, along with this bathing suit issue now. You can't be happy that things are going well with swimming. You have to ruin everything."

That's all Leah thinks about. Swimming. Nothing else matters.

"Listen," I say. "The bathing suits are a done thing. Swimming's a done thing. They can't stop us. I'm not going to stop wearing a bathing suit because nosy Mrs. Kahane opened her sewer mouth."

Leah's not convinced. She swims away from me with the butterfly stroke, splashing furiously. Her arms emerge from the water correctly, elbows first, both at once, and her body bobs, up-down, in and out of the water, quickly, cleanly. She's a beautiful swimmer.

She swims two full laps before she answers. "Wait till Father hears about this tonight. We'll see what he has to say."

"Who cares what he says. We'll do as we please. Five more laps; let's go. It's getting cold with the sun gone."

We swim quickly, and there is only our breathing and the dull sound of heavy water parting.

We dry off and get dressed silently. Walking up the block, Leah says, "Mrs. Weiss paid us today. She said to tell you she's very satisfied. She's impressed that her girls are learning so quickly."

"Judy gave me a hundred eighty. How much do you have?"

"One twenty." We look at each other.

"We're rich as Croesus," Leah says, and we laugh.

Ma's waiting for us when we get home. She closes the door behind us.

"Did you tell her?" she asks me.

I nod. She's taking this whole thing too seriously. As if it means anything. "What's the big deal? Ignore her. The others were on your side."

"They may have been on my side in the argument," Ma says, "but now they're all talking about you. Every husband will know the Benjamin girls wear bathing suits. Even if their wives never thought to wear anything else, your wearing them will mean something."

"Who cares?" I say. "Who gives a fig what they say?"

"I do and Father will. Wait until someone says something to him in the synagogue on Shabbat. Then he won't think it's fine for you to wear them. I'm warning you now. You'll have to stop wearing them."

"I won't wear anything else."

Ma looks at me. "You will if I say so. I am your mother."

We look each other hard in the eyes. I will not back down. There's no other way. I'm not going to be a lifeguard in a jumper. Imagine Mr. Gartner coming out one day and I'm sitting there dressed! I'm a lifeguard; I'm paid to watch people, to save them.

At dinner, Ma tells Father. He shakes his head. "People talking. That's not good. That's not good for your reputations. I thought they all wear bathing suits."

"They do," I say. "Every one of them wears a bathing suit. What do they want from us?"

Father sways for a few minutes; his fingers gather crumbs. "It's not so bad to be a model. Maybe we should think about this. It's an honor to be a model. It's a responsibility."

"It's important to save lives too," I say. "More important than anything else."

"Think of the opportunity. You have a chance to show people your virtue. That when questioned by even someone like Mrs. Kahane, you went back and did the right thing. You'll show your best side, humility."

I speak slowly. "I have nothing to be ashamed of. I'm proud to wear a bathing suit, and I'll continue to wear one." I look at him, hating him. Everything always depends on what he wants. Not what anyone else wants. "People talk about the synagogue too, and that doesn't stop you."

He looks up, angry. "I want you to think about this overnight. I want you to change your mind. You will stop wearing a bathing suit. The synagogue is a holy thing. Bathing suits are not. Even though I agreed to bathing suits, I said they were all right, now I want you to show good midos and character."

I shake my head. I can't believe I'm hearing this. I will definitely not change my mind. I take a deep breath. "You're just proving that the law has nothing to do with being a Jew. It's all about people. What will people say? What will people think? That's what you worry about more than the Torah. That's the truth. You live for people."

Father presses his fingertips against the edge of the table. "Everyone lives for people," he says. "We live in a world of people. We depend on people."

Sarah and Esther look at me, worried. They're afraid of what I'll say next, and of what Father will do. They're afraid there will be no more swimming and they'll have to explain it to their friends.

Ma says, "You've raised a daughter who listens to no one but herself. She does as she pleases."

"She'll do as I say. I don't want to hear another word about it."

He starts to sing "Aishes Chayil," and the words seem directed to cut, to show me what I'm not. I'm not a good woman who's hard to find. I'm not as rare as precious stones.

CHAPTER NINETEEN

''WHAT SHOULD I do?'' Leah asks Sunday morning.

"Don't ask. Say nothing and wear your bathing suit," I tell her. She looks at me, afraid. "What do you want to do, lifeguard in a dress?"

She decides to pack her bathing suit in her bag and put it on when she gets there. Sarah does the same.

Ma doesn't say anything when they leave, and I know she's just waiting for Father to come home from the synagogue, waiting to see what I'll wear. They both know Leah will do as I do.

I stay in my nightgown as long as I can, making beds, sweeping the hallway and the kitchen floor. Esther comes in and whispers, "Can I put on my bathing suit?"

"Don't say anything. Just put it on. You're not even five; it doesn't matter what you wear."

Father comes home, and Ma serves him breakfast, eggs and toasted bread. I walk past them on my way to the laundry room. I may as well get it over with. Ma is sitting at the table, across from Father. They stop whispering when I come in. Father's hand is moving slowly, soaking up the egg yolk with a piece of bread. In his other hand, like a relish, is a clove of garlic. I stay in the laundry room, banging doors and drawers, making it sound like I'm busy. I know that on my way back through the kitchen, he'll say something to stop me. It's late, and I have to get to the Weiss pool before the others. I have to test the water's pH, scoop up the floating leaves and green windmills with a net, surface dive to the bottom and clear the drains and the water pump.

I take a deep breath and walk back through the kitchen.

I'm already at the door to the hallway, when Father says, "Ruchele," and the way he says it, adding "le" at the end, I know exactly what he's doing. It's what he does when he calls Ma Tovele instead of Tova. Sweet-talking.

I stop and wait. I don't say anything. I won't bring it up. I will not help him say what he wants to say.

"I hope you're not letting me down. You're old enough to understand the importance of what you wear and to make the right decision."

He looks up at me, waiting for an answer. I keep my face still, Indian still, trying not to show anything. It's none of his business what I wear for swimming. It's my body, my reputation. I am willing to risk my reputation.

Father stares hard into my face. No answer tells him as much as an answer would.

Ma looks at me with hate in her eyes and around her mouth. "No respect for a father. That's what happens when you allow too much. Lifeguard lessons." She turns on Father. "It's your own fault. You encouraged their swimming."

I look at my diver's watch and up at the clock above the table, comparing. "I have to go. There are people waiting for me."

Father nods, acknowledging the importance of my job.

Ma says, "Go. Show yourself off nakedik. Shame your family. Go show the world what you've got. Like a whore."

How quickly she changes from one side to the other. I turn away, hating her. In my room, I see my burning face in the mirror. Even the scalp under my hair is red. I'm filled with hate. A cursed whore.

Outside, Mrs. Kahane is sitting under the tree a little too early, to prove she's right, to tell the world she's unashamed and unrepentant. She looks up, and our eyes meet. She's defiant, standing by what she did, letting me know she'd do it again. I wonder what makes her so mean. I could tear her apart, limb from limb, the way a dog would. I'm a mad dog. My tail and ears are down, and my tongue hangs out. I'm drooling. Drooling to kill. I can murder, easy. This is how people become killers, criminals in jail. Madness. I am Cain, wandering, murdering Cain.

Esther and Raisy join me, and we walk down Rita, the sun high overhead, my head burning. I feel hot. I need a dip in the pool, twenty quick laps to cool off.

Three kids are waiting at the locked gate. "It's eight minutes to one. I'll let you in at one. I have some things to do. Esther, wait with them. Raisy too. Tell everyone we open at one, not earlier."

Esther takes her position on the grass importantly, her finger in her mouth, an official look on her face. She feels important having sisters who are lifeguards. Older sisters are a reward from heaven. With an older sister, I wouldn't be the one doing all the fighting. God must love those he gives older sisters.

I close the door behind me and walk up the steps to the pool. The water is clear and blue. I dive in and swim along the bottom, the whole stretch of the pool and back, and back again. Three laps

on one breath. I exhale, spewing water. I come up, spit, inhale
deeply, and go down again. There's a tangle of wet leaves blocking the drain on the water filter, and when I lift it the water
starts rushing out, pulling. I break the silent surface and toss the
tangle over the edge. I swim laps, the crawl. Five laps in three
minutes. Another five and I'm out of breath, weak and purified.
Breathing is what matters. Breathing cleanses. I lift myself out of
the pool in one heave, my arms trembling. Lifeguards never use
the ladder.

I walk out to the fence, water streaming down my body,
streaming down between my legs. More kids have arrived. I drip
on one, and she squeals. I fling my hair at her, showering her, and
produce more squeals.

I put the whistle around my neck and let them in. They're
overheated and eager, the two-dollar entry fee crushed and ready
in their small, sticky palms. Only kids swim here. There isn't
enough room for adults to sit in the sun or stretch out on a towel.
It's a small, private pool, and charging local kids helps cover expenses. There are water costs, chemical costs, and electricity, Mrs.
Weiss says.

The kids who come here get their money's worth; they spend
every minute of the two hours in the water despite purple lips. I
know most of these kids; they're Sarah's and Esther's age, some of
them classmates. It's good to be with kids, kids without parents.
Life would be better without parents. By the age of twelve, human beings should separate from their parents, like birds and
other animals. Why do people feel so sorry for orphans?

At two o'clock, I look up and see Ma coming up the stairs into
the pool area. Mrs. Lender is behind her. Esther and Raisy are
excited. They show off the dead man's float. I stay in my chair. I
can't get up.

Mrs. Lender walks over to the deep end, to where I'm sitting. "You're making tremendous progress with them," she says. "I never expected Raisy to learn so quickly. She was always so afraid of water."

Ma's eyes are on me, on my naked legs and arms. Between my thighs. I wish I'd worn my robe, sat lifeguarding in my robe. I wish she hadn't caught me naked.

I think about wrapping my towel around me, but I hold back. I don't want Ma to see my embarrassment. I get up and stand, uncomfortably bare.

Before she leaves, Ma walks over. Quietly, for only me to hear, she says, "Aren't you ashamed? Walking around in front of these small children like that, naked. Showing everything you've got to these children."

Everything I've got. Breasts, hips, and thighs, the body of a woman. She doesn't wait for an answer. There is no answer. She and Mrs. Lender leave the pool, leave me there in my lifeguard's chair feeling ugly, disgustingly grown-up and naked, fat and ugly.

I'm in no hurry to get home. I give my students fifteen extra minutes of class time. By the end, they're all kicking their way across the pool, with their faces submerged. I send Esther home with Raisy.

I walk around in the water with the squeegee to get the dirt and silt floating and through the water filter. Leah comes by, already dressed.

"Don't you want to swim laps?"

"I got dressed at Gartner's before coming home. What happened?"

"Ma called me a whore. Then she came here, to look at me, to embarrass me."

Leah says, "When I got home, she said, 'You too. You also wore a bathing suit, didn't you? Two overgrown girls parading their naked bodies. Dov Ber's two daughters.' "

"I wish I didn't have to go home. I hate living there. I wish we could have our own place. We earn enough money to afford our own place. We could run away. We could have a small house somewhere. Where no one knows us. We could live quietly and read as much as we like and wear whatever we want."

"You're dreaming," Leah says. "We have to go to school in the fall, and we won't be earning money then. Anyway, you're lucky. You have only one more year of school. Then you can get married and do whatever you want."

When we walk in together, Ma looks at us like the enemy. "What took so long?" she says. "Planning more humiliations for your parents? Already I can't go out and face the world. I want to bury myself."

"If you are humiliated, it's your own fault," I tell her. "We didn't do anything to cause it."

"Then why am I ashamed to go and sit outside with the others? Why can Mrs. Kahane sit there all day, from morning on, without a bit of shame? And I am here, hiding behind my curtains."

I say, "Don't be ashamed. Show some pride. How many daughters do you know who are lifeguards earning good money?"

"I should be grateful. Lifeguards in the family. I should dance with joy over having raised two lifeguards. Have you saved anyone's life yet? But don't worry. You'll pay for your own sins. Everyone makes their own bed. Wait another year, when the shadchan starts calling."

"Yes," I tell her. "I'll lie in my own bed. So what are you worrying about?"

I lock the door to my room and walk forward and back in front of the mirror, watching myself, my body in a bathing suit and whistle. My thighs are too fat. I wish my legs didn't change so much from the knee up. They widen steadily, at an angle, going wider and fatter, until the top, where they meet the rest of my body and connect with a ball-and-socket joint, not a hinge, like the knee. I swing one leg in circles, slowly, searching for the one place where it looks its best, its thinnest. Some people have long, thin thighs. Mrs. Muller at Gartner's has a barrel body on long ostrich legs. She could use my thick peasant thighs to hold herself up, my thighs that look like they were meant to work the earth. Earthbound thighs. But her legs stretch so thinly up, up, and they look as if they'll break under the weight of her body. I want her thin legs. With her legs, I could walk around in my bathing suit comfortably, having nothing to be ashamed of, nothing to look at. A lifeguard should have thin legs. A lifeguard should look perfect in a bathing suit.

After we're in bed, Father tries to walk into our room without knocking, but the door is locked. He rattles the knob and bangs. I push my book under the mattress and open the door.

Stepping in, he looks at us. He doesn't sit. "Why is the door locked?" he asks.

"I forgot to open it after changing," I say.

He nods. We watch him, waiting. He doesn't say anything for a few minutes. He's never uncomfortable with silence. Finally he speaks.

"Mama is very disturbed. She's ashamed to go out and sit with the women. What will you do for her?"

I can't believe he's taking it so seriously. Ma ashamed. What does she have to be so ashamed of? Sometimes I think she's a child, younger than I am.

"Let her sit under her own tree, and everyone will join her, except for Kahane," I say. "Everyone will join Ma under her tree. Gantz, Roth. Mrs. Lender will be uncomfortable because Mrs. Kahane lives in her house and sits under her tree. But Ma will have most of the women; they're on her side anyway."

Leah says, "Rachel or I can go out and sit with her at first, until the others come over. So she's not alone."

Father nods, then speaks. "You do not make me proud, you two. You had an opportunity to shine, and you didn't. Even though I agreed to let you continue classes, to let you wear bathing suits, you didn't give anything back. No gratitude. And it is all meant for your own good, for your own reputations. That's all Mama and I want, your good. But you don't believe that. You believe you know better. Better than your own father and mother."

He gets up and straightens his tallis. The fringes swing and then stop. "Good night. God protect you."

We watch him leave the room, stop at the door to kiss the mezuzah, and walk out. He closes the door behind him, which is more than Ma does. She always leaves the door a little bit open, as if on purpose, as if to listen in.

Leah and I look at each other. No gratitude. We should be grateful we were allowed to continue classes. We should be grateful he allowed us to wear bathing suits. We should be grateful we were born. What about their gratitude? Ma's gratitude. For our help in the house. For keeping house while she was away, taking care of the children. For earning money, for paying for our own clothes. For just being us. We could have been different kinds of daughters. We could have been B and C students, like the Jacobs and the Baums. They would have liked us better if we were less smart. We would have been easier to manage. We would have been more obedient, the way girls should be.

"They don't deserve us," I tell Leah. "They should have had two idiots for daughters. I wish I'd been born in a different family."

After Gartner's the next day, I sit with Ma under the apple tree. She's doing a hem, and I'm painting roses along the bottom of Esther's new skirt. I used an iron-on pattern, and now I'm filling in with fabric paint, red for the petals, green for stems and leaves. It's boring after a while. The same colors over and over.

Ma keeps looking out of the corner of her eye, telling me who's sitting across the street, under Lender's tree. Mrs. Roth, Mrs. Kahane, and Mrs. Lender.

"So what. Don't even look that way. They're all friends. They're about the same age. Mrs. Roth and Mrs. Lender were always good friends. They're both more comfortable speaking English. Mrs. Kahane probably feels out of place when Mrs. Roth is there."

Mrs. Klein and Mrs. Gantz finally come over, bringing their chairs, and Ma feels better. I stay to listen. I want to hear the gossip. I want to hear what they say about Kahane.

Ma doesn't wait for them to bring it up. "So what's the talk on the street about me and Kahane?" she asks.

Mrs. Klein and Mrs. Gantz look across the street.

"Nothing," Mrs. Gantz says. "I've heard nothing since. She's probably angry at me too. For telling her not to talk."

Mrs. Klein knows only that Kahane and Ma had a fight, and now she wants to hear all the details. Ma starts telling her, spreading the story as much as anyone else. If she just forgot about it, everyone else would forget.

CHAPTER TWENTY

DURING SWIMMING LESSONS, when I'm waist deep in the water, teaching the kids the crawl, Esther points and screams, "Look!"

I turn around and see rolling in the water the youngest Weiss kid, Etty. She's just below the surface, bobbing up and down, and her dirty rag doll is sinking to the bottom. I stand there, not knowing whether to swim or to walk over. She's only four strokes away. I take a step and the water resists. Walking in water is slow. I push off into swimming position and do the crawl, keeping my eyes on her even though this is the shallow end of the swimming pool and there's nowhere she could disappear. It seems to take forever to reach her. On my third stroke, I lift her in my arms as I stand up. There's no reason to do anything we learned, no quick return, no carry. I just lift her and lay her down on the edge of the swimming pool. Her face is pasty pink and her eyes are rolled back. She's not breathing. I jump out of the water and kneel at her side, my wet cheek over her mouth and my hand on her wrist. Her heart is beating, but there's no breath. I raise her legs in shock victim position and call for a towel. Esther brings my robe. I turn her head sideways, and water comes gushing out. Before I can do anything I have to clear her passage. I scoop spit and vomit out of her mouth, thinking, Please breathe, please breathe. I don't want to do this. It's too easy to burst a child's lungs. I count with my fingers on her pulse, my cheek near her mouth. One, two. I have to do a quick, short blast into her mouth on the count of four. But I can feel air. Etty suddenly starts crying, and I am so happy I lift her into a sitting position and hug her. She cries, gags, and vomits all over me. I wrap my robe around her wet body and send her sister to the house to get her mother and a piece of chocolate for energy. That's what they give the victims in the first-aid film they show in CPR classes. Thank God for CPR classes. Thank God for the dummies we practiced on.

Etty doesn't want the chocolate, but she's breathing, she's alive, and her lungs are whole. Mrs. Weiss wants to give me a hundred dollars. I say no, it's my job. I'm not even sure I did anything. I'm not sure I would have been able to give her artificial respiration. I was lucky, so lucky. My hands are shaking. I tell Mrs. Weiss what I want is a latch on the inside door to the pool. Anyone can reach over the gate surrounding her property and walk in. From now on, I tell Mrs. Weiss, the plywood pool door will be latched from the inside, so there are no surprises, so that anyone trying to get in has to knock, so people can't walk in while my back's turned. My voice sounds high-pitched and thin, nervous. If I'd thought of this before, I could have put my robe on before Ma walked in.

By the time I arrive home, everyone on Rita knows about it. I am a hero. My lifeguard classes have paid off. I saved a life. The women are all gathered around Ma under our tree. Even Mrs. Kahane walks over. She doesn't bring her chair; she stands as if she's just leaving. They want to know what happened, but there isn't much to tell. It happened so quickly. I was lucky Etty started crying. Esther and Raisy repeat the story over and over; they're out of breath trying to speak so quickly, so importantly.

Leah wants to know which carry I used. I shake my head. "I didn't need a carry. I just lifted her in my arms. It was in the shallow water. It's a small pool."

She looks disappointed.

"I had to clear her passage. She was vomiting all over the place. I positioned her as a shock victim."

She smiles, picturing it. The others listen, their faces respectful, like in front of a learned scholar. It's not bad being a hero.

CHAPTER TWENTY-ONE

LATE AUGUST, MR. GARTNER stops by to say hello. I'm so
surprised I can hardly talk. I've long given up hoping to see him,
expecting him to show up. "Any emergencies?" he asks.

"Not here. Thank God."

"What happened?" he asks. His eyes on me make me warm.

"It was at my other job. The owner's child fell in during
swimming lessons, when I wasn't watching."

"And?" he asks.

"And she's fine."

He nods and puts his arm around me, around my naked shoulders. "You should be proud. Were you scared?" He looks full into
my eyes with his blue eyes.

I nod. "My arms and legs trembled the rest of the day."

He squeezes my arm where my shoulder ends, and my heart
beats and skips like crazy. All I can think is that I'm glad he's
seeing me now, tanned brown.

I can feel every woman's eyes on me with Mr. Gartner's arm
around me. He sees me look at them and takes his arm away. "Let

me give you a ride home today. You can tell me more about it. Just come inside when you're finished."

It's a good thing I wore a skirt today and not my long terry robe.

When I walk into the inn, Mr. Gartner's not around. Judy says, "Give him a few minutes. He's on the phone in his office." I wonder why she's nice to me, why she lets him talk to me.

I sit on the sofa, waiting. Ten minutes go by, and he doesn't come out. I walk over to the desk, where Judy's working. She says, "Oh, I'm so sorry. I'll buzz him." She talks into the phone, softly. I hear the word "taxi," and I know right away I shouldn't have come here. I should've gone home with one of the women, one of my regular rides. I don't belong here. I don't belong in a Jaguar.

"He says to tell you he's so sorry. He's on a long-distance conference call. I'll call a cab."

I want to say no, I'll walk. But I'm afraid to say anything. I'm afraid if I open my mouth I'll cry.

CHAPTER TWENTY-TWO

MA IS WORKING at Tabak's Fabrics. She decided that with Esther in school till three, she can go to work and earn money. She says, "It's winter, and everyone's locked up in their houses. I want to get out. And I can bring home a few dollars too."

"What for?" Father says. "What do you need that you don't have?"

"A lot," Ma says. "There's a lot I don't have. I want my own money, so I don't have to wait until you pull out your torn wallet. And I want to get out. I'm a human being too. You run around all day, even when you're home. To the bank, the lumberyard, the water department. You have a car and you go. Why shouldn't I get out a little?"

Father continues to argue against it. "Think how it looks," he says. "A mother of seven children, a Chassidic mother, selling fabric. A saleslady."

"I'm not ashamed. What's wrong with a saleslady? Better than a shnorrer. You won't see me put my hand out for money, the way you do."

"I don't ask for myself; I collect for a good cause. Your mother and grandmothers never thought of going out to work," Father says. "They stayed home all their lives and took care of the house, of their husbands and children. They knew they had everything a woman could want."

"My mother? Don't look to my mother. Your father was a farmer, he milked cows. He didn't dream of being a rebbele. What do you want me to do? Sit home and watch your building go up? Sit home until my head goes gray thinking about where all the money will come from?"

Three times a week, Mr. Tabak picks her up in the morning and brings her back at two-thirty, just before Esther gets home from school. Ma says, "They like me. I'm a fast worker. I ring up more sales than the salesladies with perfect English."

She comes home talking about Halloween. She says, "We sold out of orange felt. Public-school teachers came asking for orange felt for pumpkins and black satin for masks and witches' capes."

If Ma went out more, saw more, she'd be worse than me. She brings home yards of heavy black satin for a tall hat and a long cape, and Esther's telling everyone she'll be a witch even though we told her not to tell or there'll be ten witches in Ashley this Purim. Copycats.

Father says, "A witch for Purim? What do you want to make her a goyishe witch for? Esther should be a queen, a beautiful Queen Esther of Persia."

"She's been Queen Esther all her life," Ma says. "This is something different, something interesting. With her long black hair, she'll be a lovely witch."

In her underwear drawer, Ma keeps a money envelope, and every week she puts her pay in it.

"Let me put your money into a bank," Father says. "Money should be kept in a bank account, where it can earn more money."

Ma says, "You think I'm a fool? I'll never see it again if I give it to you. It's as if you have holes in your pockets these days."

Now that she has to dress every morning, she watches what she eats, and it shows. Farmer cheese in the morning, fruit and vegetables for lunch. She says, "I don't feel good all day if my skirt is tight. I like it hanging easy."

Not being pregnant since Esther helps too. Automatically, without dieting, she's gotten thinner. She's hoping she won't get pregnant anymore. After dinner, we take long fast walks to work off extra calories. We walk up Ashley Hill, down Ralph Boulevard, up Jill Lane, around Blueberry Hill to Francis Place. Then Ida Road and back to Rita.

"What kind of man do you want me to look for?" Ma asks when we're walking. "You'll have to rely on me to find the right one; your father has no idea."

This is her favorite subject these days.

"Not a man like Father," I tell her.

"No; I wouldn't wish on anyone a man like your father," Ma agrees. "You need iron nerves to live with a man like your father. Mine are shattered. But what did I know? I liked him. Girls today are smarter. They know more."

Liked or loved? The Yiddish word for "like" is the same as for "love." I wonder, Is there a difference?

I say, "I need someone who gets things done, someone who's on time."

"Yes, a geshikter like Mr. Lebowitz. In that family, it's just the opposite. Mrs. Lebowitz is the slow one. Her husband is always quick, quick. The way I am."

"I don't want someone exactly like Mr. Lebowitz; just lively like him."

"You're right," Ma says. "Your husband should have a head like your father and should be geshikt like Mr. Lebowitz."

I don't answer. I can think of better heads than Father's. Heads that work more thoroughly, clearly. Heads that don't care about Chassidic dynasties and about rabbonis. Heads too involved in Torah to worry about reputations. Heads that don't think about women's stockings.

Ma looks at me. "What, you don't think your father has a good head?"

"It's not that," I say slowly, carefully. "I just don't want someone who thinks rebbish like Father. I want a plain person. No rabbonis. He shouldn't be from a rebbishe family."

Ma shakes her head. "Father will only accept a rebbishe family for his first daughter. That's what he told the shadchan. He says the first one is most important. The first marriage sets the pattern for the others."

"The shadchan?" I say. "You spoke to a shadchan? I told you I'm not interested until after I graduate. I won't even hear of anyone before then."

"I know, I know. But it doesn't hurt to start feeling around. Graduation is not so far away. Chayie Brecher is already engaged. Soon there'll be others in your class."

"Chayie is an orphan. She needs a home. She doesn't count."

"The shadchan called Father," Ma says. "It's better that they call than that we should have to call them. This way you know someone put him up to it. Someone's interested." She looks at me. "Don't you wonder who?"

Her eyes sparkle. She's so excited that someone called. All she wants is a married daughter; she's excited about having a married daughter and a son-in-law.

"No, I'm not interested," I say. "I told you already. I want to teach for at least a year before getting married. I've said this at least ten times. Why didn't you tell Father to say that to the shadchan?"

She waves her hand, making nothing I say matter. "There's no reason to say it. Let the shadchan do his work. A year goes quickly. I wasn't supposed to tell you. Father said not to mention it. Maybe he was right. You go for your interview and get the job. We'll take care of things."

"What, and surprise me one day when I come home? Tell me a boy's here to see me? You better not pull any shtick like that."

Ma laughs. "Who said anything about a boy coming to see you? It's all talk right now. The boys aren't lining up at your door. Don't worry. You're not so desirable. The shadchan said there are rumors that you're modern; he asked what kind of stockings you wear. Father convinced him you wear the best. Don't worry. It won't go so smoothly, it won't be one-two-three."

She knows how to go from one side to the other with just a snap of her fingers. First a compliment, then an insult. I don't trust Father. I think he's planning to pull something off. He wants to hurry me into marriage before I know what's what. I'm only a daughter, and not one who will bring honor to this family. He wants to get to David. For David he can choose from the best.

I wear my new pale-blue mohair sweater, a long, straight gray flannel skirt, and my black shoe-boots to my interview with Rabbi Nathan. He tells me he has two grades for me, second and sixth. He wants each teacher to teach one grade in the morning and the other in the afternoon, a full day. I was looking forward to half days off, but I agree to teach both. There'll be a few meetings before the summer, he says. Before everyone goes away. This will be his first year in this school, he says, so everything will be as new to him as to me. We'll learn about the place together, he says.

I like him. He smokes a pipe, and every time he starts to talk, he fumbles, almost drops it, trying to take it out. Sometimes he leaves it in and talks out of the side of his mouth.

He says there will be two other English teachers traveling from Monhegan, both a year older than I am, both from Beth Yaakov, a better school than mine. Based on their experience, he says, their salaries will be higher.

"In the beginning, I'll be picking you up and bringing you back, since I'll be driving there anyway. The first teachers' meeting is two weeks away. The Yiddish principal wants to meet us; we're what they call the goyishe staff." He laughs. "I understand you know more about these Satmar people than I do. Perhaps you can help me out."

We don't shake hands at the end of the interview, even though it seems as if we should. I smile, and he walks me to the door of his house. I walk down the stairs stiffly, like a teacher, and, at the bottom, turn and see him still standing there, chewing on the end of his pipe watching me. He waves. "See you in two weeks," he says.

I walk home wondering whether he shook the other teachers' hands, whether he made an exception for me, knowing who Father is. People always act as if I am like Father. It is expected that I will be what my parents are.

At home, everyone surrounds me at the kitchen table. Father strokes my cheek the way he did when I was little. He's happy to have me teaching in a Satmar school, even if it's only English subjects. "Teaching is the most honored, the highest profession in the world," he says. "It's the job of every mother. A child learns his first lessons, his first words, even, from his mother."

I'm not sure I like Father being so proud. I'm not a Satmar girl just because I'll be teaching there. I tell him two girls from modern Beth Yaakov are teaching with me. He nods, not caring. He's thinking about what he can say to the shadchan: My daughter teaches at the Satmar girls' school, the best Chassidic school in the world.

Seeing Father happy pleases Ma. Leah's excited about my becoming a teacher, imagining herself graduating and becoming a teacher too. Esther pulls her finger out of her mouth long enough to say, "Imagine if one day you become my teacher."

"It could happen," Ma says. "If Rachel likes teaching, she can continue doing it after she's married. Even after she has a baby. Nowadays young women work after their first baby. They get a baby-sitter. It's better than staying home all day, cleaning and cooking. Laundry can wait. Besides, with a husband who studies, the money has to come from somewhere."

Now that Ma has a job, housework has become less important. The kitchen and hallway are mopped only every third day, and the old aluminum pots no longer shine like mirrors.

"Sarah and I can help grade tests," Leah says. "It will be fun grading your students."

"When you're married, Esther and I can baby-sit your baby," Sarah says. "It's more fun taking care of a niece than a brother or sister. Nieces are cuter."

Ma says, "You and Leah will have two little sisters to help you, to baby-sit for you. I didn't have anyone. I was here alone in America, alone like a stone."

All this talk about me married, me with babies. As if I'm already engaged. As if it's all happening tomorrow. Right now I have a history test to study for.

The shadchan calls back and tells Father people inform him I do not wear seams. That I've never worn seams. Father says, "I see her every morning and evening. She's wearing seams. I bought them for her myself. People don't know what they're saying."

Ma looks at me, into me, seeing what I don't want her to see. She walks behind Father and beckons me into the hallway.

"Tell me the truth, once and for all. What do you wear?"

I don't answer.

"Listen, it's too late to change anyway. Your reputation is your own. But don't make fools of your parents. Don't have them saying one thing when people know another."

"I wear what I want to wear. What I feel comfortable wearing. I don't wear seams."

Ma takes a deep breath. "So you don't wear seams. Do you at least wear thick stockings, stockings you can't see through?"

I nod. "Yes, I wear opaque beige and taupe stockings."

Ma leaves the room. I open my stocking drawer. She won't find anything there I don't want her to find. She'll see two old pairs of opaque tights without seams. Maybe she's already seen them.

Father comes into the room and closes the door behind him. He sits on the bed.

"Again you didn't listen to your father. For years now you've been walking around wearing what you want and not what your father wants."

"I told you then, I'll never wear stockings with seams. You want stockings with seams, you wear them." Having to tell him this makes me angry. I'm trembling. Why should a daughter wear what her father wants her to wear?

He doesn't answer. He sits for a moment, not saying anything, and then gets up slowly and walks to the door. Before he closes the door, he turns back and says, "The shadchan told me David's rebbe wants him as a son-in-law. I'm very proud of David."

So that's why he's in a hurry to get me married.

In the morning, I wear opaque panty hose over my sheer. I don't have to make believe I'm wearing seams anymore. The double layer, opaque over sheer, makes my stockings look even thicker, and Ma's satisfied.

She advises Father. "Tell the shadchan it was your mistake. That it's your wife who wears the seams. You're a man; what do you know about what girls wear? Tell him she wears thick, modest stockings. No seams. Tell him the girls in Monhegan don't wear seams."

Father keeps his head down. "Who'd want to marry a girl who lies to her own parents, tell me. We'll have to be satisfied with whatever comes. The first that comes."

Ma looks at me, bites her lip, and wrings her hands, to show me how bad things are. I don't stay to listen. I can't stand this constant talk about whom I'll marry. No matter what I say, the talk goes on. I don't care whom I marry. Once married, I at least won't have to worry about it. Married, I'll do and wear what I want. I'll be who I am.

CHAPTER TWENTY-THREE

I WALK IN from work, and Ma says, "The Sklars are breaking a plate tonight. Elke called to invite us."

I sit on my bed. There were only sixteen girls in my graduating class, but every month there's another party or wedding. And with it comes all the well-wishing: God willing, soon we'll be celebrating yours.

Should I say, Not ever, God willing? That would cause a scandal, and then it might be never. I don't know what I want.

"You don't want to be one of the last ones," Ma says. "Like that Landau girl. Who knows how her children will be."

Henna Landau waited too long, people say. First her twin brothers were in the way, then she was too picky. The shadchan stopped calling. Soon she turned twenty-six and had little choice. She married the only normal one in the Rosenbaum family.

"What about the girls I teach with? They're still single."

"So you're comparing yourself to them now," Ma says. "They come from modern homes. They wait longer. And remember David. We're not going to let Blau's daughter go, waiting for you."

David's not yet seventeen, and already his engagement is all set. They're just waiting for me. Only David knows nothing about it.

Father says, "There's no need to tell a yeshiva boy. Why disturb his studies? If we tell him, he'll get nervous, lose sleep. Without sleep, he won't study."

I wonder if David knows anything about girls and babies. About sex. Do boys in yeshiva talk about anything?

Ma says, "If we marry him off before you, you'll have real problems. As if you don't have enough."

The shadchan keeps saying, "Forget about a rabbi's son for her."

"This is why you have to be careful of your reputation," Father says, pulling his beard so hard, it is no wonder it's thin. "The Talmud says a father has a responsibility: he must give his daughter to a scholar and to a good family. It doesn't say anything about a daughter who's given herself a reputation, a daughter who's made things impossible for her father, a daughter who's better known to strangers than to her own father."

He speaks of me the way the prophets speak of whores. As if I've walked the streets, invited men into my bed.

I talk to Ma privately. "I don't need a rabbi's son. I want someone who'll work and earn a living. I don't want to be poor all my life."

She says, "Right away, as soon as you're married, you want him to go off to work? Like some coarse factory worker? Let him study for a few years. Then, after two or three children, I can understand. I also wanted your father to get a real job, bring in a salary. But not right away."

There's a lot to be said for reputations. My reputation will help the shadchan find someone for me, not Father. How else would he know whom to bring?

Ma says, "Elke's chassan is no big deal. He's no great scholar, and his father isn't either. They're plain workers and always will be."

Father would never say this, but he thinks it, he agrees. He and Ma work together, they're a team, with Ma as the bad tongue, as if it's more seemly coming from a woman.

There are advantages to coming from a regular family, like Elke's. She's free. She doesn't have to be a model for the community, to live for what people think and say. And they have a regular income. Her father works for a living; they don't have to count pennies, depend on book sales and donations. They don't have to wait for the mail, to see if there will be enough to pay for groceries. I don't want gifts all my life. Giving feels better than getting. The midrash says those who give, love. A wife gives to her husband and grows to love him. A mother gives life to her children and loves them. Takers never learn to love.

During the party, Elke takes me into her bedroom to show me what she's already bought. She's been shopping mostly in Brooklyn, where the groom is from. She shows me a Christian Dior set of sheets I've seen before, orange flowers on a white background. And towels to match. She also bought a set of white eyelet linens.

"I need two more," she says. "Everyone gets married with four sets these days."

The best thing about being engaged is shopping. A bride gets everything new, like starting life all over again. Elke's room is full of bags. I don't think I'll get as much.

"Did you see him?" she asks.

"Yes. He's so tall, and he's handsome." What I don't say is that he's not romantic, like Mr. Gartner. Maybe a man with a beard, a Chassidic man, can never be.

Elke smiles and doesn't say anything. She's in love with this man she just met, like love at first sight. Will it happen to me?

On the floor is a box containing the Sanyo vacuum cleaner Ma told me about. Elke opens the box to show me. It's a new design, beige and very shiny. Very Japanese. It looks too clean to actually clean with.

"It's the lightest vacuum in the world," Elke says. "Lift it."

"It *is* light," I say. "My mother would like it. Instead of that heavy blue Electrolux she drags around."

"I think your mother wants it for you, not for herself," Elke says. She opens the door to her room, still carrying the vacuum, and beckons Ma over. I look at her, a bride dressed in pale-peach chiffon, carrying a shiny beige vacuum cleaner.

Ma takes it from Elke and raises it, using one hand. "It is very pretty. And light. Like a toy. Will it last?"

Elke nods. "It has a two-year warranty, and it's only one hundred ten dollars. On special." She turns to me. "You should get one now. Before it goes up."

I don't answer. Elke looks toward Ma, as if I am too young to understand.

"I'll call King's Appliances and order it," Ma says.

A few days later, the box is on the floor in my closet. Ma paid for it out of her own money. I open it and imagine cleaning my own, very clean apartment. Elke found a place a few blocks away, and she's starting to decorate it. I helped her paint a coffeepot pattern on the kitchen walls one night. It was fun.

Ma's excited. She wants to start buying things and making trips to the city. She says to use my money for clothes and linens, and she and Father will pay for the rest.

"I'm not engaged yet, remember?"

"You could be. Father talked to the shadchan yesterday."

"About what?"

"What do you mean, about what? About a boy. For you."

"I don't want a boy. I want a man."

Ma laughs. "You know what I mean. Anyway, how could he be a man, at your age? But the one we're talking about is a little older. His name is Israel Mittelman."

I look at her.

"He's already twenty-one."

"What's wrong with him?"

"Nothing. He's twenty-one. You just said you want a man, yes?"

Who wants to marry a boy? But asking for a man is as good as agreeing to see one. I hear Father on the phone. They're setting something up, and I'm letting them. It's Elke's apartment. I'm beginning to want things of my own. I want to live on my own. Married is the only way I can be on my own. I have to become Mrs. Someone, Mrs. Mittelman. I try the name out on paper, Mrs. Rachel Mittelman. That's not bad. I want to fall in love, like Elke, like a woman in a novel.

CHAPTER TWENTY-FOUR

IT'S ALL SET up for Saturday night at eight. The Mittelmans
live in Brooklyn, and they're taking the first bus after sundown.

"Everyone says the best things about this young man," Father
says. "And the family: I know the father way back from Romania;
he's a good man, and the family has always had an excellent
reputation."

For Father, knowing the family makes up for their not being
rabbinical.

I'm trying not to show my excitement. I don't want to seem
eager, but I am. I'll finally find out what it's like, meeting a man.
Ma's excited too.

I act as if it's no big deal. "I'm only meeting him. I'm not
getting engaged."

"What if you really like him? You'll say no?" Ma asks.

"Everyone gets married," Leah says every time we talk about
it. "Then you can leave the dishes in the sink all day. When I'm
married, we can do things together, go shopping without anyone's
permission." She looks at me. "What? You'd rather live with Ma
and Father forever?"

We've talked about this so much, we sound like broken records. What she says is true; I can't live here forever. Still I need her persuasion. I want to be, I let myself be, persuaded. I thought I'd never get married. That I'd just move into my own house and live by myself. That I'd run my house the way we ran it when Ma was away. But that can't happen.

"Seventeen-year-old girls don't go and live by themselves," Leah says.

"But why not?" I ask. "Why can't I just do what I want?"

"You know that's not possible," Leah says. "You always want what's impossible. Concentrate on what you can get."

She plans to marry a wealthy boy from Brooklyn and wear designer clothes and high heels. Monhegan is the country, and people here look it. Leah wants to be like the Satmar girls in Williamsburg, the ones who wear mascara so lightly you can hardly tell. I am sick of lightly.

Ma talks about nothing else all Shabbat. She and I go for our walk after eating, and she's mostly too out of breath to talk. We just walk. We get along better now that I'm out of school. Maybe because I'm older. Or maybe because she's working and has her own money. She loves spending her money. She bought me a white silk blouse with French cuffs, and on Friday we had to go buy cuff links at The Men's Store. No one in our family has ever worn cuff links.

When we come back around Ida to Rita, we slow down and Ma says, "I'll call Mrs. Fogel. She can send us some fine embroidered tablecloths and napkins from Montreal. Like mine. It's cheaper there."

"I'm not engaged yet, Ma. I'm just seeing someone. And only the first one."

"How many do you think girls see? Ten? Twenty?"

"Ten is a lot more than one. There is an in-between."

"It doesn't matter. You'll need tablecloths someday. And you'll need some nice clothes. It's a good thing you've got some money saved."

Ma's so excited about tonight, about having a married daughter, I finally just let her be. I'm starting to believe I'll just get married, that this is it, that Israel's the one. I want him to be the one.

At sundown, Leah and Sarah offer to do the dishes and clean up so I can go right into the shower. I blow-dry my hair, straight, shoulder-length, with bangs. I put on my new blouse and a navy wool skirt. Ma helps with the cuff links. She's wearing her green wool dress with a matching print silk kerchief.

Ma hurries Leah, Sarah, Aaron, and Esther out to the cab. They're going to 99-Lanes on Route 59. No one's told Ma yet that bowling is modern. We took her there once, and she swung the ball hard and clean and knocked all the pins down, even though she'd never before held a bowling ball in her hand. She and Leah have always been great at sports.

The Mittelman family arrives five minutes after eight. The grandmother and an aunt too. As if we're having an engagement party. Ma leads them to the table in the dining room, and we all sit. Israel sits near Father. I can see him without looking straight at him. He is thin and well groomed. His beard is perfectly combed, and his peyess are curled and short. He wears a black hat like Father's. And a good wool suit coat, better than Father's. His hands are on the edge of the table, only his fingertips show, and they're pink with pressure. I can tell he's very nervous, and I feel sorry for him. I wonder if he's seen any other girls. It's harder to be the man, I think. He has to start talking.

There's a silver bowl filled with fruit on the table and a
pitcher of water. Father sits in his regular place, at the head of the
table. He peels a tangerine and serves it to Mr. Mittelman. Ma
quarters an apple and passes it to Mrs. Mittelman. They talk about
the one-and-a-half-hour ride from Brooklyn. There's no bus home
tonight, so they're staying over with their friends, the Kleins from
Klein's Fruit.

"Do you know them? Do you buy your fruits and vegetables
there?" Mrs. Mittelman asks.

Ma nods. "For the most part."

She looks at me and bites her lip. We're both thinking the
same thing. Too many people know about this. These meetings
should be kept secret until both sides are agreed and an engagement is announced. The Mittelmans should have rented a car or
taken a taxi.

Mrs. Mittelman asks about my teaching. She says one of my
students is a relative of theirs, Gitty Loeb.

So the Loebs know too.

During a moment of silence, Ma says, "Let's leave the children alone for a few minutes."

They make a lot of noise pushing their chairs back. Ma's the
last one out, and before she shuts the door, she smiles and winks.
The first question Father asked her was would she agree to move
away from Jerusalem. What he should've asked her, Ma now says,
is would she agree to leave her country. To that, she says, her
answer would've been no, definitely not.

I wait for Israel to speak. I won't be the first one.

"What do you do?" he asks.

His teeth are perfectly white. "I teach the second and sixth
grades at Satmar."

"What do you teach them?"

"All English subjects: math, literature, history, science."

"Would you prefer being their Yiddish teacher?" he asks.

"No. There are plenty of Satmar girls who are good Yiddish teachers. I'm good at English; I like literature."

It would help my reputation if I taught Yiddish subjects. I know this is something the Mittelmans have discussed, my teaching English. The shadchan called to ask Ma about it. I was sitting at the kitchen table with her, listening.

Ma rolled her eyes to indicate trouble. She said, "Rachel is smart and she likes to read, like her father. No matter how many Yiddish books we had in the house, there were never enough. So she read English books too. For a while, my husband even considered teaching her some Talmud, but they say women shouldn't. Anyway, it can't hurt to marry a smart girl; think of the children."

The way Ma talked, anyone would have thought she supported my reading all along.

Israel and I are talking as if neither one of us has heard anything about the other. It's all so set up. His lips, I notice, are very pink. Not like my thick brown lips. He has small features, a small nose, and thin lips, unlike mine. He's quiet, and I realize it's my turn to speak.

"Which yeshiva do you go to?"

"I'm not in yeshiva anymore. I study with the older men, in the synagogue."

I should've known that. He's already twenty-one, past yeshiva age. Most boys get married at eighteen. I can't ask, Why did you wait so long? "Do you like being out of yeshiva?"

He nods. I wait for more, for a reason. He doesn't say anything.

"Why? What's good about it?" I ask.

He says slowly, "I like not having to report to anyone and not being tested every week. I like coming and going like an adult." I watch his mouth, the way his mustache spreads so straight and black above his lips.

He mentions Gitty Loeb, who told his mother about the games I have them play in class to help them memorize. He says, "Tell me the rules of the game."

I explain the rules of Go Fish and Twister for learning body parts and colors.

He smiles. "Where do you get such good ideas?"

"From *Teacher's Magazine.* I have a subscription."

"You sound like a very good teacher."

I know he says this to flatter me. Still it works; I am flattered.

We talk about our families. He has two brothers and one sister. He tells me his youngest brother slipped and told his friend about tonight. Before they left home the phone rang. It was the boy's mother, calling to wish the Mittelmans a mazel tov. Israel laughs.

I don't think it's funny. I don't even smile. He's too sure of tonight. Who said anything about getting engaged?

We actually talk about the weather.

Then we're both quiet for what seems like forever, and I push my chair back slightly as a sign that our meeting is over.

He gets up too. I walk into the kitchen, and he goes down the hall, to the boys' room, which today serves as a living room.

I find Ma behind the kitchen door; she's been listening in.

"Well," she asks, her face happy and hopeful.

"Well, what?"

"Is it a yes or a no?"

"I don't know."

"You can't send them home like that, not knowing. They came all this way. Especially the old grandmother."

"She shouldn't have come," I say.

"You can't blame her. She's old; she wants to be at her first grandchild's engagement. They're expecting to break a plate tonight."

Father walks in. "Nu? What do you say?"

"She doesn't know," Ma says.

"That's not saying no," Father says.

"I'm not giving an answer tonight," I announce in a loud voice so the Mittelmans will hear. "I need time. Send them home."

"Shhh," Ma says and closes the door.

"We can wait till tomorrow," Father says, looking at Ma. I can tell he's warning her not to push too hard. "But you'll have to decide by tomorrow."

I say good-bye to the Mittelmans and to Israel, and just as they're finally leaving, Leah and the kids arrive home. Sarah and Aaron are arguing loudly about who's better at bowling.

Leah comes in. "He looks OK," she says. "Skinny but kind of cute. Not manly. A little like Father, don't you think? Did you say yes?"

In books, the men are always tall and dark, or tall, strong, and blond. Not at all like Israel. He does look like Father, thin and sensitive. His hair is black too. But his face is pale, unlike Father's brown skin.

"That's what I fell in love with," Ma always says. "His dark skin like a Yemenite."

"Nu?" Father prods again after the Mittelmans are gone. "What do you say?"

"Stop asking so much, or I'll just say no."

"What don't you like about him?" Father asks.

"Nothing. There's nothing wrong with him. He's fine."

"Do you still want to see another boy?" Ma asks. "Even though it won't look good for you to say no to the Mittelmans. Too many people know about this. And if you see someone else, you'll have to say yes."

"And meet another whole family? Mothers and grandmothers? Why did they have to bring the grandmother? It's embarrassing."

"There's no need to meet another family. Make this one the one. God sent you this family, a good family," Father says, smiling and trying to catch my eye.

I don't smile back, and look away. He's worse than Ma. He doesn't want to give me any choice. He wants this to happen. I could say no just to show I'm in control. But I don't know what I want. Saying no to the Mittelmans would mean I'd have to say yes to the next one. And who knows who the next boy will be. By then the Mittelmans will be insulted. Or Israel will get engaged to someone else. He's older than most boys; his parents want him married.

And if I say no to the next one, people will say I refuse boys for no reason, like the Adler girl. Everyone was saying, Who does she think she is, a princess? She finally married a boy who'd been turned down by at least ten girls because he's short and fat. Serves her right, people said. About me, they'd say worse.

I expect some sign from God all night. I don't deserve it, only the most virtuous people can hope for that, but still I expect it. I fall asleep imagining being held and kissed, and I wake up feeling thrilled. I don't remember any dreams; there's nothing to tell me what to do. But I'm excited. I try to imagine Israel in bed with me and can't. He's not the type. I can feel Mr. Gartner beside me. I can imagine Mr. Gartner doing all the things a man does to a woman. I can feel his hands on my body. I try putting Israel's face in his place. I wonder how Israel would start. How does anyone start such things?

Ma's at the kitchen counter. Father's in the synagogue. The others are in school. "Should I see another man?" I ask her.

"Not if you like Israel. After your father, I refused to see anyone else. There was a Belgian boy, from a wealthy family, and I said no because I'd already made up my mind to marry your father."

Ma had an opportunity to marry a Belgian boy, a foreigner. I'm seeing someone from regular old Brooklyn, even if he is from fancy Borough Park.

"Do you think you made the right choice?" I ask.

She looks at me, surprised. "You mean marrying your father? Of course. Look at what a beautiful family I have. Do you know how many women envy me all this?"

"What about all your complaints? You used to complain a lot. About living in America. About not having enough money. About being a rabbi's wife."

She waves her hand, making none of that matter, and sips her coffee. "Those first years were hard; it was a hard life. Feeding, clothing, and educating seven of you."

"You might have had it easier with a wealthy Belgian husband."

Ma sips and swallows. "I love your father."

Father comes home, and we eat breakfast together. We both dunk our bread in the soft-boiled-egg yolk. Ma started a new diet today; she's had her wheat germ and milk already, and now she's on her second cup of coffee. She wants to fit into her raw-silk dress for the engagement party. She wants to look as good as thin Mrs.

Mittelman, with her blond wig and her little black hat on top. Ma can never look as good in the kerchief she wears. I'm expected to wear a wig with a hat, like Mrs. Mittelman. Father says why not do even better, wear what your mother wears. He doesn't know that after I'm married, when he and Ma can't tell me what to do, I won't even wear the hat.

Ma knows. She says, "Let her wear a covered wig, and at least you'll know she'll stay with it. Not change after. Like Borough Park girls. They're more concerned with how they look than with God or their parents. It's hard to believe that after their first night with their husband they can be so hard, so unchanged, so concerned with just looks."

As if sex with a man is supposed to make you better, softer, more religious. Ma thinks that after I'm married I'll start wearing seams if Israel asks me.

She says, "Wait and see. Plenty of girls do. They're in love with their husband, and he just has to ask them at the right moment and they do it. A smart boy asks right after the first night; it's the best time to get the girl to agree."

I plan not to change one bit. I don't even want to wear a wig. I think if all women refused to shave and cover their heads, the rabbis would have to rethink the laws, change them. But I don't know anyone who agrees with me.

Leah says, "That's ridiculous. It will never happen."

When I talk to Elke, she says, "I don't mind shaving my hair. Everyone does it. You should be happy to get rid of yours. You're always complaining about how fine it is."

"I talked to Mr. Mittelman in the synagogue this morning," Father says. "He's very understanding. He suggests another meeting this afternoon, and if it's yes, we can break the plate and they can take the four or six o'clock bus home. He says he understands a young girl wanting to be more certain."

I like Mr. Mittelman for understanding. Still, what is there I could see better the second time around? You don't get to know a person sitting at a table and talking or going out on a date. It takes time. It takes forgetting that you're doing it.

Father looks at me. "So what do you say to a second be-show?"

"What for?" I say. "What else is there to see?"

He smiles and looks satisfied. He knows I'm interested. He reaches over and puts his hand on top of mine and says, "Then make this second meeting the engagement."

I call Elke's house. Her mother says she's at her new apartment.

I walk over. She's painting the woodwork in the bathroom. I sit on the edge of the tub and watch.

"Are you at all nervous, Elke?"

She puts her head to the side.

"I mean, how did you know he was the one you wanted? He was the only one you saw."

"I just did," Elke says. "He's good-looking. And he was funny when we talked. And I knew I didn't want him to see any other girls."

Things seem so easy for her. I'm too serious about things. Elke would have laughed with Israel about the phone call, she would've thought it funny.

She sits back with the brush in her hand and leans against the sink. "It's not the newest thing in the world, you know. People get engaged and married. It's not such a big deal. Just do it. We'll have fun being newlyweds."

"What about love?"

"It comes after. Everyone I know says so." We look at each other. "You think too modern," she says. "You always did. You always did things that were too modern for your family. Too modern even for the most modern girls in our class. And you're from a rebbishe family. Everyone in school talked about it. Even Leah thinks so. She says you just never know when to stop, that you have no limits."

I think it's easier for Elke because she doesn't think about love in novels. She hates reading. She doesn't know any tall, dark men in boots. She thinks only about the Chassidic way, real life. For the first time, I see a reason not to read.

I say, "It's not as if I'm about to get engaged. I'm just thinking about seeing him again."

"That's getting engaged, in Chassidic families. It happens very quickly. One day you meet, the next day you're engaged. Sometimes the same day. Just do it; you'll have to do it sooner or later anyway."

Elke is always ahead, a veteran. I used to think things would be different for me. That my life would be different. But it isn't. I teach grade school like all the others. I'll get engaged like all the others. Get married. Maybe it's better doing things the way everyone does. You know exactly how it goes. Besides, I don't even know what I really want to do that's different. Or what there is to do. Even modern girls get married eventually. They just do it later. They go out on dates instead of sitting in. Then they get engaged and married. I thought there'd be more things a person could do, more choices. But there's nothing else. People get married and start living their own lives. Married is the only way to live on my own, in my own apartment.

At four, Israel comes again. He looks exactly the same, and I wonder if he's even changed his shirt. This time, only his father is with him. The women are waiting at the Kleins'. Maybe Ma said something.

We talk. Today he looks into my eyes, and I notice his deep-blue eyes. Darker blue than Mr. Gartner's. They're beautiful. I don't know how I missed them yesterday. I ask him where he wants to live. We're looking at each other. I can see myself in his eyes, and I think maybe this is love.

He answers slowly. "Wherever you decide."

I wish his answer were more definite, a name, Borough Park. I want him to take me away to another city. I want him to be strong, a man in a novel. He isn't. But his mind is made up about one thing: he wants to be engaged to me. My reputation isn't stopping him. My hesitation, seeing him a second time, hasn't upset him. Maybe it's the family I come from. He wants to marry into a rabbinical family.

"I think I want to live in Borough Park," I tell him. "Somewhere different."

He nods. "We can. But for the summer, we should rent an apartment here. The city empties out in the summer. My parents move out to the country. It's not very nice there in the hot summer."

I think that's a good idea. I could lifeguard again. I could continue earning money. I tell him that, and he asks about lifeguarding.

"You must swim very well," he says, looking at me, admiring me.

When I come into the kitchen, Ma has that question on her face, and I know I don't want to say no, I'm tired of saying no. I don't wait for her to ask. I decide to trust her. I can trust her more than Father. "You think I should say yes?" I ask.

She nods.

"OK, yes," I say, thinking how easy it is to say it. Yes, yes, yes. There's nothing else to say when you say yes.

Ma kisses me on the cheek and calls Father. He kisses me on the forehead. Mr. Mittelman telephones his wife. I call Elke, and she quickly comes over.

Ma brings out the chipped china plate she's been saving for me, her first daughter, and wraps it in a dish towel. For some reason, we're all standing in the kitchen.

When Mrs. Mittelman, the grandmother, and Mr. and Mrs. Klein arrive, Ma hands the plate to the old lady as an honor. She looks around slowly and lifts her hands up as if she's too close to the ground. A plate that doesn't break is a bad omen. If it doesn't break, I think it will be a sign from God. A sign to say no. The plate crashes to the floor, and we hear it shatter. Everyone says mazel tov. The fathers shake hands, the mothers kiss. The Mittelmans kiss their son. The grandmother kisses her grandson, my future husband, Israel. I watch how he bends down to help her reach him. Elke hugs me. The phone rings. Everyone arrives home from school, and Leah and Sarah take turns answering and making calls. Mrs. Mittelman also gets on the phone. Aaron and Esther are underfoot. Esther wants to know if I'm going to have a baby now. Elke explains that it takes a while. Listening to her, I remember David and Levi in yeshiva. They know nothing about this. I send Aaron to tell Leah to call them. She's so excited, she's calling everyone she can think of. Leah looks at me from across the room and points to her watch to indicate it's not the right time to call. They have set hours for everything there. I wonder how long before David gets engaged, whether Father will even wait until after my wedding. I'm almost eighteen. David is already seventeen, and Father says a boy should be under the canopy before he's eighteen.

Ma unties the dish towel and hands everyone a piece of the

plate. She saves the largest piece, a piece from the center, for me. It has three tiny pink flowers. Mrs. Mittelman asks if I want it set in gold as a necklace charm. We look at my piece of the plate. It's large enough for a round or oval setting. All the brides in Brooklyn are doing it now, she says. I give it to her, and she puts it in her fancy black purse with a long strap, like younger women wear, not like Ma's old-lady bag with handles.

Ma tells Mrs. Mittelman my ring size is five. For my engagement party, I will receive a diamond ring and a big silver vase filled with roses. That's what Elke got. Bridal gifts conform to the latest trends, because mothers-in-law are afraid to differ. Receiving fewer or cheaper gifts could be taken as an insult. As a bride, I can expect a gift for every holiday that comes up between now and my wedding. I don't care about any of this, but Ma says to keep my mouth shut. She received a pearl instead of a diamond ring, and she will never let anyone forget it. Grandfather said it was because he'd seen dirt under her fingernails.

"A complete lie," Ma says. "Can you imagine me with dirty fingernails? He just needed an excuse, that stingy old man."

Ma and Mrs. Mittelman discuss a date for the engagement party and decide on a month from now, on a Sunday, my day off from school. Ma says we'll do it in the new synagogue next door, the women in the women's section and the men in their. She explains that things are still a little raw, construction isn't entirely finished, but it's large enough for the party, if not the wedding, and it's bright.

Before they all leave, Israel comes over, and Leah and Elke move away quickly. With his eyes lowered for modesty, he wishes me mazel tov and a good night. This is impressing Ma, I know. At the last minute, he looks into my face and smiles. I wonder if he's thinking of what I'm thinking. Of us kissing. Of us in bed. I can't imagine us together. I'm not sure what men think about. I always knew what the women in stories felt, I could understand what they felt, but I don't know anything about men.

Mr. and Mrs. Mittelman wish me a good night; Mrs. Mittelman kisses me, then I kiss the grandmother. Mr. Mittelman bows his head and smiles. Until I'm married, Father is the only man allowed to kiss me. Then my husband.

From the kitchen window, I watch them pile into Father's car. He's driving them to Route 59 and Maple, where the bus to New York City stops. Ma is at the front door, waving. It's a starry dark night, the moon is full and round, at the beginning of her month. I'll have to start keeping track of my month, count the days to my period and away from it. Husband and wife are allowed to touch each other only two weeks of the month. There are five to seven days of menstruating, a seven-day count of clean days, then the ritual bath. I have to find the right day for my wedding, before my period begins again.

In the Talmud, there are three kinds of virtuous women: girl, wife, and mother. I will be a girl for four more months.

PART

THREE

CHAPTER TWENTY-FIVE

SOME DAYS I think I could be married. I can be like others, like Elke. Happily married and Chassidic. Maybe living with Israel will be everything I want. I won't have to tell anyone where I'm going. I'll be free to read when I want, to stop reading when I'm ready. I'll wear anything, almost anything.

"You should be satisfied with a wig," Leah says. "Be happy you don't have to wear what Ma wears. You'll look like Mrs. Lender."

"A pretty wig looks great," Ma says. "Better than hair. It's always perfectly combed."

I should be satisfied. But I don't like trying on wigs, I don't want to have babies, I don't want to be a wife, I don't know why I said yes. Maybe just to get it over with, to get away from Father and Ma and everyone telling me what to say.

Ma says, "You don't know how lucky you are. You should be thanking God. Look at Elke, married to a bum. Look at him. Goes from place to place; the boy can't sit. He doesn't have any zitz fleish. He should get a job; he's not made for study. He won't last a full year as a scholar."

"Elke's happy," I tell Ma. When I visit, she shows me the curtains she's sewing and the latest things she did to her apartment. She's always dressed; she wears her wig even when she's in a housecoat.

"Every girl has sparkles in her eyes the first six months," Ma says. "Give her a year or two."

Rabbi Nathan wished me a big mazel tov the day after I was engaged, and we stood there and I knew he wanted to hug me or shake my hand. I wanted him to. He keeps saying he hears only good things about this boy and that he's happy for me, that I deserve the best. We like each other. During our half-hour ride upstate, we listen to news from places called Laos and Cambodia, and he tells me about the fighting there. I look them up on the map. He smokes his pipe in the car, and I like the smell. Not burnt, like cigarettes. If ever I decide to smoke, I'll smoke a pipe.

In the teachers' office, someone tells me she knows the Mittelman family, that it's a very fine family, and that the little girl, Israel's sister, is very sweet. I hate her telling me. I hate anyone telling me what a good match I'm making. I want to say, So what, who cares? What do his family and his little sister have to do with me? What does he have to do with me?

But every Sunday, Ma and I take the bus to Williamsburg and shop all day. She wants to establish a complete and comfortable home for me. I tell her I don't need so much. She doesn't listen. It's as if the more money we spend, the more she's sure this wedding will take place. As if every thousand dollars will make it harder for me to change my mind.

I select colors. I buy three pretty Barbizon nightgowns, white and pink, and, on Elke's advice, a pale-yellow one with wide sleeves, so my husband can reach in and touch my breasts. She got this advice from her sister-in-law. Feeling the soft fabric, I suddenly want to be married. I want to wear these nightgowns. I want Israel's hands under my nightgown, on my breasts.

We buy linens and towels. Three sets of each. Tablecloths. Dishes for dairy and meat. For Shabbat, I buy a set of china made in Poland, because it's cheaper.

Ma insists that I get the set for twelve, not eight. "Before you know it, you have seven children, and a plate breaks, and then if you have guests, you're short."

I like shopping like this. Buying like there's no tomorrow, Ma calls it. Buying so much it becomes work. At the furniture showroom, I look through room after room of Thomasville bedroom sets. I take home pictures, hang them up on the wall near my bed, and try to imagine how each set would look in a room. Leah likes the black modern one. Sarah likes the pale girly one, with painted flowers. Esther, without taking her finger out of her mouth, manages to say they're all nice. Aaron says to get one piece from each set, so I'll have all kinds. We laugh.

Ma says get the gold-trimmed one; that's the one she'd get for herself.

Father says, "What do you need a whole set for? All you need are two beds and a dresser."

For once he's right. It would make it easier to order only three pieces. I don't want a whole bedroom full of the same furniture.

Ma says, "Everyone knows you need a night table. Where will Israel put his alarm clock to wake him up in time for morning prayers? And since when do you listen to your father? What does he know about such things? Take it from me: it's very nice to have plenty of drawers to put your clothes in and a long triple dresser to hang a mirror over."

"What did you grow up with at home?" Father asks Ma. "Only with beds and a dresser. That was good enough for your parents and for us. Why isn't it good for our children?"

Leah agrees with Ma. "If you don't get it now, you never will. Every girl gets a bedroom set when she gets married."

I wait too long to decide and find out I won't have the furniture in time for the wedding.

When I come home with a new dress or skirt, I put it on to show Leah, and Ma takes pictures of me. She says, "Israel will enjoy seeing you looking good, still a girl. He doesn't get to see you like this."

"This is your best time," a Hungarian saleslady in Williamsburg tells me. "A young girl in her prime. You have a pretty face and a good figure. You look better now than you ever will."

Ma nods. But what she won't say is why stop the best times, why stop looking good? Everyone acts as if this is all perfectly normal and happy, everyday, like getting engaged and married and having seven or eight babies is what I was born for. No one wants to remember that I'm not the daughter who brings pleasure and pride to this family. They act as if the past was a passing phase, long forgotten now. They pretend, now I am grown up, that I have changed for the better. I can do no wrong now. This make-believe, this forgetting on purpose, is a Chinese torture. It works; it forces you to be someone else.

Early mornings, when Leah is still asleep, I stay in bed thinking about myself as a divorced woman. That makes me happy. If I can get divorced, getting married isn't so bad. I chant silently: I am engaged to be married and divorced. I am engaged to be married and divorced. Some days I believe it, I tell myself it will come true. I don't tell anyone. Someone should warn Israel. I know only one divorcée, Mrs. Glickman, but she remarried.

I'd be smarter. I'd remain divorced. People say things about divorcées, that they end up marrying and unmarrying again and again. They say such types are never satisfied, that they just haven't learned that there's both in life, good and bad. They say Mrs. Glickman is like a child, she thinks you can have only the good in life.

The Glickmans are always threatening to divorce each other. They leave home together and come back in separate cars, or they leave separately, driving their own cars, and come home together. They're always meeting for dinner to end a fight or start one. I thought for sure she'd be divorced a second time by now. That's what she kept saying when I worked there. She told me things. I'd follow her into her room, sit on her big soft bed, and watch her undress. She's short and fat and beautiful. Dark round eyes and wide dark lips. She dresses beautifully, all the way, starting with underneath. She wears black and red lace bras, black half slips, her smooth white skin overflowing. I watched her in the mirror, so it wouldn't look like I was looking. After a fight with her husband, she'd light a cigarette and say, "Men are good for nothing. If you're smart, you'll stay away from them."

Then she'd puff on her cigarette and start to smile and talk about a sexy man she met for coffee, a business associate. I knew there was no business. Her husband was the one who owned the business. She talked and talked, so fast I never had to say anything.

I watched her do her face in the bathroom. She talked the whole time. I looked to see where she put black and where blue. And when she left I tried it. Blush made me look like I had a rash, but I liked her dark lipsticks.

———

I'm afraid of the first night in bed. Of getting pregnant. Of being a married woman with seven children. Of being Ma, pregnant every year, year after year after year.

"I didn't have time to wipe my nose," she says.

When I ask her why she doesn't get pregnant anymore, she tells me about the rhythm method. "I started it after Esther," she says. "I was too tired to go through another nine months with my back and legs hurting. I take my temperature and delay the ritual bath until it comes down. Your father's a man; what does he know about such things."

"Why did you wait so long? Why didn't you start it earlier, before Esther?"

"Because you need permission from a rabbi, and when I was in Israel I went to one who's known for his leniency, someone your father would never consider going to. After seven children, the man said, God will forgive you."

Now, with all of us grown, Ma's finally happy. She works three times a week, and on Sundays we go shopping. It makes us hungry. Ma breaks her diet, and we stop at Jerusalem Falafel and order two wholes with plenty of hot sauce. Then we order two cups of coffee. We count off the things we've done and still have to do. We never get to everything, and we happily schedule next week's trip.

In stores, we see other brides shopping with their mothers and future mothers-in-law. Ma and I are happy not to have Mrs. Mittelman along.

"The less time you spend with in-laws before the marriage, the better," Ma says. "It avoids problems, insults, talk about who said what. After, it's less important. You're both stuck with each other. You can't divorce your mother-in-law."

"You never had a mother-in-law," I say.

"No, but I know what I hear. And I can tell you about fathers-in-law. Mine was worse than the worst mother-in-law. Always checking up on me, running his fingers along the dressers for dust, the old horse. That was when I was newly married and you could eat off my floors. My counters and floors sparkled. The house smelled clean. You were too young to remember. Now that I'm working, the house is neglected; there's no comparison now. In those days, all the linens were folded perfectly; they looked new. I even ironed your father's underwear. Every pile was pressed and evenly lined up and tied with a ribbon. Blue for your father and pink for me. And that old stinker your grandfather loved it. He'd come visit and open my underwear drawers without asking. He'd check the kitchen cabinets for spills. As if he ever lifted a finger when his wife was alive. It's probably his fault she's dead. He probably killed her."

Some days, sitting across from each other, sipping hot coffee, talking, Ma telling me things, I want to tell too. I'm bursting to tell someone. I want to tell her I'm thinking of divorce. I can't tell Elke; she's happily married. I stopped trying to tell Leah. She keeps saying I'm crazy. She's afraid to hear me talk. She can't understand why I'm not happy to get out of this house I've talked so much about getting away from. Not this way, I try to tell her. Not married and possibly pregnant. Why not before? Whole. Unused. Not having slept with a man. After, I will be older, taken.

"There's no other way," Leah keeps saying.

We go for fittings at the seamstress, and she says you can take a gown in only so much. Stop losing weight, she says. Ma and I smile. A bride looks good pale, thin, and fragile.

Ma worries that the gown is too plain. No embroidery, sparkles, or pearls sewn in. Plain white tafetta with quarter-inch satin trim. We bought the fabric at Tabak's, and I decided on the style.

It's costing a hundred fifty dollars, and Ma's happy about that. The dresses in Williamsburg cost over a thousand. I hated them. Dripping with lace and sparkles, they looked like old Hungarian ladies. Leah says she'll wear one of those dripping gowns and she will not get married in a gym.

Ma says, "Then you'd better plan on marrying someone wealthy, someone who can pay for all that."

I'm letting Leah down, not setting the standard for weddings in our family. I'm letting us look poor. Father wanted to have the wedding in his new synagogue, but the Mittelmans said it's too small. I'm not the first to get married in the Yeshiva gym; several nights a week the caterer turns it into a wedding hall.

"It's still a gym," Leah says.

I don't care. Weddings should be ugly, to suit what comes after. A beautiful wedding is a lie. It shouldn't be beautiful like in a book. Novels are lies, lies upon lies.

Everyone's getting new clothes. It's as if we're preparing for the biggest holiday in the world, my wedding, the most important day of my life. If only I didn't have to be there.

I asked Elke what it was like after. We were sitting in her new apartment, in the bedroom on her new bed. Everything smelled so new, and Elke showed me her nightgowns. She said you worry for nothing. It all happens as it's meant to. She said, The first night it hurts and you bleed. Then every time it gets better.

I want to ask how many times she's done it, but the bridal book every bride reads says it isn't right to share these private details. Especially numbers. There are rules for how often a couple must do it, and it depends on what the man does for a living. A farmer or other physical worker has to do it only once a week, because he's physically tired. A man who sits at work, an office worker, must do it twice. A scholar, who does not physical work, must offer it to his wife three times a week. For this first year, Elke's husband is in the category of scholar, which means they can do it three times a week, and they've been married almost three months now. I look to see if it shows.

Elke claims the hair was nothing. That she didn't even think about it. I can't imagine myself bald. And I can't imagine trying to sleep with a kerchief tied on my head. It won't happen to me. I will just not do it. I will not cut my hair; I'll just cover it. What's underneath my wig is no one's business.

Elke seems different, the way she moves, slower. She lies back on the bed, stretching and yawning. She says, "We were up so late last night, talking and talking." I think they stay awake late at night doing it.

"What do you talk about?" I ask her.

"Each other. It's like we're telling our life stories. We don't know anything about each other yet. We have to start at the beginning every night."

"Is he easy to talk to? To tell things?"

She looks at me and shrugs her shoulders. "Of course."

"Have you worn your wide-sleeve nightgown yet?"

She laughs. "He took my nightgown off on the first night. I told him about the wide sleeves later, and he laughed. He says he was lucky because he studied with his oldest brother, who's been married for twelve years. His brother said not to pay attention to what those rabbis tell young men, new grooms. They concentrate on all the things you shouldn't do. They never describe what you can do. As if a boy would know without someone telling him."

Knowing that everything your husband does is because someone told him takes away from the excitement, I think. Knowing that his brother told him to take Elke's nightgown off makes it less romantic. No one tells men in books what to do. They know.

They know more than women know. The man holds the woman and kisses her until it hurts. I'm sure no one had to tell Mr. Gartner what to do.

I wonder who's teaching Israel. He's the oldest in his family. It helps to have older brothers and sisters. Maybe if I had an older sister, I could tell her what I'm thinking about. Divorce. She could tell me they're just jitters, wedding jitters. That everyone gets them. That when it happens I'll like it, and I'll love Israel. That I'll want him to do it to me over and over. And her telling me would make a difference. It always makes a difference who tells you.

CHAPTER TWENTY-SIX

I AM SITTING at Deja Vu, with a plastic cape wrapped around my shoulders. My hair has been washed and trimmed. Now it's being blow-dried. I let my head fall forward in response to Gregory's fingers. I don't tell him it's the last time; that I'm getting married tonight. He wouldn't understand; people who aren't Chassidic don't.

Ma shaves her head every month, before any of the hairs have a chance to grow even a quarter inch. The bristles underneath her kerchief are metal gray, but maybe if they grew in, her hair would return to that light golden brown it was before she got married. In photographs, her hair is braided around her head like a crown. She says it was so long she could sit on it. I once saw her bald head on a pillow; her kerchief had slipped off. It was a ball, round and white, something you kick around on the playground.

My hair is cut China-doll style, shoulder length with bangs, the ends turned under. It will look good with the bridal wreath and veil pinned to the crown of my head.

"Use a lot of hair spray. It has to stay put," I tell Gregory.

"What's the occasion?" he asks.

"A wedding. My cousin's getting married."

"Bring a small can of spray with you. You never know," Gregory says.

I have a full-size can of All Set in my overnight bag at home. Everything else I own is already in the furnished apartment I rented for the summer. Yesterday I put my white linens on the beds.

Gregory's done. He steps away, spins the chair around, and gives me a hand mirror so I can see the back. I look. It's all perfectly turned under, and I smile my approval. He snaps the cape off and, with his hands on my shoulders, helps me up out of the chair and moves me forward, as if making some kind of offering. He's always so dramatic.

"Isn't she gorgeous?" he asks the girl who works at the desk. She doesn't answer. She just looks at me and draws on her cigarette.

"She's jealous," Gregory whispers into my ear. I hand him the three folded dollars I've been keeping in my pocket so I wouldn't have to fumble for his tip in front of him. He accepts it smoothly.

"You know, Rachel, you never say anything. You never talk. I know you're religious. Your clothes give you away."

I put on my sweater. "There's nothing to know. It's not that interesting."

He looks at me and puts his hands in his pockets. "Next time I'll ask questions and you'll answer, yes?"

At the yeshiva gym, the photographers already have their lights set up on a platform.

"Can't we do it outside, on the grass?" I ask. "I want to be outside."

Every room feels small today.

"As soon as we're done in here," says Manny from Manny Meyers Photographers.

I walk up on the platform, and Manny's assistant follows. He moves me around, this way and that. Manny shakes his head, nods, snaps. I try some with a big smile, others somber, the way a bride is expected to look on the most important day of her life. I cooperate, stretching my arms out wide, holding the corners of the veil, smelling the flowers. Father didn't want photographers. He said they're modern nonsense and that a bride and groom have better things to think about on such a holy day. But the Mittelmans insisted.

We finally move outside. Manny chooses a field in the back, where the grass hasn't been mown in months. Tall wheatgrass and wildflowers. He tells me to run through it, to hold the bridal bouquet in front of me, as if I'm chasing it. Out here, the white net gloves on my hands make everything feel unnatural. I slip them off, and Manny's assistant holds them for me. Three men, the photographers, are following my every move, and I love it. I feel the sun on my hair, the grass tickling, the men liking me.

Last night, at the mikvah, women cleaned me, wrapped me, examined me, and finally declared me kosher, kosher, kosher. Today men take care of me. I imagine Manny's assistant as the mikvah lady. He'd come into the preparation room, where I am soaking in a large white tub, and start with my fingers, looking for hangnails. He'd put out his hand for my right foot, then my left. Afterward I'd stand, and he'd wrap me in a white sheet. Everything at the women's mikvah is pure white. With the tip of a white washcloth, he'd wipe the corners of my eyes and behind my ears. I'd turn, and he'd lift the sheet off my body, examine my back for stray hairs, and his dry fingers on my neck would make my spine tingle. Then I'd follow him down the long hallway, along which other women draped in white sheets await his tickling fingers. But I am a bride, a first-timer, who gets special attention.

The first step of the mikvah is barely submerged in water, and I stand with only my ankles wet. The sheet is again removed, and behind me, Manny's assistant runs his fingers through my hair, making sure there are no knots and tangles. I step down, and down, another step, deeper, deeper into water. I look back at Manny's assistant, and he nods and mouths, "More." I can see him above me in bed, my naked body under his.

In the center, this mikvah is no deeper than six feet. I tread water.

"You shouldn't be swimming," Manny's assistant says. "Hang your arms limp."

I submerge and touch bottom.

"No, no," Manny's assistant says. "Nothing should touch at the moment of complete immersion. Just keep your body limp."

I go under and do the jellyfish, the most useful technique I've ever learned. I go under again. I know the rules: three complete immersions.

"Once more," Manny's assistant says. "The first dip was incorrect."

I go under again and wonder how Ma has managed to do this all these years. She's so afraid of water, and she can't blow bubbles. I imagine her spluttering and coughing.

I come up and say the blessing.

"Kosher, kosher, kosher," Manny's assistant says, and I walk up the stairs toward him, the water streaming from my shoulders, down my legs. He wraps me in the white sheet, now damp, and I shiver in the sudden cold.

CHAPTER TWENTY-SEVEN

IN THE RECEPTION room, a big white peacock chair surrounded by greenery on a trellis waits for me. I walk up and sit. I know I look good. I don't feel plain. My homemade wreath looks better than the three-hundred-dollar headpieces from the Bridal Shop on Route 59.

There's a long line of women in front of me, women waiting to wish me mazel tov, and I wonder, What does luck have to do with this day. I feel like dancing, not sitting here trying to look serious like a bride, receiving guests whose faces I've never seen before, people from the groom's side. They introduce themselves and shake hands. Close relatives kiss me. I try to remember names. There are so many. I remember faces, but names always come into my head only when unneeded.

The older women talk about my dress; they call it sweet, and Ma's embarrassed. I can't tell about Mrs. Mittelman, whether she likes or hates it. She's wearing a dripping mother-in-law dress, pale blue and silver. Elke comes over, and it's good to see her, someone I know. I watch her go back to dancing, and something in the way she walks tells me she's pregnant.

I want to do something, not just sit here. Knowing that the music and dancing are meant to cheer up the bride, to distract me and keep my mind from dwelling on what's ahead, makes me think more. About tonight in bed. About the groom. He has a name, I have to keep reminding myself. Israel. Soon, all too soon, he will be my husband. I look at the married girls in my class. They look different, not like themselves. Some are swollen pregnant. I don't want to become pregnant. My mind wanders. I should leave all this. When the wedding's over, I should go away. I should get up now and announce that it's over, that it was all a big mistake. That it's a good thing we didn't spend too much on this wedding, on my white dress. That that is exactly the reason we didn't spend so much.

I didn't think I'd ever be sitting in this chair. I was sure something would stop this wedding. That it wouldn't happen to me, that I'd be saved. I thought the Mittelmans would find out about me and break off the engagement; I thought of ways to make them break it off. Mornings, I prayed for a miracle. If they broke the engagement, I could claim great emotional hurt, delay another engagement. I'd return all their gifts and somehow leave home. But you need money to go away, to be free, and I spent all of mine on this wedding.

The dance music stops, the trumpet blares, and I feel wide awake, as if I've been asleep all my life, as if I've been sleepwalking. The music pounds in my head like a call, the call of the shofar. It's time for the veiling, and Ma takes the heavy white satin out of her black shiny purse. She holds it in her hand, ready to pass it to Father, who will pass it to Israel. She's my mother, but also a woman who isn't allowed to hand things to another man directly. To avoid temptation. To avoid spilling seed. Men must be so easily tempted.

The women form a long corridor in front of my chair. They clap their hands in time to the music and crane their necks to see the groom. I see Israel and his father, Father with his father, who's here from Jerusalem for this wedding. We picked him up at the airport last week. They push their way through toward me.

Ma is crying softly, and I think, not for the first time, about why mothers of the bride cry. Tears of joy, people say. I wonder whether that's what they are. I wonder, Is she sorry to put me through all this? Does she know this is wrong? I could cause a scandal. I could stand up right now, pull my wreath off, and tell the guests to go home, there will be no wedding. Not mine. I am not meant to be married. Not like this.

The men get closer, and I look up; I want to get a good look at Israel before he covers my face. Maybe seeing his blue eyes will make me want him, will excite me, the way Elke is excited about her husband.

But his shoulders are bowed and his head is down in the correct position for a groom. I can't see his face. He's right there in front of me now, holding the veil. He looks up just long enough to drop the veil over me, and I don't see his eyes. Grandfather puts his hands on my head heavily, on top of the veil, and whispers a blessing. I remember my hair and try to lower my head so it isn't crushed. His heavy hands drop lower with me, weighing me down. These are the hands that felt the dressers for dust, the hands that bought a pearl instead of a diamond ring. I look down at my diamond, a marquise cut, Mrs. Mittelman explained. It means nothing. A ring from the jewelers. I'd give it away in a minute, I'd exchange it for Ma's old pearl ring.

Ma and Mrs. Mittelman help me out of my chair and lead me,

blindfolded, to the bridal chamber. I have a few minutes to get ready for the chupah. What I do is look into my overnight bag. My everyday clothes are in there. I can change out of this white bridal dress and go away I don't know where.

I walk up the red carpet toward the canopy, escorted by Ma and Mrs. Mittelman, the tall burning candles in their hands. I am trying to walk slowly, in tune to the music, but Ma's steps are short and hurried, nervous. The heavy embroidered veil covers me like a mummy, and I feel muffled; but under cover, my face relaxes. Already the muscles around my mouth hurt from overuse, from smiling through the reception. Here, behind the veil, I'm alone.

The ceremony moves quickly. The cantor sings, and I circle Israel seven times. This has always been my favorite part of the ceremony. The slow, sad song, the groom looking serious and scared, swaying hard in prayer, the bride turning round and round her husband the way she's expected to live the rest of her life, around her husband, like the moon around earth. But now here, under the veil, the song is *too* slow, and it isn't sad. I can't see where I'm going, and I feel dizzy after the fifth time around. Ma puts her hand under my arm to steady me, and when I've completed the seventh circle, she stops me in the right place, so that Israel and I are standing side by side, bride and groom. I look down and see his black shiny shoes pointing straight ahead, and I adjust my feet, my white bridal shoes, to point the same way. The cantor calls out a name, and Israel's uncle comes up to recite the first blessing. Rabbis and relatives are honored with blessings. Grandfather gets the most important one. Then Israel puts the ring on my finger, and I don't like the way he proclaims the words that bind me to him as his wife. He announces them too loud and too clear. "With this ring you are holied and bound to me by the law of Moses and Israel."

I don't want to be bound to him by any law. But I remain silent; nothing is expected of me at this ceremony. He breaks the glass, and the music starts up again. We walk down the aisle, married, and the men follow, singing and clapping. They escort us up the stairs, all the way to the bridal chamber, where we will be alone for at least five minutes. Two witnesses close the door firmly behind us and stand watch in front of the closed door. This is one of three things that bind man and woman together forever. First there's the ring. Then these five minutes alone. And later tonight, the final one, the two of us in bed.

There's a small table set for two. Israel uncovers a tureen full of steaming vegetable soup and ladles some into the two bowls. I sip a few spoonfuls and then see myself in the mirror, my hair and wreath askew. I get up to set them right. He continues eating. We haven't yet said a word to each other. I think he looks smaller than when I last saw him, the night of the engagement. He looks shrunken, and I feel large near him.

He finishes the last drop of his soup, puts his spoon down, and says, "How are you?" I stare at his teeth as he speaks. They're too small and even.

There's a knock at the door. The photographers. They want pictures of the bride and groom together. Israel says, "In a few minutes."

"I'm nauseous from going in circles."

"Drink something." His voice sounds muffled, and I look up. He's holding a white cloth napkin to his nose, and a red stain is spreading. I don't know what to do.

"Should I call someone?" I ask.

He shakes his head no. He bends over and hangs his head between his knees, and the bleeding stops. I sip water. He gets up to wash his face at the sink in the pink bridal bathroom. I try more soup while he's in there, and I realize that I'm hungry. Brides and grooms fast all day.

Israel comes out and says, "It's finished. It comes and goes quickly."

"Why?" I ask.

He lifts his shoulders and says, "Who knows."

I hope he has some strange disease. Maybe I can use it as an excuse for leaving. He puts his napkin down on the counter near the mirror, and I think, like Ma would, What will people say about a bloody napkin? That I got my period after all?

The photographers knock at the door again. Israel opens it and waves them away.

Manny sticks his head in. "We're already working on overtime."

I suddenly don't want to be alone with Israel anymore. "I'm ready," I say and push my chair back. I pick up the bloody napkin by a corner and throw it in the wastebasket. Israel watches.

The photographers come in, bringing lights and cameras. There's a lot of clatter. They pose us this way and that. Israel won't cooperate. After just four pictures, he says it's enough and walks away.

Manny shouts, "What do you mean, enough? We've taken nothing yet."

Israel doesn't listen. He adjusts the new mink shtreimel on his head and walks out. His friends are behind the door, waiting, and they push a chair up behind him and lift him into the air, dancing and singing all the way to the men's section.

I look at Manny. He has enough pictures of me. There's nothing for me to do but go back to the women's section, alone, without Israel accompanying me to the door, not the way other brides and grooms come in together.

The musicians come forward to greet me when I enter. Someone pushes a chair under my knees, and I'm lifted up and carried
into the dance circle. I hold on to the chair. On the other side of
the screen, in the men's section, I see Israel, still in the air. He
doesn't see me. When I'm lowered back to the floor, Israel's
mother is there with open arms, ready to dance. She's so ac-
cepting, so believing, so happy to have a daughter-in-law. I feel
like a liar. I dance with everyone: Israel's grandmother, his aunts,
cousins, and family friends. I don't know half of them. I'm glad we
don't have many relatives here in America. I dance with my
friends. The music gets faster and faster. I'm out of breath. Someone brings a chair and tells me to sit in the center and rest.

Ma hands me a glass of water and says, "Save your strength."

Finally the caterer speaks into the microphone and asks the
guests to take their seats for the main course. I sit at the head
table. I am mostly thirsty now. I sip water and look around the
room. The tables are covered in lavender cloth and white lace, and
the tall white calla lilies look good in the center.

There is a bud vase in front of me, and I bring it to my face,
feel the soft petals. There's hardly any smell, that fresh grass smell
is missing, and I feel like crying.

Ma looks at me, sharp, like she can tell. "What's wrong with
you?" she asks.

I swallow. "Tell Esther not to let people take all the flowers. I
want them."

"Fine. But that's what you're thinking about now? A few
flowers?"

Gita Pal comes over to wish Ma mazel tov. She kisses me and
whispers, "Everything will be fine. Don't worry. It's perfectly
normal to be nervous."

I want to throw my arms around her and never let go. She
looks at me.

"Here, eat a piece of challah," Ma says. "It's delicious, it's still warm."

I put a soft piece in my mouth and chew. But it won't go down, I can't swallow, and I spit it out into my napkin. The music starts up again, and I leave Gita with Ma. They're both watching me. I go back to the dance floor and don't sit down until dessert is served. I can keep dancing all night. My legs are tired, but I'm afraid to sit down. It's almost over; people are saying good night. Only close relatives stay for the last dance with the bride. Fathers, uncles, and brothers. Each one gets the chance to cheer up the bride and delay what's to come on this night. Wouldn't it be better to just let the bride and groom get it over with? Only Father and Israel hold my hands when we dance. Israel looks down, shuffles his feet for two seconds, and lets go. No one could call that romantic. I want to shake him or hit him or something. Father takes over, and he pulls me along all over the room with his eyes closed, until Ma gets up to stop him.

"Enough," she says. "You're tiring her."

Grandfather and Mr. Mittelman use a napkin. They don't touch me, a woman. I hold on to one end and they pick up the other. They shuffle from side to side for a few seconds and then go back to dance in the men's circle. David is called up for his turn, and he doesn't use a napkin or his hands. Before beginning, he opens a book and reads the text and explains that it says to dance in front of the bride, not with her. He dances in front of me, moving back and forth. Levi joins him, and they hold hands and run up and down in front of me, singing, always facing me. Father's proud of David, of his engagement to his rabbi's daughter, of this new interpretation. He joins them, and together they move forward and back in front of me, in front of the chair I'm sitting in. The other men stand in a circle, clapping, smiling, and watching. Israel's brothers too. They look just like him. Someone pushes

Aaron up, and Father holds his hand, and he too runs back and forth in front of me laughing. Ma's sitting on my right, and her eyes are wet. Mrs. Mittelman is on my left. Leah sits behind me and laughs at David and Levi, two yeshiva boys in black hats and black coats. Israel's little sister and Esther are running around gathering flowers. They're both excited about their matching white eyelet dresses, the flowers in their hair and on their wrists. Sarah and her friend Toby are sitting in the back, talking and giggling. It's two in the morning, and the musicians and photographers are gone.

Israel helps me in with the flowers. We have to make two trips. Then he turns left at the door and goes straight to the living room. I watch him walk down the hallway. He's not there to carry me over the threshold. Or to help unbutton me. I walk to the bedroom, close the door, and take off my gown. Good thing it opens with a zipper and not hundreds of tiny satin-covered buttons. My new nightgowns are in the bottom drawer of a dresser that's not mine. Only the dishes, clothes, and linens in this furnished apartment are mine. There's a bookcase filled with books for me to read, the landlord's son's books. This was his bedroom once.

I choose the white nightgown, with smocking and embroidery on the front, and cuffs on the sleeves. Tonight I don't want to be touched. I get into bed with a book and wonder how it will happen.

He knocks on the door a half hour later, undresses in the dark, and comes into my bed, still wearing his long, floppy underwear like Father's, and I wonder how he'll manage. He moves on top of me, flattening me, then kisses me on my forehead. He says my name, Ruchel, and it sounds strange coming from him. He has never said my name. I haven't said his either, not aloud. I love you, he says in Yiddish, and that also sounds strange. I just lie there quietly, waiting. This is either too real or completely fake, I'm not sure which. I feel him between my legs, pushing, but he doesn't go farther. He reaches for the extra pillow and puts it under my hips. Someone must have told him to do this; maybe he learned it from his father. He directs my legs up so my knees are bent, and it works; he seems to fit between my legs now, and I don't want him to. I bring my knees in closer. He pushes at me again, and I feel him soft and warm against me. It's not a bad feeling. He stays there pushing. I am facing up and can see light begin to come in through the window.

"We're not supposed to do it in light," I say softly.

He moves away from me and kisses me again on my forehead and goes back to his bed.

CHAPTER TWENTY-EIGHT

ISRAEL WAKES UP at eight. I feel his eyes on me, but I keep my breathing regular and my eyes closed. I'm not ready for him. I need time. I'm tired. I want to just sleep now; put today off forever. He dresses silently and quickly, and leaves.

I get up and put on a white robe. I make my bed and then Israel's. He should make his own bed. I straighten his sheet and blanket, lift his pillow, and find blood on the new white case. He must have had another nosebleed. I take the pillow out of the case, and there's a stain on my new down pillow.

In the bathroom, I look in the mirror above the sink. Nothing's changed. I brush my teeth and splash cold water on my face, looking up into the mirror between each splash, making sure I'm still there, I'm still me.

The kitchen is new and strange. There's milk, butter, eggs, and bread in the fridge. Ma thinks of these things. Should I make breakfast? I wonder. I don't even know how he likes his eggs.

The doorbell rings, and I think it's him, my husband, home from the synagogue. Should I say something about his bleeding?

It's Ma.

I stand there, not welcoming her. It's strange seeing your mother like this in the morning, realizing you still have a mother after you've been in bed with a man, after everything. She doesn't have a right to be my mother now.

She walks in past me, goes straight to the bedroom, and takes the old electric razor out of the box she's carrying under her arm.

"Where's the socket?" she asks and, without waiting for an answer, finds it behind the dresser.

"I am not shaving my hair," I tell her. "You can pack up that razor and take it home."

"What do you mean, you're not shaving your hair? What will the Mittelmans say? And your father."

"I will give myself a short haircut. I don't want to shave my hair."

"You will shave it. I will do it for you. You're a Chassidishe daughter. I told Mrs. Mittelman she can go home, that I will see to it. How can you worry about such nonsense after last night? Don't things ever change?"

She looks at the beds, and I'm glad I made them and that I put a fresh pillowcase on Israel's bloody pillow. Protecting Israel, not letting anyone know that he couldn't, makes me feel close to him suddenly. That's what she's looking for. Blood as a sign that I'm no longer a virgin. Her looking disgusts me.

"Hurry up. I don't have all day. I must get home. Think of the scandal. Rabbi Benjamin's first married daughter with a full head of hair."

She always knows when to say the words "scandal," and "reputation," and "what people will say." She pulls up a chair, but I don't sit. "Look. It's the first time. I'll use the number ten attachment on the razor so it won't be that short. We won't tell anyone. It'll look just like a short haircut."

I sit on the edge of the chair, not fully trusting her to keep the attachment on. I can't think of anything to say or do. I hear the drone of the razor begin. It vibrates on my scalp, and a chunk of long hair falls in my lap. I jump up. The razor falls and wriggles on the floor.

"You could've broken it," Ma says. She bends over to pick it up.

I run into the bathroom and lock myself in. In the mirror above the sink, my eyes are wide open. I'm different now. There's a big hole where my hair is missing. Yesterday's hair spray is there on my scalp in big white flakes.

"Open up." Ma bangs on the door. "Let me finish and go."

I swallow hard and say, "Go. I'll finish it myself."

"It's too hard the first time," Ma says. "It will take me only a few minutes."

I open the door, push Ma aside, and walk into the bedroom. She stands back and watches me turn the razor on, throw my hair forward over my face, and shave from the back, moving up all the way to the crown of my head. I move quickly, nape to crown, around my ears. Then I'm finished, and I snap the motor off. Thin loose strands of hair stick to my wet face.

"An expert already," Ma says. "I wanted my mother to do it for me, and not just the first time."

I stand there looking at her, hating her.

"Don't stand there bareheaded, naked," she says. "Put on a kerchief."

I don't move.

She looks at me, her eyes searching. "What's wrong? How did things go last night?"

I don't answer. I won't tell her a thing. I know not telling her will hurt more than anything. I've heard her tell enough stories about young couples, about a bride who ran home to say her husband is a dirty pig, about a groom who tried to enter his bride the wrong way. I won't give her something to laugh at. I pull the cord out of the socket and pack the razor into the box. She just stands there. I push the box into her hands.

She takes it and says, "Since you're so good at doing it your-self, I'll order a razor from King's Appliances. Israel will need it too."

I don't answer, and she walks down the hall. She stops at the door and looks at me, suddenly softer. "Was it that bad? You can tell a mother."

I hold back hard, and it hurts. I don't want her to see me cry.

She doesn't move. "Listen. Don't be a fool. You get used to it. Everyone does." Her voice is hard again.

"Good-bye," I say, opening the door for her. I know I'll hear about this, a daughter throwing her mother out of her house. Such thanks after all the expenses, the wedding, the trousseau.

I lock the door behind her and walk into the bathroom. Now I try to cry and can't. I look like a boy without peyess. I've never seen my head like this. Round and small. Bumpy. Like Jews in concentration camps. Like Mrs. Sklar must have looked. I run my hands over my head and feel nauseous, like I'm pregnant. I stick my finger into the back of my throat and choke, but nothing comes up.

CHAPTER TWENTY-NINE

ISRAEL DOESN'T COME home for breakfast. He calls to say he met Father and Grandfather at the synagogue and went home with them. He says, "Your mother says to get dressed and walk over."

I say, "I'm not hungry. Eat without me."

"Then I'll see you later this afternoon, around four. Your father wants to spend some time with me, and then your grandfather and I will study together. He says he's here from Israel for only a week and he wants to get to know me."

I hang up. Already they own him. No groom spends his first week studying. During the first week, Elke and her husband took walks and talked and talked. They went food shopping and set up house together. They unwrapped gifts, gathered all the checks, and went to the bank. I'll go to the bank on my own.

Father and Israel together. Father will ask questions, and Israel will answer. He'll answer every one, tell all, and I feel hot thinking of what he will say. Then I think about Father's advice, telling Israel how to do it properly, how to penetrate me, his daughter. Why not have him in bed with us, to show us, to just do it to me, and what then do I need Israel for, lying in bed uselessly beside me?

Ma calls and says, "If you don't want breakfast, walk over in time for lunch. They'll come in from the synagogue again then."

"I'm not hungry," I tell her and hang up.

She calls back. "What's wrong with you? Treating your mother that way? Pushing her out the door, hanging up on her? Even your own husband you don't treat well. Don't you want to come and be near him?"

"No. You can have him. You like him so much, keep him." I hang up again.

The phone rings ten times before I answer. It's Leah. "What's wrong? Do you want me to come over? What are you doing?"

"Reading. I'm reading a novel I found on the shelves. I don't want anyone to come over. This is my apartment, and I want to be alone."

"You don't sound so happy alone."

"You wouldn't be happy either if Father decided to stick his nose into your married life. He's probably telling Israel about rabbonis and what stockings I should wear and about wigs and about every other crazy thing he's got in his head."

"I told you not to live here in Monhegan. That's exactly why I won't live here after I'm married. Not even for half a day. I'll live in Borough Park, away from Father."

"Where are you? Which phone are you on?"

"The kitchen. Ma went next door to talk to Father. She's not here."

"I'm not staying married."

"You're crazy. In one day, you make up your mind. You're absolutely crazy. Ma's coming. I'll call you later."

Father brings Israel home for lunch. The thought of them deciding that they'd better bring him home to me, and Father driving
him, taking him everywhere, deciding everything for him, makes
me want to scream and laugh. But I'm afraid to start, I'm afraid my
laughing will turn to crying that won't stop. There is something in
my throat, ready, waiting, waiting so hard that any sound coming
out will turn to sobbing.

Israel walks in, and the way he walks, so importantly, makes
me hate him. I don't look up. He stands there watching me read,
watching me lie on the green tweed couch in the living room, the
book hiding my face.

"You want to eat lunch together?" he asks. "Your mother
packed a lunch for us. It's on the table."

"No. You eat it." My voice shakes as I speak, and I try to
harden it, to make myself angry.

He walks into the kitchen, and I hear the unfolding of a bag
and then of aluminum foil. I hear him opening drawers, rattling
silverware. He comes back. "Come and sit with me anyway. You
can have a piece of melon if you're not hungry. Your mother wants
you to eat something."

He promised to see to it that I eat something. After lunch,
when he goes back, he'll say, She ate a piece of melon. Like I'm a
child, a patient. I suddenly realize that they'll say I went crazy,
that I had a nervous breakdown. I must be careful not to let them
think I'm mentally ill. Diagnosed, I'll lose everything; I will lose
my right to go out alone and breathe air. I'll end up in a mental
hospital with the thirteen-year-old Vieder girl. A community fund
pays to keep her there.

I put my book down and walk into the kitchen ahead of him.

I'm still in my nightgown and robe, and under the wig styled to look like my hair, shoulder length with bangs, my scalp is hot and itching. I'm so uncomfortable I want to scream. Israel washes his hands for bread and sits across from me, at the small table for two in the kitchen. He eats, keeping his blue eyes on his food. I look at him and then stare out the window, seeing nothing. I wonder how he can eat at such a time. I should be talking to him, getting him on my side, but I don't want to. I don't want to fight for him. I don't want him. Not now, with Father and Grandfather teaching him, and him sitting blissfully beside them.

Getting to know each other. Grandfather doesn't begin to know me, his granddaughter. At the airport, I walked toward him to greet him, expecting something. He looked at me, his oldest grandchild, and smiled and kept his hands down at his sides. We couldn't kiss or hug. We couldn't touch. Grandfather or not, he is a man and I am a woman.

Israel eats. He's skinny, even though it seems he's always eating. Ten years from now I'll still be sitting at a table watching him eat, the way Ma sits with Father. We're both silent. We'll never talk, not the kind of talks Elke and her husband have. We'll only say the everyday things, the comings and goings, the weather and the time.

As if agreeing, Israel says, "Your mother said to remind you that the sheva brachas begins at seven. She wants to know whether we can walk there, or whether to have your Father pick us up."

"Since when is my father such a willing chauffeur? I don't need his services. I can walk. If you want to, ask him for a ride."

Israel stops chewing and looks up. "I'll walk with you. I'll come home at five to get dressed." He looks at me. "Aren't you going to put something on your wig? Don't your parents expect you to keep your wig covered?"

I don't answer, and he looks down. "I want you to. My mother wears her wig covered."

I don't care, I want to say. Who cares what you want. What about what I want? It's my head, not yours.

"I want you to cover your wig," he repeats, and this time he looks at me, waiting for an answer.

"If you'll wear long pants instead of those short pants my father got you to wear, I'll wear my wig covered."

He answers slowly. "I'm wearing short pants because your father asked me to. I'm doing it for your family. My father wears long pants."

"I didn't ask you to. But I now ask you to take them off and wear regular pants, like your father, like most of the world. You surprised me last night with those short pants. I didn't expect them from you. You're not from a rebbishe family."

"But your family is, and I married into it. Your father wants them. He's an important man in this community, your father. He says your brother will wear them too. It's important how his son-in-law dresses."

So that's it. That's how they spend their time together. I say, "What my father wants is not the same as what I want. Who do you think you married, me or my father?"

Israel doesn't answer, and I feel sorry for him. I'm ruining his first day of marriage, the day that should be the happiest of his life. He doesn't understand any of this.

He wipes his lips with the napkin and says, "What you are asking is that I change for the worse. I am asking that you change for the better. Your father warned me that you'd try this, that you'd want to be modern. I gave him my word that I would stand firm."

I smile. He's such a fool to tell me this. Knowing definitely that Father is behind everything, pushing, controlling, makes me stronger. I know I can fight harder. I will not remain within Father's grasp.

"And what else has my father told you? Better still, what have you told him?"

Israel blushes. I'm making him hate me. I want him to hate me as much as I'm hating him. I hate his simpleness. I hate his listening to Father. I hate that I can be so mean to him, that he's letting me be so mean.

"How would you like it," I ask him, "if I called your mother and told her everything about last night?"

"I wouldn't mind. I have no secrets from my parents or yours."

I look at him. He's telling the truth. He doesn't have any secrets. He's not ashamed about last night. He doesn't know the things Ma will say later. He's a two-year-old. I'm married to a baby. Even David would have more shame. He'd know better. He would know not to blab.

"Tembale kishke," I say, using Ma's expression for an idiot. He looks at me, questioning, but I don't explain. I push my chair back and ask him whether he's finished. He nods, and I take his plate to the sink. He reaches into his pocket, takes out a little prayer book, and sways, whispering the after-meal blessing.

I wash the dishes with my back to him. It's not his fault he ended up with me. He could have been happily married to anyone else. For some reason, he has terrible luck, and I wonder why. What did he do to have such bad luck? Why is God punishing him? If only I could forget about everything and just be happy. Like Elke. I could enjoy what I have. My own apartment, my own kitchen, my own husband. I can't go anywhere without hair on my head. I am stuck, married and stuck.

Israel gets up, unfolds his caftan, and tightens his belt. He lifts his shtreimel to adjust it, and there's a red dent on his forehead.

He rubs it. His head must be tired and hot, wearing the heavy fur hat all day. Does it itch the way my head itches?

"What will you do this afternoon?" he asks at the doorway.

"I'll go down to Route 59. to the bank and to buy a radio. I listened to the news every day this year going to teach, and I miss it."

He leans on the door. "A radio? Do your parents have a radio in the house?"

"No, my parents don't have a radio in the house."

"Don't buy it today. Let me think about it first. If I say yes to a radio, will you cover your wig?"

I look at him. He thinks he can tell me what to do, that he is taking Father's place. He thinks that because he's a man, I'll listen. "You mean you want to ask about it, not think about it," I say. "Everything you do, you have to tell them about. Well, you can tell them there's no bargaining. I'm married and I'll do both."

He looks at his watch. "You don't have much time today. Wait for me. Maybe we can go tomorrow. I don't think a radio is so bad; my parents have one. But your parents don't, and I don't know what they'll think. If we buy one, it should be a good one. We can ask my mother which one. We'll be in the city next week. It will be cheaper there."

There's a short beep from a car outside. "Your father," Israel says. "He's waiting."

Everywhere I turn, there's Father. But I don't have to see him. It's easy sending Israel into his waiting arms, into the lion's den. I smile, thinking of Israel in the lion's den.

"Good day," I say. Israel looks up, happy, as if my smile and greeting have already made his day better. I'm a mean shrew, a bitter hag without teeth. One day of marriage, and I'm worse than Ma already. I'm beginning to understand her better.

Why did she stay? I wonder. Why did she leave Jerusalem

with Father in the first place? And when she had the chance, when she went for a visit, why did she come back?

"Only for my children," she said when we asked. "I came back because of you."

I didn't believe it. I was sure she was back for Father. I laughed at her love of Father. I try to picture for the hundredth time Father's face above Ma's, and for the first time I can see him there. I can see him in place of Israel last night, and now it is as if he were above me there in the dark, my father above me, in bed with me, in the dark. I suddenly wonder whether Ma really loves Father. What should she have done? What she didn't do I must do. I must get away, far away, where Father and Ma and Israel and the world can't reach me. I want to go where no one knows me, a place where I won't know myself. I want to forget that I'm married, that I belong to a man, that my head is shaved. Remembering my hair makes my face red, as if I've been found out, as if I've been caught without anything on, bald.

In the closet, there are hardly any clothes I recognize. I always wanted something new for every day of the week. Now that I have it, I want something old. I hate this new person in the closet, this newly-married, with all new clothes.

At night I wear my new pink chiffon blouse and silver-gray flowing skirt with the purple sash. I'll go down looking better than ever. When people start talking, they'll say, And she looked so good married too. What was bothering her? Why did she leave?

Ma meets us at the door and kisses me and looks back and forth, from me to Israel and back to me. She's trying to see us as a couple, as newlyweds. Her eyes search mine. Leah is behind her, also looking. I keep my face blank, refusing to give anything away.

"The men are in the synagogue," Ma tells Israel. He nods and smiles and goes to join them.

"You look great," Leah says. "That skirt looks beautiful, very Williamsburg."

Ma nods. "You look good. Why don't you feel good? Why did you spend the day pissing your eyes out, giving me something to worry about?"

I walk away, not answering, up the hallway into my old room. It's strange seeing my bed, perfectly made, unslept in. I sit on it and feel the bouncing springs. All my life, sleeping here, I've wanted to be elsewhere.

Leah follows me in and watches me bouncing. She sits on her bed and looks at me.

"Are you feeling better than this morning?" she asks.

I nod. I can't talk. What does that mean, feeling better? How could I feel better? My life is all wrong, a mistake.

"The guests will start arriving any minute," Leah warns and speaks slowly. "You'll have to go out and greet them. Are you tired? Ma made all the kids take a nap this afternoon. Sarah's still getting dressed."

She speaks as if to a child. I want to remind her that I'm the older one, I am a married woman now.

"I wish there weren't this party tonight," I say. "I'm already sick of them, and this is only the second. Tomorrow it's at the Loebs' house. Then all the visiting. Friday we're going to the country, to his parents'. Next weekend, we have to go to his grandmother in Borough Park. The only good thing is that we'll go early on Friday so I can buy a radio. I want to make sure I have a radio from the beginning. Israel says we'll ask his mother which brand."

"So he's not so bad," Leah says. "He's letting you buy a radio."

I nod. Letting me. Why do I have to depend on people's letting me? Why am I telling her about the radio? I'm not even sure Israel has agreed. I'm babbling to make myself feel better, to convince myself that I'm getting what I want.

Esther comes in. "They're here. The Mittelmans are here. Israel is outside talking to them already."

I get up to go and greet them. It is expected of me to go and kiss Mrs. Mittelman and talk. About what should I talk? Now that I'm her son's wife, with possibly her son's baby inside me, she'll think, she will want to get to know me. I stop in front of the mirror and stretch my mouth wide and force it into a smile. It hurts. So much smiling instead of crying.

Mrs. Mittelman wears a little navy-blue hat perched on her blond wig. I'm wearing an Yves Saint Laurent gray-and-pink scarf. Silk. The girl in the store said that it was new and that everyone will be wearing it.

"I'm happy you changed your mind," Israel said when I came out wearing a kerchief.

I didn't bother explaining. What do I care about a kerchief when everything else is wrong, when I know that I should leave everyone and everything? I'm in a leaving mood. I can get up right now and walk away from Israel, from Ma, from the Mittelmans, from Leah, from sweet Sarah, Esther, and Aaron. From Levi and David, who are back in yeshiva anyway. From the Torah. I'll leave Father and the Torah. I'll leave them all behind. Who cares about a kerchief when there's so much to leave? Will permission not to wear a kerchief satisfy me? Will a radio on the night table be enough? They're steps, tiny steps. I want to leap the whole staircase and be done with it. How slowly life moves when you're dead. Another day, another hour, another night in bed. I want to live awake. I've been sleeping. Sleepwalking. Awake, I will not have to kiss people I hardly know, and talk and smile and smile. And smile.

Ma serves a beautiful dinner, stuffed cabbage and roasted chicken and warm apple strudel on the side. Leah and Sarah help. As the bride, I am expected to sit in my chair and smile and eat. When I get up to help, I'm forced back into my chair. Sit, rest, eat. Like an invalid. A goose being fattened for the kill. Ma's face is flushed from the oven, the flushed face I remember from David's and Levi's bar mitzvahs, the big moments of her life. David's wedding is only four months away, and I wonder, Will I be here? The married older sister. I shake myself. I'd better not be here. If I'm still here then, it will be to stay. I swear I'll miss David's wedding. David, I say silently, apologetically, and I'm surprised and pleased that it hurts already, missing my own brother's wedding. I want the pain of missing, I deserve it, my punishment for leaving. I've known this pain, thinking of myself far away, separating myself. I want it to become a familiar pain, a daily pain that will let me know I'm free.

Israel comes to my bed again. He tries and tries. I feel like a thing he wants to break through. He sighs and presses against me, soft warm flesh against soft warm flesh. I'm curious about how good it feels, about how much I want him to enter me. I want to feel him inside me. When he moves, he loses me, and I guide him back. But he loses his place again, and finally we stop trying and he stays at my side for a few minutes. I lie there stiffly, not moving. I feel sorry for him. He seems tired, and after a few minutes he returns to his bed and leaves an empty place near me, in me. I want him beside me, I want him to sleep with me all night. But he's curled up, and his face is turned to the wall. I stare at him, hoping he will feel my eyes and turn to face me so I can say come back. I don't know why I want him back; every second he's near me, I'm in danger. He doesn't make a sound, and his back is white like the sheets. Finally I fall asleep.

In the morning, I wake early, before Israel, and make coffee. I drink it at the counter, in front of the window, looking out on backyards. There are old trees and fallen trees between the houses, and down the hill is where Saddle River Road begins. There are so many houses here, all in a row, one after the other. I used to want to live in this part of town, close to Main Street, where the girls in my class lived. I can get dressed and walk to the bakery for fresh bread every morning. I hear Israel move around in the bedroom, and I stay there at the window, sipping coffee. He comes into the kitchen, and I turn toward him and say, "Good morning. Did you sleep well?"

He smiles and nods. "And you?"

"I made coffee. Do you drink coffee?"

"Sometimes. I'll have some if you made it."

I pour his coffee, and we both stand leaning against the counter, looking at each other. His eyes are beautiful in the morning. Clear and deep. Oceans. Deeper than Mr. Gartner's.

"I'll go to Main Street and buy fresh rolls for breakfast. Do you like scrambled eggs?

He nods. "We can walk down the hill together. If you're ready."

He looks at me. I'm wearing my nightgown and robe and a terry turban over my bald head.

"I can get dressed quickly."

I go to the bedroom. I like this, getting up in my own apartment, making my own coffee, walking down the hill with my
husband. I wear my new wine-color skirt, the matching print shirt,
and matching sheer hose. On my head, the China-doll wig, without a kerchief.

"You look very nice," he says. Someone told him this is what
to say when your wife gets dressed.

I smile, and we walk out together. He either didn't notice the
missing kerchief or decided not to mention it today. Maybe he's
getting smarter. We walk down the hill, our shoulders side by side
but not touching, the steepness of the hill pushing us forward,
down, our legs moving on their own to the same beat, left-right-
left-right, announcing we're together. He asks about the history of
Monhegan and where the yeshivas, mikvahs, and schools are. I tell
him Monhegan was the name of the Indian chief who ruled here,
and I take him a block out of our way to show him the Revolution-
ary War memorial on Saddle River, near the firehouse. I tell him
about the old war heroes' cemetery on Maple and how I always
wished I were an Indian, with beautiful straight black hair and a
name like Lightning Foot. He smiles. I tell him where the bus
stop to the city is, on the corner of Maple and Main. At Frank's
Bakery on Main, we part. He continues on to Father's synagogue.

Mrs. Frank is not there, and I'm glad it's her husband serving
me, not recognizing me. I buy four hard rolls. The street is very
quiet this early in the morning, before traffic picks up, and I walk
home slowly, down Lane Street, onto Saddle, and up the hill to
Evan Lane and my furnished apartment. After all the celebrating,
it feels good doing this daily thing, buying groceries on Main
Street. Life is in the everyday.

I reheat my coffee and prepare the eggs for scrambling. I'll
cook them when Israel gets home. I butter a roll and take it into
the living room with me. I can read while I eat and whenever else

I want to. There are questions the characters in this novel ask that I've never heard asked. Is there a God? Would a God allow so much suffering? The two boys each want what the other has. It's always this way, I think. You want what you don't have. If I know that, can I just live with what I have?

CHAPTER THIRTY

AT BREAKFAST ON Friday, Israel says, "I haven't said anything about the kerchief the last few days—I thought maybe it
was too warm in the house—but you will wear it when we visit my
parents today, yes?"

So he hasn't learned a thing. It's still all about kerchiefs. I
shrug my shoulder.

"Which bus are we taking?" I ask. "There's a twelve o'clock
and a two-thirty."

"Two-thirty," he says. "I want to lie down. I'm tired."

He's thin and pale. What did Father say this morning? I wonder. Last night, Israel drank a glass of red sweet wine, and then he
didn't feel well. In my bed, he tried for maybe five minutes. I look
at him. His blue eyes are red. He's been crying. He looks strained,
and I feel sorry for him. Should I stop, should I just wear a
kerchief and be what he wants me to be? People will start talking,
seeing me with a kerchief one day and without it the next. I was
planning to pack one to wear at his parents' house, the way I do
when I go home. But his eyes are red, and looking at them, his

beautiful blue-red eyes, I say, "You want me to wear a kerchief today, I'll wear a kerchief."

"I want you to wear a kerchief every day."

I nod and he smiles, and already, I think, his eyes are clearing up. As long as I can read anything I want to, who cares about the kerchief? I went through the bookshelves and pulled out five books. They're in a pile on the table in the living room, and looking at the stack, five more books, I think I can stay awhile.

Mr. Mittelman meets us in front of the bungalow colony where we get off the Red & Tan. He greets me and says to put my suitcase down. I put it on the ground and he picks it up and we walk up the dirt path together. He points out the swimming pool and says it's a pity we didn't come earlier so I could enjoy a cool swim. "Maybe Sunday," he says. "Why not stay with us a few days, even a week?"

He's so friendly and good-looking in his dark suit and white shirt, his blue eyes deep and smiling. I like him. I wish Israel were more like his father. He looks pale and thin next to this strong man. But maybe Israel will change, maybe it takes time for a son to look like his father. Already he seems happier, more comfortable, more himself. I look at him and see that he's been suffering, that he's afraid of Father, of his father-in-law the rabbi. He looks up and sees his little sister come running, and he smiles and opens his arms. His sister runs into them, and he holds her and kisses her.

Mrs. Mittelman and her younger son meet us at the screen door to their bungalow. She and I kiss, and she stands aside to let us in. Mr. Mittelman shows us our room and puts the suitcase on a chair.

He opens a closet door and says, "You can hang your dresses in here. Maybe take them out now so they won't be wrinkled."

I look at him and smile. Father would never think of saying anything about dresses wrinkling. Ma would be the one to show a guest the room and closet. I look at Mrs. Mittelman. She's shy and quiet, blond and pale. What if Israel is more like her; what if he takes after his mother? But he has blue eyes and black hair, like his father's.

They step out of the room, and before he closes the door, Mr. Mittelman says, "When you're settled in, come sit with us on the porch and drink something cool."

Israel takes off his suit coat and hangs it in the closet. I hang up the two dresses I brought.

"Will you be comfortable here?" he asks.

I nod. They're all so nice to each other in this family, so polite. We go out and join the others. Mrs. Mittelman sits near her husband, smiling, letting him do all the talking. We drink iced coffee and watch the sun drop lower in the sky. Husbands and sons, just off the bus from the city, walk up the dirt path. They come out carrying towels and go to the pool for a swim before sundown. On Friday afternoons, Mr. Mittelman explains, the swimming pool is open for men only because they're not here during the week. He jumps up to do a few last-minute things and lets us know how much time to candle lighting. I give him my fold-up silver traveling candlesticks, and he looks at them admiringly and sets them on a side table in the main room. I explain that it's an old gift from Father and that this will be the first time I use them. It still feels strange, me a married woman lighting candles.

The men go to the synagogue, and the women go for a walk on the country road outside the bungalow colony. Mrs. Mittelman introduces me to friends and neighbors, who are also out walking.

By myself with shy Mrs. Mittelman, I have to do more of the talking. Israel's little sister, Dina, walks between us, holding both our hands, and I ask her about friends and day camp.

Dinner on the screened-in porch, half inside and half out, the nighttime sounds of insects in the trees, and the deep voices of the three men singing make me happy. Mr. Mittelman gets up to serve; Mrs. Mittelman remains seated. I want to help, but he won't let me. He does everything in this house. I wonder, Does she even cook? Israel sings along with his father and talks a little to his mother and brother, but he doesn't get up to help. Mr. Mittelman serves the fish, which look like the pale slices from Meal Mart. The challah is store-bought too. I look at Israel to see if he's noticing the differences. He never says anything about Ma's cooking. He's eating without looking up, the way he always eats. I look at his mother; she eats the same way. On Israel's left is Dina, and her eyes don't leave him. I wonder what it is she so likes about her older brother. I wait for Mr. Mittelman to sit.

He asks us some questions about what we've been doing, and I'm embarrassed that there isn't much to say. I explain that my grandfather is here and that Israel spent most of the week with him, getting to know him.

"How long is he staying?" Mr. Mittelman asks.

"He's leaving tomorrow night," Israel says. "We won't be there to see him off."

"Good. Then you don't have to hurry back. You can stay a few days. I go back to work early Monday, but there's no reason for you not to stay."

"We're expected back," Israel says. "Her father said he and I will continue studying together mornings."

"Every day?" Mr. Mittelman asks.

Israel nods.

I wait for Mr. Mittelman to say that every day is too much, but he doesn't.

I say, "Next Friday, we're going to Borough Park. I hope it isn't too hot there."

Mr. Mittelman smiles. "Yes, Babishu is very happy you're visiting her," he tells Israel. "Talk to her when you're there, try to persuade her to come out here for a week. Fresh air would be so good for her."

Mr. Mittelman clears the table and washes the dishes. I dry. Mrs. Mittelman says she's tired and goes to bed. The rest of us go for a short walk, and when we come back, Mr. Mittelman makes a pot of hot tea, even though it's June.

It feels as if I've been awake a whole week by the time we get to our room, and getting ready for bed, I realize I've been wearing my wig for hours without thinking about it. For hours now I didn't remember there is a wig on my head and no hair underneath. Maybe I'll get used to it. It's possible that around people who don't know me any other way, the wig feels normal.

When I wake up in the morning, the men have long since gone to the synagogue. I get dressed. Mrs. Mittelman is sitting with her prayer book under a tree in the front yard. I make myself a cup of coffee and sit on the porch with a book. The cool morning air feels good on my skin. There isn't anything in the world as good as sitting here drinking coffee and reading my book. I want to stay and do this forever. I'll tell Israel I don't want to go back tomorrow. I'll tell him to call Father and say we're staying awhile. It will be good for Father to know he's not in control and that we can get away if we want to. I stretch my legs out on the chair across from me and lean back and close my eyes. This family is so much quieter and gentler than ours. Here I can rest; there's no one trying to control me every minute of the day. I can see why Israel is not used to the fighting and why he has a hard time with Father. It would be good to live in such a house, where no one's pushing for something. I look at Mrs. Mittelman, with the prayer book in her lap, her face smooth and calm, her lips moving slowly. This is what's expected of me, the new woman in this family. I should be sitting under a tree turning pages of prayer, not the pages of this book full of non-Jews. I watch her praying and think of Mr. Mittelman's face reciting last night's blessing and the parts of his face in Israel's. This family is so good, so pure. What am I doing with them?

CHAPTER THIRTY-ONE

ISRAEL INSISTS WE leave on Sunday, even though there are no rides. Workingmen with cars leave late Sunday or early Monday morning. I say I'd rather go by car than by bus.

He says, "Bad enough I'll miss Sunday morning."

He seems happy here, and I don't understand why he wants so much to leave. He won't call Father. I say I'll call, and he says no.

"I know your father will say it's important that we're home Sunday night," he says, and then I understand. Father wants him to consummate our marriage before my period begins. This is why it's important that we're home Sunday night. I decide to say I'm menstruating when he comes to my bed.

We say good-bye to the Mittelmans and walk down the hill to the road and stand there not knowing whether we've just missed a bus or not, whether we'll be here waiting a half hour or more. The sun is overhead, and I'm hot and angry. The suitcase weighs a ton. Israel's carrying his shtreimel in a box and his tefillin bag. I could be sitting in the shade or swimming in the pool. Instead I stand in the hot sun, in the dusty road, seething. What's worse is Israel's suddenly trying to keep a few paces ahead when we walk in public. Father always walked ahead of Ma, but Mr. Mittelman doesn't do it. He and his wife walk side by side.

I tell myself not to follow, to sit down on a rock or just walk the other way, away from him forever. Finally I can't stand it, and I walk up to him. But before I reach him, he takes three steps away. I sit on the dusty grass and wipe my face. I will not move an inch.

A car pulls up, and the driver, a Chassidic man, offers us a ride. Israel opens the front passenger door and gets in. I don't move. The driver backs up and stops in front of me, and I can't breathe in the dust and pebbles the tires raise. They sit there looking at me, waiting. The driver looks at Israel and says something. He's feeling sorry for Israel; everyone will feel sorry for Israel, stuck with a shrew. I get up and brush myself off slowly and get into the back seat, leaving the suitcase standing on the grass by the road. Israel gets out and picks up the suitcase. The driver shakes his head and pops the trunk. I look out the window and try not to smile. I didn't know I could be so mean.

By the time we arrive home, after four, I find that I won't be lying about menstruating.

Israel goes to the synagogue. I unpack our suitcase, and then the phone rings.

It's Leah. "Elke and I are going to the mall. You want to come?"

"I don't know," I say.

"Israel can eat dinner here. Father can tell him."

"When are you leaving?" I ask.

"Right now. Elke's father's taking us. We can pick you up. I called earlier, but you weren't home."

"I just got back," I say. "It was the worst and hottest day of my life."

"How was it there?" Leah asks. "Ma wants to know."

"That part was good. I wanted to stay. I like Mr. Mittelman."

"We'll pick you up in five minutes," Leah says.

I look at myself in the mirror and take my kerchief off. With a kerchief, I'd rather not go at all. Leah will be uncomfortable seeing me without it, but she won't tell Ma. Still, with or without the kerchief, I'm married, a Chassidic wife expected to live with this man, to have children with this man. It doesn't matter about the kerchief, or about Israel; it has nothing to do with Israel. He just happens to be the one I married. It could have been anyone.

Elke wants to buy a needlepoint. She says, "I sit under a tree with the other women every afternoon, and I could be doing something useful in the meantime. A framed needlepoint will look good on the wall in my bedroom."

Leah and I say we wouldn't have the patience, but Elke is pregnant and everything about her is slower, slow and calm and satisfied. If I got pregnant, maybe I'd be satisfied too. Maybe that's what Father wants. Pregnant and sitting under a tree with the other women, I wouldn't worry him.

At the store, Elke debates between a still life of a bowl of fruit and a scene of a meadow with trees. "The meadow will go better in the bedroom," I say.

There's a sale rack of tiny crewels, and I decide to buy one even though I never finish these things. I choose a picture of an old cast-iron Franklin stove, something American. I could try being happy, I could try sitting under a tree like other women, embroidering. This could be the test. If when I finish this crewel I'm still not happy, I'll leave.

"Come over tomorrow morning and we'll start them together," Elke says.

Leah looks at us jealously, two wives buying nice things for our homes. "You're so lucky, you two," she says.

"What makes us so lucky?" I say.

They look at me. I look at Elke. Her once smooth skin is red and pimply, and in her wig she looks ten years older. It's been five months, and already she looks like an old married woman.

"You mean you don't think you're lucky?" Elke says. "I feel lucky. I don't understand what you want, what would make you feel luckier. What do you want that's different from what you have? You're already not wearing a kerchief; that should make you happy. What more do you want?"

"Don't listen to her," Leah says. "She's crazy. My mother says she'll have to get over it, she'll just have to learn to be satisfied with what she has."

"Wait till you get pregnant," Elke says. "You'll see. When you're pregnant, you'll be satisfied. Even though you're sick at first and you can't eat, still you feel happy. That's what you need."

That's what I need, she thinks. I'm sorry I said anything. She'll never understand. Leah won't either. It's not the kerchief or a radio or any one thing I want. They're things I want to have and forget about, things not worth fighting for. I don't want to fight for anything. I want to just be and do, with no one saying they're letting me.

CHAPTER THIRTY-TWO

ISRAEL SMILES WHEN I tell him. He starts talking about the weekend and about the people he met in the synagogue. I watch him so suddenly light and happy. He doesn't have to come to my bed tonight. He's free for the next twelve days.

Father picks him up after breakfast, and he doesn't come back until four in the afternoon. Then he sleeps for an hour. I prepare dinner for the two of us. Skillet-stewed chicken with plenty of Hungarian paprika. Flat round American burgers in a bun, not like Ma's fat oval kufteles. Everything served with ketchup on the side. After dinner it's time for evening prayers, and I walk Israel to the synagogue. It's the only time we talk. If I'm wearing a kerchief, he's in a good mood.

Tuesday, I go to Elke's house. I take the shortcut up Route 306. I don't want to be seen. Cars speed by. Everyone has someplace to go. This road is all uphill and it is sunny, and the weight of the sun and the wig on my head makes me crazy. Underneath, my scalp is so hot, so itchy, it's like running a fever. I turn to walk back. But I don't want to go back. I turn again. Cars keep passing me, a crazy person who doesn't know which way to go, who can't decide what to do with herself. It's true, I can't decide what to do. To stay or to go. It's this wig. It makes me crazy. I can't think in this hot dead wig. My head is burning. I have to get to Elke's house. I have to soak my head in ice water. I run.

"Take aspirin," Elke says. "I heard some women get headaches. Wigs take getting used to. It didn't bother me much."

In her bathroom I swallow four Bayers. I take my wig off and scratch my scalp with a comb.

"Did you put it on right after you showered?" Elke asks.

I nod.

"Your scalp was still wet. Next time wait a few minutes. When I'm in a hurry, I use my blow drier."

"You blow-dry your scalp?" I ask.

"Just to dry it," Elke says. "What's so strange about that?"

"Nothing. I just wouldn't have thought of it. Anyway, it's better now. It was the sun. Let's sit in the shade."

She picks up her needlepoint. "I started separating the threads. I think I'll start with blue, with sky. Where's your crewel?"

I open my bag. Elke smiles. "It's so small, you can finish it in one day."

"You think so? That would be great. I'll stay here all day just to finish it. You know I never finish these things. You feel like sewing all day?"

"Why not?" Elke says. "My husband doesn't come home for lunch."

"Israel doesn't either. Let's start. I want to start and finish. Before I even start I want to be finished."

"If you like doing it," Elke says, "you can buy another one, a larger one. Bring that chair."

She slowly makes her way down the stairs, one hand on the

rail. She walks like a pregnant woman. I walk behind her, slowly, waiting. We settle under a large maple in the backyard. I watch Elke wet the end of the thread and concentrate, putting it through the needle. Then her face relaxes. The needlepoint lies draped over her new round belly. She is happy, happily married and pregnant.

I pull out the black thread and start with the body of the round crewel stove. I sew slowly, carefully. An hour later, only a small corner is done. I have to work faster. I push and pull the needle, in-out. The fabric bunches up in my fingers. I'm pulling too tight. I go back and loosen the stitches. It's important to move quickly but loosely.

Elke puts her sewing down and yawns. "Let's stop for coffee. I can't sit so long. I need to stretch."

I follow her inside. I can stay up and sew all night if I have to. I can sew before dinner and after. I will be free all night. Tonight Israel will not come to my bed. Tonight and eleven more nights. Twelve nights of no risk. I can stay till then, decide by then.

"How about lunch?" Elke says. "We can make a batch of blintzes. I have the ingredients."

It takes us more than an hour to make blintzes. We do it carefully, keeping the kitchen clean. Elke brings out one ingredient at a time. She measures every amount carefully, wipes the bag, and puts it away. She makes cooking seem fun. This is the good part of marriage. Having your own kitchen, cooking what you want to cook, doing what you want. But why do we need husbands; why not without husbands, without marriage and children; with hair, not wigs?

It's two o'clock by the time we sit down to eat. We talk about Elke's baby.

"I wonder if it's a girl or a boy," Elke says. "A girl first is better for the mother, they say. Girls help when they're older."

"Do you feel ready for a baby?" I ask.

"I'm pregnant," she says. "Obviously I'm ready. You think a year from now would be different?"

"I don't know."

She looks at me.

"I don't know what's wrong with me," I say. "I'm not ready for anything. I'm not happy. I'm not happily married like you. I'm enjoying this, today. But I don't want anything else. I don't want to be married, I don't want to live this way."

She's not surprised, and suddenly I think it's possible Ma spoke to her.

"But how do you want to live?" she says. "What would make you happy? You could talk to your husband, even your parents. Certain things could be changed. They could compromise."

"But I don't want compromise. I don't know what I want. I have to find out what I want."

"Then find out and then talk to them," Elke says. "No one can help you if you don't know what you want."

She doesn't understand. Why should she? I don't understand. I don't know what I want. But I know what I don't want.

Elke looks at me. "You want to come again tomorrow? There's another day's sewing in that crewel."

CHAPTER THIRTY-THREE

THURSDAY NIGHT, WITH only the red tip of the crewel stove left, I stay up late and finish it. This is the first time I've finished any kind of embroidery. I stretch the square of muslin on my knee. Is this a real test? Should I stay or go? I don't know where to go. I fall asleep on the sofa in the living room, not knowing.

In the morning, Israel and I leave early so there'll be time to buy a radio.

At the bus stop he says, "I thought about it. I think if we buy a radio, we should do something to make up for it. I'd like it very much if you started wearing seamed stockings, like my mother. We can buy several pairs in the city."

My face turns red. I could kill him. I could grab him by the throat and choke him. "And you have the store address right in your pocket, don't you? My father wrote it down for you on a piece of paper."

He nods, and I stand there looking at him. He's a pure idiot. He's the stupidest person I've ever known. He tells me everything. He tells Father everything. I walk up the steps into the bus, he steps up behind me, and then we're separated by the curtain that divides the men from the women. For once I'm happy with the curtain, I thank God for the curtain. I don't want to see any men. I want to live in a world with no men: with no fathers, no husbands; a world free of men.

I sit at a window, watching the trees on Maple and then the traffic on Route 59. He's probably asleep again, I think. He's one of those people who sleep away their lives. I kneel on the arm of my seat and look above the curtain. His eyes are closed. How could he sleep at such a time? I could reach over and strangle him. If only he suddenly died. I'd be free, a widow. There's hardly anyone on the bus, and I have the whole seat to myself. I don't have to talk to anyone. I look out the window. I pick out people in cars and wonder about their lives. I make up their lives. To non-Jews, I give happy lives. In one car, a man has his arm around a woman. She's sitting close, near him, her head on his shoulder. I can imagine Israel's heavy head on my shoulder, but never mine on his. It's as if I'm the one who's older, as if he's the child, but he expects me to listen to him, to obey him because I'm a woman. Everyone expects me to obey my husband. Father must think Israel can accomplish more than even he has in all these years.

At our stop, on Eighteenth Avenue, I am the first one off the bus. Other people get off, but not Israel. He's such a shlepper, always the last one out. The door closes, and he hasn't gotten off. I start to lift my arm to stop the driver, but I don't, and the bus keeps moving, taking Israel away, and I think God is on my side. My stomach leaps. I'm happy, grateful. I almost wave. I don't want Israel with me, here in the city. I don't want him with me at all. I turn off Eighteenth, onto Forty-ninth Street, and walk quickly to Seventeenth. I don't want to be found. I'm free. I untie my silk kerchief and put it in my bag. If I had hair on my head, I'd pull my wig off and throw it away.

I don't know where I'm going; I just keep walking quickly, past Sixteenth and Fifteenth. Numbered streets make strangers in a place feel safe. I know where I am. I'm on Forty-ninth Street. One block down is Fourteenth. I walk there and turn. Fourteenth Avenue has all the fancy shops. Ma and I came here once, but this time I don't stop to look in the windows. I've shopped enough for a lifetime. I used to like shopping. I used to think I could go shopping every single day of the week. Now I don't want to walk into a store. I walk past Fifty-fifth and Fourteenth, past the Parker Hotel, and stop, turn around, and go back. I need a place for tonight, for Shabbat. I have my checkbook with me and money in the account, all the gifts from the wedding. I look up and down Fourteenth, making sure no one knows me, no one sees me, and I open the door. I'm trembling. I'm scared. I am in the city, completely on my own. I walk up to the desk and ask for a room.

"A single or double?" the man asks, looking at me.

"A double," I say. "My husband will join me later." I want him to think I'm with someone, not alone, not a woman alone. This is like a novel. I, the heroine, walk up to the desk and ask for a room. A double.

"How long will you stay?" the man asks.

"Two or three nights. It depends on some things. Do you need to know for sure?"

He shakes his head and smiles. "I'm putting you down for three days, so we don't book that room. How will you pay?"

I open my bag and take out my checkbook. I didn't know you had to pay in advance. "By check. Do you want it now?"

"It's forty-five a night. Why don't you pay for two nights. If you stay a third, you can pay for that later."

I write the check, and he comes around the desk, carrying keys. He walks ahead of me, and I follow with my small bag. This

week I packed light, so instead of a suitcase I carry a vinyl hand-
bag. Israel has his clothes in a garment bag.

In the lobby, there are mostly old people, sitting on tweed
chairs that look too hot to touch on such a warm day. But in here
it's cold, it's air conditioned, a different world with different
weather. I feel eyes on my back as I follow the man to the elevator. He pushes the button and turns to face me, smiling. "You're
getting a lot of attention. We don't often get a pretty young
woman like you."

I smile and the elevator door opens and I don't have to say
anything. He holds the door for me and then the door to my room,
number 33. I stand in the middle, not knowing what to do in front
of him. This is me he holds the door for, smiles at, compliments. I
think I'm dreaming. He walks around quickly, drawing open the
curtains, setting the thermostat. He waits and smiles and then
moves toward the door.

"I think you'll be comfortable," he says.

"Thank you," I say, and he pulls the door shut behind him.

I stand there in the middle of the room and wait and listen.
The floors are so padded with carpet you can't hear his footsteps
or anything, only the hum of the air-conditioning. It is so closed in
here, I feel safe. I'm here for at least two days. I can stay here
forever, and no one would know. There is a color television in my
room, and I turn it on. I sit on the bed, and it's so springy I bounce
up and down. I reach for the remote control, and climb higher on
the bed, leaning on the padded cloth headboard. I jump channels,
the way I've seen Mrs. Glickman jump, one after the other, not
stopping for long. I could stay here until my money runs out.
Forty-five dollars a day. I can stay over Shabbat, till next week. I
could go out and come back, maybe only after dark, so no one
recognizes me. I don't want to be seen or found. In two days,
everyone will hear about this. The wife who disappeared after two

and a half weeks of marriage. When a husband disappears, the wife remains alone, an agunah, hoping, waiting. She can't remarry. But the man whose wife disappears finds ways.

I wonder what Israel is doing now. Probably calling Father. I laugh. There is nothing Father can do now except call the police. But he'll wait before causing a scandal. He'll wait until after Shabbat. I sit there watching television, not listening, just seeing things on the screen, thinking, What now? What's the next thing that happens in this novel, my life?

It's too quiet for what I've done. I expect to hear banging on my door. I expect to hear Father and Ma behind the door, saying, "What's with you? Have you gone crazy?" I expect to hear Leah beg me to open up, to come back. I hear Sarah crying, afraid; David saying, She wasn't taught to respect a man, her husband; Ma looking at Father, telling him with her eyes that I belong in an asylum.

I watch a show called *General Hospital*, and I don't know who's who, but I'm interested in this man and woman kissing, in how stuck together the man and woman look when they're kissing. I watch for a while, and then I read my book with the television still on, and when I look up again, it's dark outside. There are no candles for me to light, and with no candles there's no Shabbat. I fill the sparkling white tub and take a hot bath with the door open. There's no one to close the door for. This is what it's like, living by yourself. You read in the bathtub until you're a prune and your book is swollen with soap and damp. Then you step out and dry yourself in a big white towel. There's no reason to get dressed, even. I remain wrapped in the towel.

I'm suddenly hungry, and I remember the two Danishes in my bag. They go down quickly, one after the other, not the way a Danish should be eaten, in small bites between sips of coffee. I'm still hungry, but I'm afraid to go out for food tonight. I've never been out alone at night in the city. I'll have to get to know this place in daylight. I stand at the window and watch the lights and cars. I look across the street, into apartments across the way, and I can see people move around. I suddenly worry that someone will see and recognize me, and I draw the curtains.

I sleep well. In the morning, I'm in the center of the big, wide bed and I stretch out, feeling my skin on the crisp white cotton sheets, my naked body under the covers. When you live alone, you don't need nightgowns. The telephone is on the nightstand, and I turn to face it and wonder whom I could call. I'm dying to talk to someone, but it's Shabbat, and no one I know will answer the phone till sundown.

Downstairs, I worry about the man at the desk seeing me, knowing there isn't a husband after all. I cross the lobby to the door, keeping my eyes straight ahead, feeling his eyes on my back. But when, at the door, I turn my head, there is no one at the desk after all, and now I am disappointed not to see him.

In the sun, I am happy again, glad to be outside, breathing real air. I decide to continue yesterday's walk, heading up Fourteenth Avenue, to Fifty-sixth Street, then Fifty-seventh, Fifty-eighth. I am finally going somewhere.

I have to be careful with my cash; I have only twenty dollars, and there's no Union Savings Bank in Brooklyn. My stomach feels empty, like after a fast day. I have to find a place to eat breakfast. Kosher restaurants are closed. That's better, I decide. I'll eat where I won't be recognized. I walk more blocks, and soon there are fewer Jewish people. I've walked out of the Jewish neighborhood. There's a place with a sign that says "$1.99 Breakfast," and I walk up to the door. The smell of coffee and fried eggs is strong. I sit at a table in the back and order scrambled eggs and coffee.

"With sausage or ham?" the waiter asks.

I look at him. I can't eat meat with eggs fried in butter. But on the griddle behind the counter, the eggs and the meat fry together, and the cook is using the same spatula for both. I'll be eating the fat of the meat with my eggs anyway. Already I've turned the television on and off on Shabbat and ridden the elevator down to the lobby. Also, I'm carrying money.

"Sausage. And bread, toasted rye."

The plate arrives with two fat sausages, fatter and shorter than hot dogs, and I look at them, not sure I want to eat them. They smell so strong. I move them to a corner of my plate, so they don't touch my eggs. I start eating slowly and finish quickly. I'm so hungry I can eat another whole round of eggs. I try a sausage and gag on my first bite. I spit it out in my napkin and quickly sip coffee to get rid of the taste. Now that I've tasted sausage, I know this coffee shop stinks of it. I finish my toast and ask the waiter for more bread. I can fill up on bread.

After breakfast, I walk around the neighborhood. The signs are in Spanish. No one knows me; among these people I'm safe. It's a warm, sunny day, and women sit on the stairs, talking, watching their kids play. I wish I could join them on the stairs in the sun. But I don't speak Spanish, I'm not a mother, and I don't live here. I have to head back to my room and think about what to do, whom to call. Ma's cousin Frieda used to live here in Brooklyn. I saw her once in a black velvet dress all the way down to the floor. I was ten and we were at a wedding, and with her red hair long and loose, she was a painting.

Father criticized. He said her dress was too long, too noticeable. And why wasn't her hair braided and knotted in the old way, like our foremothers?

Frieda laughed, a high giggle. "It's in style," she said, spreading the skirt of her dress. "There's mini, midi, maxi. This dress is maxi."

I said I'd wear mini, and Frieda laughed again.

If I could find her, she would show me how to live the way she does, alone.

I look in the phone book. There are many Brauns, but no Frieda Braun. Maybe she went back to Israel. Maybe Ma's right and Frieda wasn't so happy living alone; an old maid with gray hair, Ma called her.

I think of calling Mrs. Glickman because she's been divorced, because she's the only divorcée I know. But I'm not sure about her; I'm not even sure I like her.

I thumb through the white pages. On a map of Brooklyn I find Sea Gate. I could go there tomorrow. I could take a train to the ocean. I could live there. But first I must call home. I must tell Ma I'm alive.

I turn on the television again.

After a while, I can't stand to watch, and I read. But I need to go out again; I'm bored staying in this room so long. I feel like moving around. I walk down to the lobby, and everyone is sitting there watching television, not talking. I wonder why they bother leaving their rooms, why they don't just watch alone in their rooms.

There is a woman at the desk now; that man still isn't there.

I take the elevator back to my room, where he could be sitting, waiting in the chair beside the bed, his legs crossed. How do men find it possible to sit with their legs crossed? I've never seen Father sit that way. Chassidic men keep both feet on the ground, a foot or so between them. And with the flaps of their long coats over their baggy hips and thighs, there isn't anything to see.

I turn the key in the lock and open the door and cross the room into his arms. He uncrosses his legs and puts his arms tight around me. I sit feeling him, feeling him near me, almost in me, with only the dark wool of his pants and the thin cloth of my skirt, and the nylon and cotton under it, between us.

How does it happen without having to stop and take it all off?

It will happen, and then he'll be there in me, a man deep in me, far in me, reaching, aiming, spilling in me.

CHAPTER THIRTY-FOUR

I'M HOME BUT not home. I look at Leah, Sarah, Aaron, and Esther. David and Levi are in yeshiva. I can never be one of the children again. I'm a stranger in this house. Esther follows me around with her big brown eyes, questioning eyes. I help her with what she needs no help in: homework. I don't belong here.

Now that Israel is gone, Ma's saying he was a bit of a tembel, that he had to be told everything, that he didn't have an ounce of common sense.

If I'd stayed, they would have done nothing about it. But at the table, Ma would have said, "Unfortunately Rachel is married to a tembale kishke, a nice boy but a little slow to catch on."

Father would have smiled. "A tembel is not so bad. Who says it's good to be smart? The smart ones are less happy. Better a tembel than a boy with open eyes."

They would have said this to Leah and the others, smiling, shrugging it off with: We didn't know. I would have been someone to pity, an unfortunate sacrifice.

The building next door is almost finished, and Ma's talking about moving in.

When I ask what happened to not wanting to live above a synagogue like a rebbetzin, she says, "What's done is done. It's nicer and larger than this old bungalow. What should I do, continue living in this hovel and rent that out?"

With new families moving in, the synagogue has become useful. People come when it's late or raining; mornings, they pay to use the mikvah. Everyone likes a synagogue conveniently nearby. Even Viznitzer Chassidim come, and there's a rumor they want to buy the place from Father, that they're prepared to pay a quarter million for both properties.

"It's more than it's worth," Father says. "I can sell here and buy elsewhere. I can build a synagogue in a better spot, away from Viznitz, in a place with more acres, with room to build houses for all my children."

"You're out of your mind," Ma says. "Your children don't want to live near you. David will stay near his rebbe and father-in-law, Leah will live in Brooklyn, and I am not moving. Now that I have neighbors, you want to drag me off again. Tell Viznitz I will not sell for a whole million. I have some say over this land too; I own this land as much as you do. You wanted to write a book, you wrote it. You wanted a synagogue, you built it. Enough is enough. Now you'll do a little of what I want."

"Don't be foolish. They want it so much," Father says, "we can ask for a half million. That's more than pennies. We own real estate worth a half million."

"You're the fool," Ma says. "Don't you see they think you'll want to sell out with all your problems? They're rejoicing in your troubles. They're sitting with their hands folded on their fat stomachs and laughing at you. A divorced daughter on your hands. Plenty of debt."

I won't be here, on their hands, for long.

I watch Ma light candles, and a spreading glowing pain is in my chest. Father's kiddish hurts. I love them and I don't. I know this is what I'll miss when I go: the children at the table, Ma lighting candles, Father's kiddish. Aaron sits across from me, on the boys' side. I look into his face, his pale skin and green eyes, and he smiles and I smile and he looks down at his plate. He starts to giggle, his shoulders move up and down silently, and I think it's because I'm still the same that he's laughing. I'm still his older sister, back home, where he's used to having me.

We stand for kiddish, the story of creation.

When God created the sun and the moon, they were the same. The moon said, One of us should be larger. God agreed and shrank the moon until she was less than an eighth the size of the sun. The moon hid all day and came out only at night. To make it up to her, God gave her the stars.

"But the moon is still ashamed to this day," Father says. "She doesn't like to be looked at, and if you stare at her too long, you climb walls during the night."

I watch the moon hanging above my bedroom window and hope to climb walls. It is blue dark outside, and the moon has a nose and eyes. I whisper to her. I wonder how high I will get before I fall.